ROAG'S SYNDICATE

Gentle, bland, scheming Mr Hammersley thought he was on to a good thing, until Simon Good emerged from the yellow fog to remind him of an alcoholic confidence made in the dim and distant past... Roag's Syndicate are not drenched in the blood of terribly mutilated victims, nor are they filled with juvenile delinquents. Reference *is* made, however, to nice, comfortable adult delinquents. From an Anglo-American insurance company in Fetter Lane, the action moves from Temple Station via New Scotland Yard, down to St Ives, along the colourful waterways of Amsterdam, right into the dock ... at the Central Criminal Court.

ROAG'S SYNDICATE

ROAG'S SYNDICATE

by

George Davis

Dales Large Print Books
Long Preston, North Yorkshire,
BD23 4ND, England.

British Library Cataloguing in Publication Data.

Davis, George
    Roag's syndicate.

    A catalogue record of this book is
    available from the British Library

    ISBN   978-1-84262-803-4 pbk

First published in Great Britain
in 1960 by Chapman & Hall Limited

Copyright © 1960 by George Davis

Cover illustration © Colleen Farrell by arrangement with
Arcangel Images

The moral right of the author has been asserted

Published in Large Print 2011 by arrangement with
George Davis, care of Watson, Little Ltd.

Dales Large Print is an imprint of Library Magna Books Ltd.

Printed and bound in Great Britain by
T.J. (International) Ltd., Cornwall, PL28 8RW

'An insurance contract is one requiring the utmost good faith on the part of both parties.'

CONTENTS

1

Dead Slow in the Temple

Mr Hammersley came up from the depths of Temple Station into the grey wintry bleakness of the Embankment. Red neon signs across the river glowed smudgily through the mist which hung like a pall over the Thames. The mast and funnel of the training ship *Wellington* stuck up through the fog like a gaunt icy finger and thumb, cocking a snook at the world in general and him in particular. A tug, nosing its way up-river on the flood tide, hooted mournfully, and Mr Hammersley shuddered. There was a bleakness in his heart which matched the weather.

The bright lights of the snack bar at the entrance to the station attracted his attention, and he pushed his way through the swing doors into the steamy interior. The smell of the sausages, onions, and coffee made his mouth water. He ordered a coffee and a hamburger, made his way over to a high stool in the corner, and there, whilst consuming his refreshments, considered the implications of the threatening missive now reposing in his wallet.

Charles Hammersley was a short, plumpish, round-faced gentleman who eked out his sight through a rather ancient pair of National Health glasses. It may have been a trick of the lenses, but the grey, watery eyes wore a slightly bewildered expression which seemed to convey that life to him was full of faint surprise, and gave the impression that he was doing his pathetic best at great odds – although privately he considered he was one of the Jacks who were all right.

The letter which had arrived by that morning's post had nevertheless come as a great shock to his nervous system. He had read it and re-read it a dozen times during the morning without arriving at a satisfactory solution as to the sender. At first he had been inclined to throw it in the garbage bin but had had second thoughts. Was it a hoax, the humour of which escaped him? Knowing what he knew about himself, he doubted it, and possibly that was why the more he re-examined the letter the more conscious was he of the little pulse of alarm in his throat, of the slight constricting of his chest muscles. In all his forty-five years he had never failed to heed those warning signals. And so, far from throwing the letter away, as the afternoon came around he found himself actually carrying out its instructions, catching a train at Mortlake for Waterloo in good time for his appointment.

The warmth from the coffee urns and the appetizing smell of the pans of food on the hot-plate thawed him out a little, and with the advent of animal comfort the iciness in his heart melted until it was almost difficult to believe his equilibrium had been so profoundly disturbed.

He felt for his wallet and once again got out the letter. He examined the envelope carefully under the glare of the strip lighting. The paper was of good quality, but the imprint of a firm or company had been either scratched out with a sharp penknife, or erased with a hard ink rubber, from the flap. The address was typed, as was the letter itself, and above the address was an official 'Postage Due' stamp. The latter point rankled. Having to pay double postage for the doubtful privilege of receiving a threat seemed the height of indignity.

He extracted the actual letter, holding it carefully by one corner, and flipped it open disdainfully. It was typed on a sheet of quarto typing paper, and read:

'My Dear Hammersley (I address you thus because I know how you hate being called Charlie)

'If you wish to hear something to your disadvantage (as our clever legal eagles say) meet me in the Inner Temple, at the top of the steps leading to the fountain in Fountain

13

Court, at 3 P.M. today.

'Doubtless you will debouch from Temple Station in good time so as not to keep me waiting: I loathe being kept waiting. I suggest you proceed through Temple Gardens, dwell for a moment at the statue of that awfully brainy chap, John Stuart Mill (no *s*, you notice), cross over to Milford Lane, pass through the wrought-iron gate and so to Garden Court ("There is a door through which I cannot see" – although you can see through this one, of course), up the first flight of stone steps to the lawns on the right, and so to the second flight which leads to Fountain Court.

'I shall be there.

'Even if you *don't* want to hear something to your disadvantage, you will nevertheless meet me there as directed.

'Yours very sincerely,
Simon Good.'

The signature, flamboyantly executed in green ink, was further embellished with an extrovert flourish.

Simon Good? He knew no Simon Good. The name meant absolutely nothing to him, although he had a vague feeling that the *style* of the letter was familiar, that there was something about it which should give him a clue as to the writer, and yet the answer eluded him. It was most irritating.

He bit off a mouthful of hamburger and chewed thoughtfully. So Mr Simon Good, whoever he might be, intended to watch his victim's approach to the rendezvous from the vantage point of comparative height, the top of the steps. Well, well! Too many people had done too many things to Charles Hammersley as from a great height for him to be caught that way again.

He was now feeling more at ease, the effect of the coffee and the lingering savoury flavour of the snack had given him a sense of well-being. He glanced at his watch – 2.30 p.m. Plenty of time. Brushing the crumbs from his lips, he got down, pushed his way past some chattering typists, and went once more into the bleakness of the afternoon.

At one end of Temple Gardens, adjacent to the Underground Station, there is a large illuminated map-and-guide to the locality, provided by a benevolent Local Authority. To this Mr Hammersley made his way. He turned the knob at the side and brought up to his own eye level the area containing the Temple, and studied it carefully.

The scale of the map was rather too small to show all the intricacies of the Temple's alleyways and buildings, some old, some new, some with the mellowness of a more gracious age, some with the stark look of post-war rebuilding, but the plan was large enough to confirm what he had in mind.

Those who know the Temple and its environs will be aware that Fountain Court can be approached either from the foot of Milford Lane, in which case one passes through the Temple car park to Garden Court (O where are thy fig trees now?), up some steps, past the lawns on the right, and up a broad flight of fifteen steps (by all means count them if you wish) to the southern aspect of the court; or, alternatively, by walking some two hundred yards farther along the Embankment it is possible to proceed up the gentle incline of Middle Temple Lane until one reaches the eastern side of the court, well away from the actual fountain. Further, by skirting this side of the rectangle, one can reach Brick Court, and pass through an old covered passageway into New Court, which abuts directly on the northern exit of Fountain Court.

The suggestion in the letter was for Hammersley to approach the fountain from the south, up the flight of fifteen steps aforementioned, apparently so that he would be under observation. For all his outward mildness, however, he was a calculating man, and in spite of the 'do-it-or-else' tone of the letter, he decided to carry out a right-flanking movement and to approach from the north, thus possibly being able to observe the observer. Mr Hammersley was not without military experience – if only in the role of batman.

He felt for a cigarette, lit it, and flipped the match expertly into a near-by litter basket. Then settling his scarf more comfortably round his neck to keep out the damp and fog – he enjoyed his creature comforts – he turned right on to the Embankment and proceeded purposefully along to the gateway to Middle Temple Lane.

Now that he had settled on a plan of attack, the neon signs across the river took on a positively friendly look through the damp, yellowy mist. The tower with its glowing red OXO literally emanated warmth, as did a sky sign for somebody-or-other's Ale.

Turning left under the arch, he made his way up the easy gradient of Middle Temple Lane until he drew level with the stone posts at the eastern boundary of Fountain Court. At this higher level the fog was rather thinner on the ground, although the yellow pall overhead cut off what wintry daylight there was and necessitated the lighting of the street lamps.

He peered cautiously towards the fountain. A splodge of light from an octagonal lamp threw into hazy relief the thick bole of a tree with its skeletal branches. It was just possible to see the stone edging of the round pond into which the fountain plashed gently.

He scanned the wide area very carefully. Occasionally a hunched figure scuttered through the nimbus of light to be swallowed up again by the fog wraiths. So far, nobody appeared to be waiting to make a rendezvous with him; everyone was more intent on reaching the fuggy warmth of the chambers and offices which surrounded that fog-blanketed smokeless zone.

He was momentarily tempted to move farther in to make a closer examination, but a certain military caution, instilled so long ago now as to be almost an atavism, held him back in the shadows. Two could play at waiting and he was in no hurry. Lack of movement, however, soon caused the chill to seep into his bones, freezing the very marrow. He stamped his feet and rubbed his hands to restore the circulation, and then decided to walk a little farther up Middle Temple Lane and back, lighting another cigarette on the way.

A vagrant breeze crept hesitantly round from Pump Court, driving the fog before it so that it moved first in one direction and then another in a vain endeavour to escape. The lights from the traffic in Fleet Street were just visible through the ancient archway at the top of the lane. At times he could make out the DEAD SLOW traffic notice painted on the wall, and he wondered cynically if this could be descriptive rather than a command.

Finishing his cigarette, he tossed the butt away in a glowing arc, and strode back briskly to the north-eastern corner of Fountain Court, and at this point his caution returned.

The fog was thinner, and the lights from the hotch-potch of buildings at the western end were discernible in warm, comforting diffusion.

A stillness had descended. Even the crumpled newspaper placard which had drifted limply down the lane from the news-vendor at Temple Bar was now a damp, exhausted mass in the gutter; and the incautious zephyr which had urged it thither was a forgotten sigh which had stilled itself suddenly because of the enormity of its indiscretion at the seats of the mighty. Like an indelicate belch at the Lord Mayor's Banquet.

Nothing stirred in Fountain Court. The water of the fountain no longer tinkled – a couple of turns of a stopcock had cut off the fairy music. From his vantage point Hammersley carefully searched the gloom for any movement, but a nightmarish stillness pervaded everywhere. Although the lights from the surrounding offices cast a certain amount of warmth over the scene, there appeared to be no movement within. And there was certainly no movement without. The legal brotherhood was sleeping peacefully, taking advantage of the blanket of fog.

DEAD SLOW! Oh yes, it was descriptive,

all right! But, he ruminated grimly, the legal brotherhood often appeared to be sleeping peacefully, and when you yourself woke from a deep miasma of false security you found the Statute of 1677 was there all the time, and the Law in all its majesty sat up, yawned, and sent you down for another couple of years.

The Law Courts' clock chimed out the quarters and reluctantly struck three o'clock. If anything, Hammersley relaxed a little, although at the back of his deceptively mild eyes there lurked the glint of an animal at bay. Well, here he was at the appointed hour, within a stone's throw of the rendez-vous, and there was not a soul in sight to meet him. Was it a hoax?

Ice-cold maggots suddenly wriggled up his spine and settled uncomfortably in the nape of his neck. From the smudgy shadow of the bole of a lofty plane tree, a mere twenty paces away in the middle of the court, a large man emerged and drifted over towards the steps that led down by the lawns. As the figure passed within range of a lamp bracketed high on the corner of one of the buildings Hammersley noted the trilby hat tilted at an outrageous angle, noted the well-set shoulders and lack of greatcoat in spite of the raw cold. And as the shape was swallowed up in the maw of the fog, there was something about the walk that was disturbingly reminiscent of – *what?*

Was this the keeper of the rendezvous? He searched his memory back over the years for a clue, but remained baffled. Simon Good. Simon Good. The name didn't ring a bell. But the little sensory warning flutter remained. No, it wasn't a hoax. He was dealing with a coldly calculating somebody who had found out, somebody who knew his secret, not officialdom, for this was not the approach of an official.

He carried out another rapid flanking movement. By retracing his steps to Brick Court and thence to Essex Court, he could pass through the old covered passage into tiny New Court, whose six or seven steps led back down into the north-west corner of Fountain Court. He would thus be nearer, and behind, his adversary – adversary? – and gain the vantage, as all good flanking movements did, without sweat and toil and loss of blood, and Mr Hammersley was all for this.

He broke into a discreet trot, feeling he was desecrating the sanctuary of the dozing Temple. Whipping round through Essex Court, he cut through the draughty little passage, debouched into New Court, and took what little cover there was behind an old wrought-iron lamp standard at the top of the steps. His eyes searched keenly beyond the fountain for the figure of his unknown quarry. Although the fog was thinner, the natural light was failing, and the halo cast from the lamp immediately above him made visibility beyond that point almost as difficult as when the fog was at its height. He fancied he could make out a dim, indeterminate form over to the right of the fountain.

And then that warning pulse suddenly fluttered in his throat as a sixth sense impelled him to whip round a fraction of a second before a well-modulated voice said:

'My dear Hammersley!'

Speechless, he gazed up incredulously into the smiling eyes of the vibrant character beside him.

'Major Meek!' he gasped at length. 'I thought you were dead!'

The taller man smiled tolerantly.

'And why should you think that?' he inquired.

'That afternoon at Hondschouwen–' (such was the power of teaching by numbers that Hammersley almost automatically added 'sir') '–we all thought you'd bought it immediately after you liquidated those two Spandau nests, up the road from the factory we were supposed to be occupying. We saw you give chase to a man who made for a truck, and just after you vanished over the brow of the hill there was an almighty explosion, and, so far as we knew, you'd had it. And after the war, I heard you'd been awarded a French decoration, post-post–'

'By post?'

'Posthumorously – if that's the right word.'

'It isn't, and you know it isn't, but never mind. Still the same old Hammersley, posing as the half-educated moron, bluffing your way along just like you used to when you were my batman. I'm willing to wager you live in a luxury flat filled with Picassos and Henry Moores. Am I right?'

Hammersley wasn't listening, he was peering round over his shoulder at the figure near the top of the steps. It appeared to be a young woman in a light macintosh.

'You seem very jumpy, Hammersley,' said the other, watching him closely.

'I thought you were dead, I didn't expect to see you.'

'I can appreciate that. But now that you have seen me, what about a cup of tea?'

'I'm – I'm waiting– I'm meeting someone here.'

'Ah! Do I detect a romance? An assignation? A woman? The young lady over there by the fountain?'

'Woman my foot!' was the indignant rejoinder. 'You know me!'

'Yes, I know you.' The tone was very gentle. 'Rather better than you imagine. And I also know when I'm not wanted.'

'Well, it's not like that,' said Hammersley uncomfortably. 'I'd like to have a talk about old times, over a cup of tea, but it's – well, it's just not convenient at this moment.

Some other time, perhaps. I'm supposed to be meeting someone here at three o'clock. Business.'

'Here? At this point? Behind this lamp standard?'

'Well, not exactly here – over there, at the top of the steps.'

'Over by the young lady?'

'Yes.'

'Extraordinary! Then why peep through all this wrought-iron work over here?'

'Well, I was...' Hammersley's voice trailed off.

'If you ask me, Charlie, you were carrying out a flanking movement.'

'In a way, yes, I suppose I was,' confessed the other.

'Just as I thought you would,' said Major Meek.

'As you thought I would?'

'Yes, that was why I was able to come up behind you. Clever anticipation. I wanted to see what sort of a customer you'd grown up into. You got my letter, of course?'

Hammersley's jaw dropped and sheer dis-belief sparked in his eyes. 'You!' he managed to jerk. 'But the letter was signed–'

The other doffed his hat in an old-world bow.

'Yes. Me. You see before you Simon Good.' The hat was replaced with a flourish. 'Peter Meek – rest his soul – went up, or down, with the explosion you just recalled. Best part of the road went up, too, as I went over the brow of the hill that day, blazing away like a lunatic, with a Bren at the hip position. Must have been mad. Good job there were no stoppages, I could never remember what to do when. If ever the brutal soldiery asked me, I used to inform them that that was the subject of a later lecture. It was a tip I picked up on an ABCA course.'

Hammersley's eyes glinted with the excitement of recollection, and a certain amount of relief flooded his being. This was some form of a joke, after all! His warning system had gone astray for once. Words began to tumble out excitedly.

'I can see you even now,' he rattled, 'you lit your pipe first – do you remember? And you said "Well, chaps, we're almost out of ammo, and unless we silence those two Spandau nests, we've had it – not that there's much future in anything else anyway." And Sergeant – what was his name? Lake? Blake? Yes, that's right, Blake – started to sing "You'll get no promotion this side of the ocean..." And you said "You'll get none the other side, either!"'

'I said that?' said Simon Good, in mild surprise.

'You did,' said Hammersley, his eyes still gleaming, 'and you said it as if you meant it. But what happened to you? I remember you lit your pipe, stuck the Bren at the hip position – an awkward position, if ever there was one – said cheerio, and walked straight up the middle of the road into the astonished fire of those Spandaus. You didn't open up until you were almost on them. How they never hit you, I just don't know – it was miraculous. We saw you silence both guns and then vanish over the brow of the hill, still blazing away like fury. A couple of seconds later the whole landscape was thrown up into the air in one awful shattering roar. Upset me quite a bit.' The mild, grey eyes filmed over momentarily. 'I thought you'd bought a dozen Teller mines and they hadn't wrapped them up very well. Sergeant Blake ordered us forward, we found the Spandau teams knocked out, and over the ridge there were half a dozen craters filling in with flood water from some German-engineered inundations. But you'd disappeared. And whilst we were looking for you, the tide of war swept on and we were ordered to join some armour and task troops who were pursuing the retreating enemy column. Where on earth did you get to?'

Simon Good considered.

'I went over that ridge firing blindly. There's something about an automatic weapon – once you squeeze the trigger and get the feel of the thing, you're very reluctant to stop firing until it jams up or, to your surprise, the ammunition runs out. I once saw a bloke firing an Oerlikon at a gunnery practice at Severn Beach, and instead of taking it in bursts, he kept his thumbs on the firing plate, and the gun ran away with him. The barrel went through ninety degrees over his head, showering shells up like a firework display. He nearly broke his back trying to hold it. And all he had to do was to take his thumbs off the firing plate. The Naval Officer in charge nearly tore his hair out. And the plane towing the target belted off over the Severn to South Wales and was never seen again. Just shows you. Never carry an automatic, Hammersley.'

'I can assure you I don't,' said the other, 'but you still haven't told me what happened.'

'Pardon the digression. One of the crew of the left-hand Spandau broke cover, made for a truck parked off the road, hopped in, started to back it in a quick turn, and went slap over a mine. Either it was linked to others straddling the road, or they went off in sympathetic detonation. For a few moments I didn't know whether it was Wednesday or Piccadilly. When the noise died down and the smoke cleared a little, I found, to my astonishment, that I was still standing. The Bren was as heavy as lead, it was covered with mud and slime, and the barrel was draped with weeds. I remember cursing long and loud because, of all things, the bowl of my pipe had gone, and I was just sucking the stem. For a while I didn't know what I was doing, I was lucky to be alive, standing up in the middle of it all. Funny how one reacts, I bent down and started to grope around for the bowl of my pipe! And, curiously enough in all that chaos, I found it. I've still got it. I stuffed it into my pocket and staggered off the road half dazed, until I sank exhausted in the cover of some partly submerged bushes at the very edge of the floods. And then I passed out. It's a wonder I wasn't drowned.

'And as you so aptly put it, the tide of war passed on. I was left, poor little me, alone, dreaming blissfully of home and other impossible things – like promotion to Lt-Colonel – so you can imagine what a rude awakening it was when I came round and found that even the war had passed me over. There was I doing heroic deeds, and as soon as I took my eye off the ball for a few seconds, the very war itself rushed off somewhere else, ignoring me completely. Most annoying.

'I sat there nursing my resentment up to fever heat, and suddenly I found myself blaming everything on to my *name*. Meek! *Meek!* A name like that always conjured up the wrong sort of image of me, and so I never got anywhere in life. That was how it presented itself to me at that moment.'

'You must have been round the bend,' said Hammersley.

'Maybe, but nevertheless I decided to discard the name of Peter Meek for ever, and then was as good a time as any to do it. Identity discs went straight into the swamp. All other means of identification had been handed in before we went out on that particular operation, as you probably remember, and amnesia did the rest. It took me a couple of days to catch up with the war which was running away from me as fast as it could go up into N.W. Europe.

'I dwelt a lot on what to rename myself. "Peter" – "a rock" – had never gone well with "Meek", and as I've said, I didn't like "Meek" anyway. And then for no apparent reason through my head went the biblical phrase "Simon called Peter". Why not "Peter called Simon"? I rather took to the name.'

'But why Simon *Good?*' queried Hammersley.

'Because I decided that unless things turned out my way in future, I was going to be an utter rogue – within limits – and like so many other people, take what I wanted. And "Good" seemed to fit the bill.'

'You certainly *were* round the bend.'

'Why? If one intends henceforth to be an utter rogue, it seems fairly sound to start by changing one's name. Don't you agree?'

'Could be,' agreed Mr Hammersley. 'Of

course, I remember you were always anxious for advancement, even in those far-off days. I couldn't fathom what your worry was, I was quite happy as a mere batman. I should have thought you had plenty of opportunity to demonstrate your ego without this crazy talk of changed names and roguery. Tell me, is all this some kind of a joke?'

'For me, yes,' said Simon Good, lighting a cigarette. 'For you,' he added, between puffs, 'no.'

'Then perhaps you would be kind enough to let me into the secret,' said Mr Hammersley, with dignity. 'I am not without a sense of humour.'

'I know that!' replied Simon Good quickly. 'Oh, yes, I know that! I, too, am not without a sense of humour.'

'And does your brand of humour include not putting stamps on your letters? Or was that accidental?'

'Oh, no! Quite intentional.'

'But why no stamp? Surely it's a small enough thing to do when one is writing to an old friend to make an appointment to talk over old times?'

Good regarded him with amusement.

'I would like to take you up on those points in the reverse order,' he said gently. 'First of all, I don't want to talk about *old* times – I want to discuss present times. Secondly, when we've talked about present times, I don't think we'll be old friends. Thirdly, for those very reasons, I wanted to be certain you received my letter. So I didn't stamp it.'

'Are you sure you're feeling all right?' queried the other anxiously. 'You wanted me to get your letter so you didn't stamp it. I should have thought it would have been preferable to register it.'

'At the present exorbitant rates? Not on your Nellie, as the vulgar are apt to say. No, Hammersley, the cheapest and safest way to ensure a letter reaching its destination is *not* to put a stamp on it. The Postal Authorities then guard it like mother hawks. They pass it lovingly from official to official, never losing sight of it for one moment. A few coppers are owing to the Inland Revenue, and public criticism is always set strongly against public waste. And so they detail a special man to look after it, to deliver it personally, to see who this mean recipient is whose friends don't put stamps on letters, to see if he will be so very mean as to refuse to pay, after all the loving care they have bestowed upon it.'

'They do all that?' said Mr Hammersley incredulously.

'They do all that,' said Simon Good.

'It just shows you the lengths some people will go to,' said the other obliquely.

'How right you are,' agreed Simon Good, gazing steadily at him. 'There are no lengths to which some people *won't* go.'

His measured tones seemed to imply a special meaning to Mr Charles Hammersley. 'You're not hinting at me, are you?' he jerked.

'And *you* were not by any remote chance referring to *me?*' countered Mr Good.

'I was referring to the Postal Authorities,' said Hammersley indignantly.

'Well, of course, if you've any reason for dissatisfaction you can always refer the matter to the Postmaster-General.'

Hammersley's alarm system was now working overtime. The talk was too smooth and was leading nowhere, anywhere. He was beginning to feel very chilly again, and the fog was in his throat.

'I once complained to the P.M.G. about the high registration rates,' went on the other. 'The Appropriate Department replied. Most polite. They couldn't do anything about it, of course. So for important letters I now use the special Postage Due Service. Cheaper than Registration, and not liable to be stolen like the registered mail. And something of a personal service, I feel. Of course, it works out a little more expensive for the recipient, but I don't really mind that.'

'I must remember all you've told me when I send you a Christmas card,' said Mr Hammersley coldly.

'When you hear what I have to say, you won't want to send me a card of any kind – other than one inscribed with "R.I.P.".'

'I'm beginning to think that Teller mine took its toll after all,' said Hammersley carefully. 'You *are* round the bend. And halfway round the next.'

'You think so?' Simon Good smiled tolerantly, but there was little humour in his eyes. And running parallel with the banter was a steely overtone which Hammersley didn't fail to note. 'If it's anything to go by, I'm as sane as you are, but twice as big a rogue. We're going to get along together famously.'

'*We* are?'

'Yes. What are you doing for a living at the moment?'

'I'm – I'm–' (Why should I even consider answering such a question, thought Mr Hammersley. Who's Peter Meek, or Simon Good, or whatever he calls himself? I might have been his batman once upon a time, but all that has faded into limbo. Without his uniform he's just another civilian with no more than equal rights. To the devil with Peter Meek!)

'You were saying–?'

Hammersley quailed before those mocking eyes, and words rose unbidden to his lips. 'I'm – I'm connected with Insurance.'

'Connected? You mean – *in* Insurance?'

'Well – in a manner of speaking.'

'You don't mean that you are an inspector, or an agent, or that you work in an office, do you?'

'No – oh, no. When I came out of the Army, I put all my savings and my gratuity into the business. A man I knew in the City advised me to. He told me insurance was a good business to be in provided you didn't do insurance.'

'Come again.'

'Well, for example, if you're an insurance broker, you earn your money *from* insurance, but you don't *do* insurance. You've got responsibility but no *lia*bility.'

'And you are an insurance broker?'

'Well, no.'

'Then may I ask how you manage to live, if it's not a personal question?'

'You may, and it is. I live on – er – the dividends from my investments.'

'You might say, then, a man of independent means?'

'You could put it like that, I suppose,' said Mr Hammersley doubtfully.

'You know, Charlie, even as a batman you were fond of gracious living.'

'I did my best to share with you what little gracious living I could acquire in those dark days,' said Hammersley.

'As you will continue to share with me in these even less enlightened days,' responded Simon Good. 'You must be in a better position to do that now, than say before the war, when you travelled Europe in a circus.'

Hammersley's mouth and tongue went dry.

34

'Cir-circus?' he stammered.

'Yes, circus, don't you remember telling me? You were a little tiddly at the time, I think you'd been at my whisky allowance. I haven't betrayed your secret to a living soul, I have regarded the confidences made to me as an officer and a gentleman with all the solemnity of the confessional. You told me you travelled in a contortionist act before the war. What you didn't tell me was how you could dislocate your shoulder at will, and how you had dislocated it regularly in the four units you had been in before you came to us – presumably to avoid irksome guard duties and fatigues. I discovered *that* part of it quite by chance when looking through your posting papers a couple of days after your alcoholic reminiscences. I didn't split because you were too good a batman for me to lose, but I often laughed myself silly in the long watches of the night.'

Charles Hammersley tried to say something, but the fog seemed to be suffocating him.

'You might almost say,' continued Simon Good remorselessly, 'that you've got to be something of a contortionist to get anything out of an insurance company.'

'Oh, I don't know,' gulped the other, 'insurance is a bit of a gamble anyway.'

'Not the way you do it – the insurance

companies can't win.'

'I think I could do with a cup of tea after all,' said Hammersley abruptly.

'Yes, you do look a little pale – probably the shock of seeing your old O.C. alive and well when you thought he was dead. Hot sweet tea, they say. There's a nice little place in Devereux Court. Come along, I'll show you. The legal fraternity use it quite a bit – if we get stuck on any fine points of law, they may be able to help us out.'

2

Utmost Good Faith

Mr Hammersley's knowledge of insurance was in certain respects rudimentary, but he had read somewhere that the comparatively small individual premiums of the many paid for the losses of the few. This, he felt, was a good idea, and his knowledge of first principles never progressed much past this point.

They were soon settled near the fire on the first floor of a comfortable little restaurant which served afternoon tea, each with a cup of steaming liquid before him. The red shaded lights added a touch of intimacy, not that Mr Hammersley wanted any such touch. He fingered the frames of his glasses nervously.

'Perhaps you'll come to the point quickly,' he said, glancing round to see that they were out of earshot of other customers.

'Yes.' Simon Good dropped a couple of knobs of sugar into his tea. 'You were once a contortionist in a circus, and you had the ability apparently to dislocate your shoulder. I gather this wasn't part of the act, you merely could do it amongst your other contortions, and you could perform realistically enough to fool a string of M.O.s during the war. Oh, yes, it was light duties only for Rifleman Charles Hammersley. The manipulative treatment, the massage, the simulated painful after-effects, the valiant endeavours to lift a rifle – all beautifully carried out, until you were practically excused everything except living. And you've been using your peculiar talents since the war to live a life of ease at the expense of a number of insurance companies. Just how many, I don't exactly know. I could find out, but if I took the necessary steps, things would be exceedingly unpleasant for you, to say the least. If you are reasonably co-operative, I will not take those steps.

'The usual Personal Accident policy covers – apart from the capital sums in the event of death, or loss of one or two limbs, or the loss of one or both eyes, or (a rather neat permutation this) one limb and one eye – a hundred-and-four weeks' total disablement benefit at between twelve to sixty pounds per week, depending on the premium paid. It is also possible to obtain modified benefits for partial disablement at a moderate additional premium. You are at present making a claim in respect of total disablement on at least one unsuspecting insurance company. Do I make myself clear, so far?'

Mr Hammersley nodded miserably. Simon Good was making himself all too clear.

'In that case, my dear Charles, it was very naughty of you to keep this appointment with me today. As a totally disabled man you should have kept yourself tucked up in front of the fire in your cosy little flat at Mortlake. The insurance company wouldn't approve of you wandering about in the chill air at their expense. Don't let your tea get cold.' He took a satisfying gulp at his own, 'I gather from certain papers I went out of my way to borrow, that your procedure is to have a fairly long period of total incapacity at the high rate of benefit, followed by a short period of partial incapacity when you struggle manfully to get about your business again. I need hardly point out that the reason for the shortness of this second period is the greatly reduced benefit; and the business you are so keen to get back to seems to be looking for the next company to fleece. Yes, Charlie, you've certainly been living on the fat of the land.'

'I come from a good family,' remarked Mr Hammersley, holding his cup daintily so that his little finger seemed to have no connection with the others, 'and, as you've already remarked, I'm used to gracious living. There's nothing wrong in that, is there?'

'I doubt if the insurance companies would actually foster gracious living by encouraging fraudulent claims.'

'Fraudulent claims!' Mr Hammersley seemed horrified. 'The policy covers incapacity, and when my shoulder is out, I am incapacitated. What's fraudulent about that?'

'The incapacity must be caused accidentally – don't you read the policy conditions?'

'The policies have conditions?' said Mr Hammersley incredulously. 'Well, well!'

'The injury must be caused by violent, accidental, external, and visible means. Yours isn't. It's by manipulation. It's self-inflicted. It's not accidental.'

'It is the way I do it. You should see some of my claim papers!'

'I have. But disablement directly or indirectly due to intentional self-injury is specifically excluded from the policy.'

Mr Hammersley removed his glasses and polished the steam off with his pocket handkerchief.

'Well, now,' he said, 'you have a point

there. If I put my shoulder out, I can just as readily put it back, so there is no self-injury. But if I slip in Oxford Street, as I have done so many times, and my shoulder is put out, and I make no attempt to put it back but leave that to the medical profession, what then? A score of people have seen me fall, and have witnessed my helplessness. A score of people have seen the ambulance take me away. A score of people have seen me at the hospital, and some have even seen the painful treatment I've had to put up with, the manipulation, the massage, the electrical treatment to stimulate the nerves and sinews after inactivity, and the shock – above all, the shock. Primary shock. And secondary shock. A nasty thing, secondary shock. Can last for ages. Very difficult to pin-point. Almost as good as amnesia for a claim.' Mr Hammersley replaced his glasses carefully. 'But sometimes I wonder if it's all worth it.'

Simon Good smiled pleasantly and reached for the ashtray.

'I've listened carefully to all you've had to say,' he said, flipping open a gold cigarette-case and proffering it to the other, 'but I still find there is an intention to defraud, and that is not nice. An insurance contract is *uberrima fides*.'

'You-bury-me-what?' said Hammersley, fascinated.

'*Uberrima fides*. Latin. "Of the utmost

good faith."'

'But I have the utmost good faith,' declared Mr Hammersley. 'I've got good faith in the companies I deal with, I've got absolute faith they all have sufficient funds to pay me with, and I've got the utmost good faith none of them will welsh. In fact, you might say I've got good faith of the very utmost.'

'Unfortunately that's not the sort of good faith Lord Mansfield had in mind when he made his famous utterance about contracts of insurance in *Carter v. Boehm, 1766.*'

Hammersley said doubtfully. '1766? That's a long time ago, isn't it? Surely things have progressed a little since then?'

'You make me wonder. You see, the good faith has to exist on both sides. If you are in possession of facts which might influence an insurer either to increase the rate, or impose certain restrictions, or possibly decline the proposal altogether, then these *facts* must be declared. Conversely, an insurer must not accept premium for a risk he knows no longer exists.'

'I should think not,' agreed the other emphatically.

'Now, for every policy you've taken out you've had to fill in and sign a proposal form. *This* form is the basis of the contract, is incorporated in the contract, and is the very essence of the contract. The contract itself makes that clear. And the declaration you sign on the proposal form states that you have not concealed any circumstance which ought to be communicated to the insurers.'

'But I haven't *concealed* anything,' remarked Mr Hammersley. 'To conceal something is positive. I merely haven't told them, that's negative. And as for the phrase "which *ought* to be communicated to the insurers" – the interpretation is apparently left to me, and if in my ignorance I don't labour the point with the insurers, and then unhappily meet with a chain of painful medical and therapeutical circumstances such as I've just outlined – arising you will note, *accidentally* (usually from a fall in Oxford Street) then who am I to be blamed? The fact that the medical profession incapacitate me in their efforts to put right in a matter of weeks, months, what I can do in three seconds, is not my fault, is it? Especially in these days of pre-cradle to last-post welfare. Who am I to criticize? The legal aspect is not without interest.' Hammersley appeared to be getting into his stride, to be staging a comeback. 'Perhaps some of your law friends would be pleased to express an opinion,' he added daringly.

'I've no doubt they would,' agreed Simon, 'but you wouldn't be pleased to hear it. Tell me, how do you normally answer the question on the form which says "Have you any physical defect or infirmity?"'

'No.'

'You mean you won't tell me?'

'No, I mean I always answer "No".'

Simon raised an eyebrow.

'I can only assume you didn't hear the question,' he said.

'And I can only assume you don't know what a physical defect is,' said Mr Hammersley. 'You see, to me my shoulders are perfectly normal – yours are the defective ones because they're not like mine.'

'Then what about your eyesight? Would not that come within the scope of this question?'

'Eyesight? Never been better!' declared Mr Hammersley stoutly. 'It's got to be good to stand up to these National Health glasses.'

Simon Good permitted himself to chuckle.

'And what about "Have you any other Personal Accident Insurance? If so, state the name of the Insurance Company or Underwriter and the amount insured"? Did you put a truthful answer to this question on every Personal Accident proposal you've ever completed? Be careful how you reply – I may have seen some of the actual forms.'

'But of course! I can assure you the very quintessence of truth went into this answer on every single proposal form.'

This time both of Simon Good's eyebrows shot up.

'Quintessence! And this from a man who pretends never to be able to remember "posthumously"'! Come out from behind those glasses, Hammersley, and tell me the worst. What did you put?'

'I said "No".'

'No. And you call that the very quintessence of truth! How morally decadent we're becoming!'

'Well, it was the truth, as it happened.'

'How could it be? Surely there came a time when it *wasn't* the truth? – when you did have other Personal Accident insurances running concurrently

Mr Hammersley smiled in a superior fashion.

'They're *all* running concurrently,' he said, 'and the answer is very simple. When I originally decided to invest in insurance I took out all the policies with different companies at *exactly the same time*. By so doing, I figured there wouldn't be time for me to appear on the companies' Black Lists, and literally there wasn't any other cover in force because none of it had then so far been accepted. I had to be very careful, because there are well over a hundred companies transacting Personal Accident business, and many are allied, or part of a group, with possibly the same underwriting clerk dealing with proposals coming in to several apparently different companies. It would have been rather awkward if I'd unwittingly sent three or four applications to the same underwriter, wouldn't it? However, an insurance almanac gave me all the information I required, it was well worth the fifteen bob I paid for it. I might tell you the original policies cost me a pretty penny, I could ill-afford it at first because I had to wait a considerable time before I could reasonably have an accident. Of course, things became easier as the benefits became payable. I usually allow a policy to lapse once a company has paid a lengthy claim – that is, I normally renew it once more after the claim is discharged to show there is no ill feeling. In fact, I make a practice of paying for the renewal out of the last payment from the company.'

'There's good faith for you!' said Simon Good.

'That's the way I look at it,' agreed Mr Hammersley. 'After all, you must remember that I've paid, and still do pay, premiums to quite a large number of companies who still regard me as a good risk.'

'Until the proper authorities get to hear about it.'

Charles Hammersley looked shrewdly over the top of his glasses. 'Then you're not the proper authority?' he said. It was more of a statement than a question.

'Would you like another cup of tea?' said Simon.

Hammersley drained his cup. 'I think I would,' he said. 'And I wouldn't mind one of those biscuits wrapped in coloured foil. Over there in the glass case.'

'You shall have one,' promised Simon, snapping his fingers at the waitress. 'Jenny! Two more teas, please. And a couple of Pelicans.'

The waitress brought the teas over, together with two chocolate biscuits on a saucer, and retired once more to her knitting.

Simon unwrapped his Pelican meditatively. 'I wonder what strange quirk induces you to pay out a further year's premium,' he mused. 'It seems unnecessary. Conscience?'

'Good lord, no!' choked Mr Hammersley. 'It's merely a rather fine psychological touch. And I never know when I might really need the cover. I mean, I might meet with an accident that would *prevent* me from dislocating my shoulder, and then I certainly would be in trouble. I might even be faced with having to work for a living.'

'Dreadful!' agreed Simon, in mock horror. 'I take it that if you were compelled to work – I mean, of course, outside any of H.M. Prisons – your occupation would be vastly different from the way you styled yourself on the proposal forms?'

'Yes, I don't know what I'd do if I wasn't a man of independent means,' agreed Hammersley. 'The middle classes – and I am not snob enough to pretend I am more than middle class – living on fixed incomes, have

46

been crippled by taxation, as everybody knows.'

'I don't suppose the tax-man sees much of your money, Charlie. What do you tell *him?*'

'What I tell him is nobody's business.'

'Certainly not yours,' agreed Simon.

'I found the question of fixing an appropriate occupation quite irksome. I thought, first of all, that "Accountant" might be a nice clean sort of profession to put down, I was always accounting for something or the other. But then there was the aspect of being reminded too much of income tax. I then considered being a "Potter". I'm always pottering about. To my dismay, however, potters are Class 3 risks, and Class 3 risks carry double the premium of Class 1 risks. It had, therefore, to be a Class 1 occupation, and it had to be something sufficiently vague to get by the average inquiry that might be made. Something like 'Secretary'. I studied the lists kindly provided by the insurance companies, and finally decided on being a "Factor". In life there are many factors, and I was one of them.'

'So you're a "factor", are you?' mused Simon. 'I've often wondered what factors did for a living. I had no idea they swindled insurance companies. I must confess, however, that it must have required a lot of organization to put your plan into operation.'

'Yes,' agreed Mr Hammersley modestly, 'it

47

did. For obvious reasons all the proposals had to go through different agencies; the agencies had to be far enough apart to avoid the possibility of friendly agents discovering I'd effected cover through more than one of them, and thus starting off an awkward train of inquiry; then there was the choice of precise venue for the accidents, bearing in mind the hospital I was likely to be taken to, or the doctor who might be called.'

'Ah, yes, the doctor! I take it you haven't a regular National Health doctor?'

'But I have!'

'And all your claims go through him?'

'Oh, no, I use him for coughs and colds, and such-like. After all, we pay enough for it. But for serious things, like dislocations, I find you can't beat the private doctor. I must be on the books of dozens of 'em. I first consult them about my catarrh and hay fever. And they usually give me little white tablets with a line down the middle – one to be taken at night and one in the morning – although I've never discovered what the line down the middle was for.'

'And do they do you any good?'

'Most efficacious. In fact, I'm in danger of *not* getting hay fever. I've had to curtail my consumption of the wretched little things. I've got a big jar full of them, at home. If you ever get hay fever, let me know, and I'll send you a year's supply. I've had to start taking sugar because I'm always mixing 'em up with my saccharines.'

'I gather that after "recovering" from one dislocation, and before "suffering" from the next, you make it a practice to have hay fever, or some such allergy?'

'That's right.'

'And I think I see the reason why.'

'You do?'

'I do. On the claim form there's a question regarding when you last received medical attention prior to the accident, and what was the nature of the complaint. The answer is "Hay fever". Or "Catarrh". Very troublesome! "–A regular patient? Well, he hasn't been with me for long, but from what he's told me, he seems to have been exceedingly free from sickness and accident, and has very little use for us sawbones. Although he's had to fall back on us for common or garden hay fever! I suppose we all have our little weaknesses, well, well!" Am I right?'

'Uncannily so. You are very perceptive.'

'Yes. And whilst on the subject of claim forms, there is another question which must cause a man of your peculiar integrity some disquiet. It asks whether you are insured with any other Office for Personal Accident benefits, and if so, to give particulars. What little gem do you put here for an answer?'

'I usually write "Fire Policy No. 09990 with Midland Fire Insurance Co. Ltd, and

Burglary All Risks Policy No. 12340 with Equity & Marine."'

'But that doesn't answer the question.'

'I know. Nothing could be further from the point. But they all accept it as an intelligent answer. It's never failed. They either think I'm very naïve, or that I'm so anxious to put down every policy that I've got that I couldn't possibly have another Personal Accident policy or else I would have put it down. I'm afraid they don't know their business very well. But they've been in it longer than I have, and I wouldn't be presumptuous enough to attempt to put them right. I'm not that sort of a man.' Mr Hammersley toyed with the tinfoil biscuit wrapping, smoothing out the creases, and then starting to make a little boat. He suddenly looked up at Simon Good. 'I still feel we haven't come to the real point,' he said quietly.

'How right you are,' replied the other. 'I know you are very shock prone, and liable to dislocate a shoulder on the slightest provocation, so brace yourself very firmly. Within the next few days you are going to have another "accident" – this time on my behalf. You will be good enough to supply me with a complete list of your insurance – investments, shall we say – and I will advise you which one to claim under for my benefit. Give me the complete list, it will be less embarrassing than if I have to set in

50

motion official inquiries.'

'But I can't make another claim yet!' exclaimed Mr Hammersley in an agonized voice. 'I've already got two going now!'

'Then get three. It will be good practice.'

'But if I make too many claims at once I might get found out!'

'You have been found out.'

'That sounds like blackmail to me!'

'From where I'm sitting it sounds like a fairly steady income.' The bantering tone had fled, the eyes were like granite. 'I gather you are insurance-minded?'

Mr Hammersley shrugged his shoulders miserably. 'I suppose you might say that,' he agreed.

'I do say that. Then regard what you're going to pay me as something in the nature of an insurance premium. At a very moderate rate, too, though there might have to be some upward revision on renewal. We shall see.'

'This is all very disturbing,' said Mr Hammersley.

'It's one of the disadvantages of not changing your name,' commented Mr Good. 'If you had taken that elementary precaution, "Charles Hammersley" wouldn't have stuck out like a sore thumb on a soap plate, and you wouldn't have been detected. Take my case. I'm Simon Good. Nobody knows I'm Peter Meek.'

There was an almost imperceptible silence.

'Except me,' said Mr Hammersley, and his voice was as soft as silk. The silence was more perceptible this time. Long enough for the icicles to form.

'I, too, dislike the word "blackmail",' said Simon Good at length. 'And that sounds very much like blackmail to *me*.'

'From this side of the table,' said Hammersley suavely, 'it sounds like stalemate.'

Simon Good smiled wolfishly. 'How come? Simon Good is Peter Meek. So what? Neither person has done you any harm.'

'Intent to blackmail is not regarded very highly at the Old Bailey.'

'Then I suggest you tell the Recorder your story. He will be very interested.'

Hammersley thought this over for a bit.

'I'm inclined to agree with you,' he said at length. 'Together, we'd make a nice pair of rogues.'

'I'm glad you see it my way. Now we can speak frankly. I take it you are not averse to picking up a bit of money by any means whatever?'

'Anything short of violence.'

'Anything?'

'Well, almost anything. I have a certain code. Some things are just not in the calendar.'

'All very right and proper. Knowing you as I used to, I feel our ethics will dovetail very neatly. We can call ourselves Robin Hoods, robbing the rich to pay the poor. We are the poor. Charity begins at home. But first I must put you on probation.'

'I don't like the sound of that word either,' said Mr Hammersley.

'I want to see how you behave. We'll start with the discipline of your having to bring me a complete list of your insurances. Do you know the Public Record Office?'

'Vaguely. It's in Chancery Lane, isn't it?'

'Yes, at the bottom end, near Fleet Street. Meet me inside the Museum at one-thirty tomorrow.'

'The Museum?' queried Mr Hammersley. 'Where's that?'

'Go to the main gateway in Chancery Lane, and there you will see, either side of the entrance, identical notices tastefully executed in brass, or some such alloy. Read one of them. And then read it again. You will have to, because at first you'll wonder if it quite makes sense. It does, but it's rather on the lines of an old Act which once read "The Board of Guardians will meet on the last Tuesday of each month, unless such day falls on Christmas Day, Boxing Day, or Good Friday". From then on, follow your nose and the arrow, and you'll find yourself in the Museum. You'll have to sign your name on a form at a desk just inside the building, but I'm sure that will present no difficulty. Signing names on forms is your strong point.'

'What sort of a place is it?' asked Hammersley doubtfully.

'It's a small museum containing much of the documentary wealth of the nation. There, history unfolds itself. It reeks of tradition. You will enjoy it. Ask the attendant to direct you to the Magna Carta showcase, and study the information concerning this great document. You will find it most interesting. For example, did you realize that although King John and Robert FitzWalter, to say nothing of six earls, six barons and what-have-you, signed the charter in 1215, it was Henry the Third's re-issue on the 11th February, 1225, which was the final, definitive form of the Charter of Liberties?'

'I must confess I didn't.'

'Then study it, and keep on studying it until I come. I don't want to be seen outside with you. I will make the approach. Don't speak until I speak to you. And above all, be casual. Do you want any more tea?'

'No, thank you.'

'Just as well. It's quite expensive.' Simon Good rose and reached for his hat. He looked round for the waitress. 'Jenny! My friend here will settle the bill. And don't forget,' he said, leaning over close to Hammersley's ear, 'your freedom today depends on Magna Carta. And me.'

With a cheery wave, he was gone...

3

Old Fred When Young

Simon Good left the tea-shop and strode
briskly through the Temple via the Cloisters
to Mitre Court, coming out into the lights
of Fleet Street at the foot of Fetter Lane.
Crossing 'the Street', he proceeded up
Fetter Lane, past the back of the Public
Record Office, to a point where there was
evidence of much new building on either
side of the narrow roadway. He made his
way to a monstrous building which reared
itself up into the fog, a building which he
always regarded with some horror, because
of the cold utility, or futility, of it all. It
seemed to consist of a number of giant
boxes, each containing a larger number of
smaller boxes, each containing yet a larger
number of smaller clerks, each and all with
their lives tucked away in still smaller boxes.
Too horrible to contemplate for more than
a few seconds at a time. He paused for a
moment to buy a newspaper from Old Fred
at the main entrance to this building.

'Old Fred' had sold papers, man and boy,
from a convenient nook in the pre-war

building before it had been razed to the ground in the blitz; he had sold them from the brick wall of the bomb-site which at one time was seemingly never to be cleared; and now he carried on business from a niche in the architecture of the modern building, a niche which was never designed for the sale of newspapers. The curious thing was that nobody objected to Old Fred's crude shelter – a cunningly adapted orange-box covered with roofing felt – which he somehow managed to make stay put against the building in inclement weather, although obviously the architects had made no allowance for it in their original plans. It was equally obvious that the outstretched arms of the plump and inadequately dressed female figure in Epŏg Jebstein's 'Nuclear Age' – a symbolic poem in stone incorporated in the main entrance – were not designed to accommodate the surplus midday racing editions, although mylady's lap was considered by the van-boys to be fair game for the Late Night Finals.

Presumably Old Fred once had a surname, but nobody knew what it was. It was lost in obscurity. It was doubtful if he knew it himself, although he remembered Gamage's when it was just a little shop at the mouth of Leather Lane. He had even appeared in a television panel game merely as 'Fred', and he had walked away with a considerable cash prize because he had well and truly baffled the experts. He had achieved this by giving the wrong answer to his conception of every question, and the panel remain utterly foxed to this day.

Simon Good glanced at the headlines and the stop-press. 'What's new, Fred?' he asked.

Old Fred inclined his head conspiratorially. 'That 'orse I mentioned, guv'nor – didn't come up.'

'I said what's new?'

'Now you've bought a paper, I'll tell yer. Nuffing. No satellites. No plane crashes. No murders. Nuffing. Except p'r'aps that wealthy South African bloke – what's 'is name – van Meyer, has had his diamonds pinched. Forty farsand pounds' worth – so it says 'ere. Serves 'im right, shouldn't 'ave that much money to play arahnd wiv. 'E's a nasty bit o' work by all accounts. I expect they're insured anyway – 'e's probably making a packet on the insurance.'

'I expect you're right,' agreed Simon, and passed into the brightly lit vestibule of the new office block.

A large man standing casually at the cigarette kiosk to the right of the entrance hurriedly stuffed a packet of Player's into his pocket, grabbed his change, and moved swiftly through the plate-glass doors in Simon's wake. In the vestibule he paused uncertainly. On one hand, two automatic lifts were at different floors on their way up; on the other, the indicators told of one lift in the sub-basement, and the other stationary at the eighth floor. The mock-marble stairways were empty. The vestibule was almost devoid of people, it was certainly devoid of Simon Good. Two clerks, slipping out for a cup of tea through the staff door of bank premises on the right, glanced at the large man quizzically, wondering if they could help him, but before they reached him he had turned tail and was out once more in Fetter Lane. Moving over to Old Fred, he produced sixpence and asked for a late *News*.

'Do you know that man?' he asked casually, holding out his hand for the change.

Old Fred looked up swiftly. 'What man?'

'The man you were chatting to a moment ago. Bought a paper and then went into this building.'

Fred thought for a moment. 'I don't *know* 'im, guv. I seen 'im abaht.'

The large man gazed at him speculatively. His eyes were cold and steady. 'Do you know who *I* am?' he asked.

Fred flicked an all-embracing eye over the other. 'I don't know 'oo you are,' he rasped, 'but from yer build, yer looks, and the size of yer boots, I know *what* you are.'

'Right! Tell me all you know about the man who just bought a paper.'

'Like I said. I seen 'im abaht. Going into

the building.'

'And where else?'

'Coming aht agin.'

'Does he work there?'

'I wouldn't know, guv. I don't ask no questions. I might ask the wrong bloke the wrong question at the wrong time and get kicked orf me site. Before the war I used to pay a bob a year – sort of grahnd rent – but since this new building's bin up nobody's asked me for it and I ain't paid it. I kind of think we're foxing each other, and when I reaches the Age of Retirement and goes down to me Stately 'Ome in Sussex, I don't reckon they'll let anyone else 'ave this pitch. But I got me roots 'ere, see? And I feels they respect me, and I ain't one for abusing a privilege. So, like I said, I don't ask no questions.'

The other listened patiently. 'Do you *think* he works in there, then?'

'I try not to think, it 'urts me 'ead, and I get brainstorms, and then everybody's upset.'

'Does he buy his papers from you regularly?'

'On and orf.'

'As the fancy takes him? Not regularly?'

'More or less.'

'For how long, more or less on and off?'

'Cor stone the crows, guv, don't tie me up. I'll be giving customers the wrong change, and then you'll 'ave me for fraud.'

'For how long,' persisted the other.

59

'I don't rightly remember, guv, honest.'

'Days? Months? Years?'

'Listen, guv. I don't worry abaht for how long 'ave I 'ad this customer or that – all I worry abaht is 'ow many coppers I've got in that there bowl at the end of the day. I'm just a lily of the field, as yer might say, without a flipping care in the world, toiling not nor spinning, as me old Sunday School teacher used to say.' The rheumy old eyes glazed over for a moment. 'When I was a lad I used to go to a little chapel orf Lamb's Conduit Street. 'Ad a boys' camp in the Isle of Wight in the summer. Them were the good old days. I takes me hat orf to the geezers that used ter run that chapel, they did what they could for us poor little perishers. All kicks and no ha'pence.' He expertly flicked a paper into a neat fold and thrust it into the hand of a customer. The coppers were flung into the wooden bowl which served as a till. 'No, guv, at my age you don't look for trouble, you just live from day to day.'

'You've certainly done that all right – for the last hundred years or so, I should guess!'

'Maybe you ain't so far out at that! I remember when the Old Bell in Holborn was all red geraniums and white posts and chains–'

'And yet you don't remember how long that fellow has been going in and out of this building?'

'No, that's right. Me memory's not so good as it was. Funny, I can remember things that 'appened sixty, seventy year ago, and yet orften I can't remember things that 'appened last week. Rummy, ain't it? And even the Old Bell's gorn, now. But that bloke can't have been going in and out all that time, can he? The building ain't been up that long, and 'e certainly didn't work on the bomb-site, if you get my meaning.'

A flicker of annoyance crossed the other's face. Of course, this particular office block was part of the City's rebuilding scheme, and had only been occupied a matter of – months? Even now it was obvious that parts were not yet fully equipped.

'Did he buy papers from you at this point before the new building went up?'

'You didn't ask that before,' said Fred quickly.

'I'm asking you now. Did he?'

Another paper flashed out and more coppers rattled into the bowl.

'You've been very helpful,' said the large man. Fred missed the delicate nuance.

'I always aim to please,' he said. 'After all, what's life if you can't 'elp each other at times? Nuffing!'

'I'll remember you,' said the other, turning away.

'I bet you won't ever forgit me,' agreed Fred, his mind leap-frogging back to the days in Sidmouth Street, King's Cross, when he enjoyed removing policemen's helmets by stretching string head-high over the pavement to a convenient lamp-post.

4

Transmogrification of a Major

There was nothing miraculous in the way Simon Good had vanished from the vestibule a few minutes previously. Blissfully unaware that he had excited the interest of the large man who was now striding down towards Fleet Street, he had just managed to dive through the closing doors of one of the automatic lifts and had been whisked up to the third floor almost before the other had made up his mind to enter the building.

Proceeding along one of the corridors, he came to a room with 'Guarantee & Reinsurance Department (World-wide)' emblazoned in gold-leaf lettering on the door. He paused for a moment, irresolutely. Anyone observing him closely would have noticed a subtle change come over him. The flamboyancy of the man outside the office seemed to drain away and leave a tired, bored husk of something that had once promised brilliance but had had the glitter knocked off. He pushed the door open, and with a feeling almost of revulsion, passed through into the humdrum atmosphere of the room where he once more became a very small cog in a very large wheel.

The pneumatic arm shut the door behind him with a slight hiss. He glanced quickly round the room, where a number of people were working at separate desks, for the offices of the Tyburn & New York Insurance Company, Ltd, were furnished American style. Unobtrusively putting his hat on a peg, he made his way over to a desk in the corner by the window.

'Simon – the G.M. wants you,' said Pemberthy, glancing up from his work.

Simon stopped in his tracks. 'Wants *me?* The General Manager?'

'Yes,' chipped in young Jim Laker, the departmental junior. 'Promotion at last, I shouldn't think.' He was something of a cynic.

'Wonder what he wants? Did he buzz or ring?'

'Came through on the internal phone. Laker answered it.'

'What did he say, Jim?'

'Actually he wanted His Moronic Highness.' (His Moronic Highness was the Head of Department – Mr Moran.) 'I told him he was away ill, suffering, unfortunately, with

63

nothing more serious than a severe chill, and then he asked for you.'

'How long ago was this?'

'Just now – a few minutes ago.'

'Where was I?'

'Fixing some reinsurances in the City. That's what I told him. I don't know if that answers your question.'

'Pretty good, Jim. You ought to go far. Probably as far as the Old Bailey. Did he ask how long I'd be?'

'No, but he asked what time you went out.'

'And you said?'

'I told him we expected you back at any moment.'

'Thank you. I'm afraid it will be the Old Bailey.'

Jane Seymour, one of the specialist typists the department possessed, was busy with cups and saucers in a partially concealed corner behind some filing cabinets. 'Don't be long, Simon,' she called over her shoulder. 'I've made the tea.'

'I'll tell the General Manager not to keep me,' promised Simon. 'Did he give you any inkling of what he wanted, Jim?'

'He started to say something about the new Global Reinsurance Treaty, and then he changed his mind, and said to tell you to come up and see him as soon as you returned.'

'Oh!' Simon started for the door. 'Keep the pot warm, Jane, my love.'

'I expect you've already had a cup of tea while you were out "fixing up the reinsurances",' said Miss Seymour primly. 'We've been waiting for ours till you came back.'

'I've actually had *two* cups,' corrected Simon. 'However, I pay you an exorbitant sum weekly for two cups per day of very indifferent liquid, and I intend to get value for money.'

'You get your fair whack,' said Jane, bending over and stirring the pot vigorously.

'You'll get a fair whack, too,' threatened Simon, pausing to pick up a ruler.

'Don't you dare! I'll sue you for assault!'

'The police have already been here once today,' said Jim.

Simon Good stood very still. The grin on his face remained, but the humour had faded. A tiny pulse hammered in his jaw. 'The police?' he said. 'Here?'

'Yes, a plain-clothes man from Scotland Yard.'

Simon Good took a grip on himself. 'What have you been up to, young Jim? Stealing the Crown Jewels? What did he want?'

'Ha, ha, no. He was only inquiring from the Personnel Manager as to whether somebody or other worked here or not. One of the typists told me – you know, the snazzy one with the big, innocent eyes.'

'Keep away from snazzy typists with big, innocent eyes, young Jim. They are a snare and a delusion.' Simon forced himself to ask the next question, although he asked it casually enough. 'Who was he asking for?'

'She didn't say.'

'Some delinquent female who's run away from home, I shouldn't wonder.'

'Oh, no. It was a man he was after.'

The pulse in Simon's jaw quickened. 'A man?'

'Yep. But whoever he was, he didn't work here anyway. He'd committed monogamy. Or bigamy. I forget which.'

Simon relaxed and made his way up to the Executive suite on the fourth floor.

Sounds of the General Manager's voice raised in anger came through the open door of his room. It was evidently not one of Jullien Fane's better days. Simon Good withdrew to a discreet distance. He had picked up much useful information in those carpeted corridors with the doors that were generally half open.

The G.M.'s private secretary, Miss Quenella Mansfield, came out of the room in a hurry, and stopped dead when she saw Simon Good. Simon flicked an appreciative eye over her trim figure, and was inclined to agree with the opinion of the junior male staff that the G.M. could certainly pick private secretaries, and this recent acquisition was no exception. But then, Simon Good knew what he knew. When he got back to her eyes he found her regarding him with faint disapproval.

'Would you mind leaving just my shoes on?' she asked in dulcet tones. 'My feet give me agony otherwise.'

'I beg your pardon,' murmured Simon. 'I wasn't thinking.'

'I thought you *were*,' said Miss Mansfield. 'I could almost hear you. You can get psychiatric treatment for that sort of thing, you know.'

'Only if you're worried by it,' said Simon, unabashed. 'I'm not worried – I rather enjoy it.'

'At your age you ought to have something better to think about, Mr Good.'

'At my age, Miss Mansfield, there *is* nothing better to think about,' said Simon equably.

She regarded him frostily. 'I advise you not to go in there yet,' she said at length. 'Mr Fane's got a phone call that isn't agreeing with him.' She went on her way to the small private room where she did her typing, and Simon admired the lithe swing of her body as she went along the corridor.

The G.M.'s voice rose and fell, and apparent anger gave way to hard steeliness; his part in the conversation deteriorated into curt monosyllables with ever-lengthening periods between, until finally there came a faint *ting!* indicating he had hung up. Simon waited a little longer and then made for the door, tapping lightly and entering. He was just in time to catch the grim look on the well-fed face of Jullien Pane, a look which was replaced almost instantly by an expression of bland inquiry.

The General Manager of the Tyburn & New York Insurance Company was a man in his early sixties, with soft brown eyes seemingly full of compassion (as befitted a man at the head of a company which profited by other people's liability to suffer misfortune) and an unexpectedly soft, well-modulated voice – not quite out of the top drawer, but certainly the voice of experience. At first encounter, one was conscious of a detached friendliness – if things were going the way the G.M. wanted them to go. If by any remote chance they were not going that way, one soon became aware of the flimsiness of the velvet glove and could feel the granite upon which was draped the thin veneer of gentle benevolence.

Simon Good was very much aware of the rapier-like keenness of Jullien Fane.

'Ah, yes, Good. I really wanted to see Mr Moran, but I understand from the astute young gentleman who answered the telephone in your department that he is away ill.

I also gather you have been fixing up some reinsurance in the City. I hope you were successful.'

'Not entirely, sir,' said Simon, equally smoothly. 'I'm having some trouble in placing a foreign risk – the Pakistan Jute Mills Trust. The market's rather short because of the riot situation.' (There'd be a riot if you *knew* the situation, thought Simon Good.)

'I hope we're not carrying too much overnight?' said the G.M. anxiously. 'Have we explored the Lloyd's market?'

'We have, sir – most of the larger syndicates are reluctant to take any more until the riot position eases. They're already heavily committed because several leading companies effected facultative reinsurances a week ago – that's why I've had to tap the Company market.'

'H'm, I suppose it can't be helped,' said Jullien Pane, 'but do what you can, as soon as you can. I wanted to see you about a matter in the Home field. As you know, Mr van Meyer's mansion at Reigate was partly gutted last night, and I've asked the loss adjusters to rush us a report by tomorrow morning. You appreciate that here a directorial connexion is involved – an important one at that. For your private information – and kindly refrain from broadcasting this, even though it may be an open secret – Mr van Meyer is about to receive an appointment on our London

Board. I mention it to give an indication of the degree of importance attaching. As you know, we already benefit by the large blocks of gold and diamond mine business he puts our way in Johannesburg, and we hope to get a foothold on the insurances of his London concerns. He is over here for six months looking into those interests, and now he has the misfortune to have a wing of his house burnt down.'

'Yes, it is indeed unfortunate coming on top of his bad luck in the City,' commented Simon politely.

Jullien Fane regarded him steadily for a moment. 'You can't believe all you read in the papers, Good,' he said quietly.

'Unfortunately a lot of people do, sir, especially what they see on the City page. The *Financial Chronicle* has not been without comment.'

The G.M. changed the subject.

'You're not here to discuss other people's financial troubles with me, Good. I have to think of our own. I am informed by the Fire Department we hold Mr van Meyer's mansion one hundred per cent. As soon as you get an estimate of the loss from the Loss Department, I want you to work out our net position under the new Global Treaty. And I want that information first thing in the morning.'

'And what about the diamonds, sir?'

70

Jullien Fane froze in his leather swivel chair.

'What about what diamonds?' he said at length.

'The van Meyer diamonds. I gather he's reported the loss of forty thousand pounds' worth. It's in the evening paper. In the stop-press.'

'Do you mean he's had them stolen?' said the G.M. slowly. 'Or were they lost under the debris of the burnt-out wing?'

'I really don't know,' replied Simon. 'It doesn't make it clear. The newspaper man said something about them being stolen, but my paper merely says "Van Meyer diamonds valued at £40,000 lost". I suppose they could have been stolen.'

Fane looked thoughtful for a moment. He reached out for an internal telephone and dialled a number.

'This is the General Manager. I want to know what jewellery Mr van Meyer has insured with us – van Meyer – Mr van Meyer.' An irritable frown creased the G.M.'s forehead as the recipient of the message failed to comprehend immediately. (He's probably been dragged away from his Pools, thought Simon.) 'Ring me back as soon as you have the information. It's important.'

Jullien Fane replaced the receiver gently.

'This presents another problem,' he said thoughtfully. 'If it's a burglary it will come under another section of the Global Treaty. Are the terms and conditions the same?'

'No, sir, the Treaty Fire terms are better, and in any event there's probably a limitation as to amount under the fire policy unless the diamonds were insured for full value as a special item.'

'Well, let's hope the experts decide they've been lost in the fire, and not stolen,' grunted the G.M. 'Anyway, I expect the Press has exaggerated the value.' The telephone rang in muted tones. He lifted the receiver. 'Fane,' he said, and listened. 'You've been quick.' (Praise, indeed, thought Simon Good, but flattery will get you nowhere – at least, not much further, there are only two places left for you now, and you won't be going to heaven.) The G.M. listened a little longer. 'Let me have a note of the position first thing in the morning,' he said, and hung up.

'Well, Mr Good, it appears that whilst we have all Mr van Meyer's overseas jewellery covers ourselves, through Johannesburg Branch, the stuff he and his wife have brought over to this country has been placed with other companies and Lloyd's. We are on only by guarantee and possibly by inwards treaties.' He paused before rounding off the interview. 'As regards the information I want from you, I must have it first thing in the morning.' (*First thing almost any morning now*, thought Mr Good.)

'Yes, sir,' he said, and left the room.

At five-thirty sharp, Simon Good left the office and made his way to Temple Station, where he caught a train to Richmond. There he had a modest bachelor establishment in an ancient little house overlooking the river.

5

Ghosts and Coincidences

The Commander (Crime) New Scotland Yard, looked up from his desk at Superintendent Lingard, and frowned. 'What's the matter with you, Lingard? You look as if you've seen a ghost.'

'I have, sir,' said Lingard.

'I don't believe in 'em, myself!' chuckled the Commander.

'I may have been mistaken.'

'If you saw a ghost, you *were*,' declared the other emphatically. 'However, there are ghosts *and* ghosts – suppose you convert me. I've got a few minutes. Sit down, and you may smoke if you wish, although you may think that for the brief time I'm allowing you it will be scarcely worth lighting up.'

Lingard looked doubtful as he sat down.

He didn't light up, because he knew the Commander well enough to know that this looked like being a 'quickie'.

'It goes back rather a long way, sir – to the latter days of the war, and that's a long time ago.'

'It is, indeed.'

'In those far-off days they were calling for men with linguistic ability, and in view of my flair for European languages, the study of which was then a hobby of mine, I left off being a policeman, and found myself in the Army Special Investigation Branch. I was pounding the beat then,' he added apologetically.

'Even I was a policeman once,' nodded the Great One sagely.

Lingard was momentarily disconcerted. The Commander smiled suddenly, and the sting went. 'But I was,' he declared. 'And glad of the experience, too.' He glanced at his watch. 'Don't let me delay your tale of the supernatural.'

Lingard hastily reassured him. 'I shan't be long, sir.' (After all, the Commander had *asked* him for the story.) 'Towards the end of the war I was detailed for an Intelligence-cum-interpreter job with a unit whose objective was a German-occupied factory dominating a perfectly straight mile of railway line. Allied troops had to cross this line at one particular point daily, and in spite of changing the routine, Jerry always seemed to get wind of it, and the Spandaus and 88 mm. guns which were trained straight down the track on to the crossing-point, would open up dead on target every time.

'At the actual crossing there was a notice which read "At this crossing there are only two kinds of soldier – the quick and the dead". Corny, but true. The number of steel helmets hanging from wooden crosses at the roadside added point to the observation.

'The factory was a modern one constructed of concrete and steel, and had defied destruction from the air and ground. And it remained a thorn in the flesh of the local commander.

'The job of the company to which I was posted was to take it by storm. We were given the help of part of a French Armoured Brigade, who were going to cover our advance, together with a company of Polish shock troops – war-toughened veterans who had an almost personal hate of the enemy. The attack was timed for 0530 hours. Disaster set in almost from the start. Once again Jerry had got wind of the operation, and almost overnight had cleverly devised tank traps. The French armour belted forward in the half-light without opposition, followed immediately by the Polish shock troops, whose job it was to winkle out the enemy and cause enough confusion to cover our consolidation. Then disaster. The tanks, advancing over-enthusiastically, without hindrance, practically reached the factory and suddenly found themselves trapped in such a way that they couldn't elevate their guns enough to give any covering fire. The waves of shock troops were enveloped in a welter of cross-fire, and only a handful ever reached their objective. The force which was to consolidate found itself pinned down by Spandau and mortar fire, and was ordered to dig in.

'The factory was held by comparatively few of the enemy, but they and their weapons were placed with Teutonic efficiency. During the ensuing day they almost annihilated the half-dug-in force, which was ultimately obliged to withdraw under cover of darkness with very heavy losses. Four out of the five officers were killed.'

'And you?' queried the Great One.

'I happened to be with the handful who got through to the factory.'

'It was safer inside?'

Lingard's hackles rose. 'It certainly was,' he said, as mildly as he could, 'having once got there. We very soon found out why we had managed to make it. It was a more or less isolated part of the factory complex, and apparently undefended. This puzzled us.

'We were only a dozen British troops, under the command of a Major Meek –

Major Peter Meek – a cheerful extrovert if ever there was one. The gods must have been in a facetious mood when they sent him to the *Meek* family.

'He soon organized what men, arms and ammunition there were. Thirteen Poles had got through, and there were twelve of us. A quick recce showed we were in this cut-off section of the factory. There were three parallel underground passages leading to the main building. One of the Poles attempted a recce along one of them and was promptly killed by a booby-trap. That was the secret of the undefended building – each passageway was booby-trapped to high heaven. It was the one clear, inviting way into the main building, and the one way where casualties would be devastatingly heavy.

'Meek himself made a cautious examination – they told me he'd been on several mines-and-booby-traps courses at the Army school at Knocke – and he came to the conclusion it'd be sheer suicide to attempt to negotiate any one of those long concrete passages.

'Outside, the half-dug-in men were gradually being wiped out with German precision. Meek did what he could to support them, but we were so placed that in spite of all effort it didn't amount to much. We were low on ammo. Our arms consisted of rifles, a Bren and a Piat. We wrought a bit of havoc with the Piat until we were down to the last two bombs. As the day wore on it was apparent we were lucky to be where we were, at least we had superficial protection. The food and water situation was somewhat acute, although things were too hot at first to worry about that.

'During the night, the remainder of the men outside withdrew with their wounded under cover of darkness. And in the morning there was an unholy quiet. Everything was still. The sun came up over the scene of this private little war. To the outside world this was just an unimportant episode in a world war. To sixty-eight poor devils lying in grotesque positions in the morning sun, this was the whole war. Even the birds were quiet. Death had stalked that way, and was now waiting to point at some other living, breathing thing.

'We kept on the qui vive, expecting some sort of attack from the main building. A special watch was kept along those booby-trapped underground passages, and we searched for other possible surprise ways in. The men were in a pretty poor state from lack of food and water, some with wounds – but Major Meek kept up morale by his constant effort and example. From what little I saw of him I felt they'd follow him through fire and water. And yet – and this was curious – he struck me as being utterly unscrupulous, although I couldn't lay a finger on it. I remember thinking it was a good thing he was on our side.

'All through the morning the tense stillness persisted. There was not a sound from the other parts of the factory. "They've cleared out," decided Meek finally. "Probably the place was only lightly held and they expected us to call up reserves over the W.T. and counter-attack. One of us will have to make a recce into the main building and find out what they're up to. I think it'll have to be from the inside along one of those corridors. It isn't going to be a piece of cake, and whoever goes will probably be saying good-bye to his next Brussels leave. I want a volunteer."

'Meek's men came forward to a man. I explained the position to the Polish sergeant, and after he'd put it to his men in their own language, they, too, all came forward.

'"That makes all of us," said Meek, "because I've just volunteered too. Has any one of you a good knowledge of booby-traps? Has anyone been to the school at Knocke? You know the school's motto that faces you everywhere you go – in the classroom, in the mess, in the practice area, everywhere – 'You only make one mistake'."'

Lingard absent-mindedly pulled out his cigarettes, caught the Commander's eye, and put them back again.

'Well, it appeared that although everyone was prepared to have a go, nobody, apart from Meek, was really qualified to delouse – or even recognize, for that matter – any boobies. "It looks as though I've earned myself a job," he said. "That's what comes of volunteering. Hammersley's" (yes, that was his batman's name, Hammersley – Lord, how it all comes back!) "Hammersley's always telling me it's unwise to volunteer for anything in the Army, and by the Lord Harry, he's right!"

'He proceeded in a calm and detached way to delegate his orders to a British sergeant – what was his name, Blake? – yes, Blake, in case things went wrong, and then ordered everyone except the look-outs to spread and lie flat – Jerry had a warped idea of humour with booby-traps, often the action of delousing a very obvious trap would blow sky high the only available decent cover fifty yards away; oh, yes, they were great guys at using F.I.D. – fuse, instantaneous detonation – and then Meek selected one of the underground corridors, and went cautiously on his way down the slight ramp.

'Dim light came in through heavy glass squares set at intervals in the roof of the corridor, and from where I lay I could see his slow progress along the passage, as he picked his way with infinite care over and around the many objects which cluttered up the place, apparently haphazardly.

'Once he stopped, lowered himself flat on his face, and examined something with the utmost caution. He appeared to be tracing the path of a piece of wire, and we knew, as well as he, that one false move meant death or injury. For fifteen tense minutes he fiddled and manipulated, and then stood up, stretched himself, and gave us a silent thumbs-up. He went on with even greater caution, well aware that often the next step taken after the elation of delousing one booby-trap was the fatal one, because you walked straight into the next.

'He reached the end of the passage, and without looking round again, slowly mounted the ramp at that end and vanished into the main factory.

'The minutes dragged by reluctantly. We waited tensely for a shot to ring out, or for the shrill blast of a thunderer whistle, which Meek said he'd give if he was in sudden danger of being captured. But nothing happened to break the tension, and we sweated it out for nearly an hour.

'And then, larger than life, he came striding back across the intervening courtyard which ran over the three underground passages. A sentry helped him through a shattered window, and he immediately called us together. "They appear to have hopped it," he said, "unless they were hiding from me in the cellars. I've had a quick look round, and I've been up on the roof to their observation post. And what a fine O.P. it is! No wonder they were dead on target every time! The only sign of life I could see, however, was about a couple of hundred yards up this road to the left, that leads away from the courtyard. There are a couple of machine-gun posts, one on each side of the road, and they seem to be manned."

'"It's a wonder they didn't open up on you as you crossed the yard, sir," suggested Sergeant Blake.

'"Maybe I was mistaken, and they aren't manned," replied Meek. "Anyway, that concrete gatehouse over there with the cycle-shed restricts their view somewhat, and they couldn't have seen me for more than a few seconds. There's one thing I must tell you, however. If they've definitely vacated that building, I've a feeling it won't be with us much longer. There are demolition sets all over the place, and they all seem to be wired up and primed ready for use. They may be sappers up the road waiting for a signal to blow the lot up. And we're the saps."

'As he spoke, there was a muffled roar, and the walls of the building across the way started to sag outwards and collapse, showering masonry over the courtyard. Explosion after explosion followed, great mushrooms of smoke rising from the wrecked building, the atmosphere thick with choking dust as the rubble settled. When the air cleared a bit and the singing in our ears had given over, it was surprising to see how much of the main factory still remained apparently untouched.

'"I must be psychic," commented Meek.

'"You were just out of it in time, sir," said the sergeant.

'And at that moment a series of shattering roars opened up *behind* us, one after another, each one nearer than the last.

'"Sergeant," said Meek sadly, "why did you have to open that parade-ground mouth of yours? Look what you've started – they're demolishing this place now. Scramble!"

'We piled through all available openings like greased fishes. The ground was vibrating violently with the shock-wave of each explosion, and the last few men were literally rocked out of the building. And we were no sooner out in the open than we were met with a withering hail of machine-gun fire from the guns up the road. Fortunately there was no shortage of cover – there were huge chunks of rubble strewn all over the place. Three men made a dive for the concrete gatehouse. "Not the gatehouse!" roared Meek, spotting them too late. They reached it just in time to go up with it.

'"They'll never learn," said the sergeant laconically.

'"I'm afraid they won't now," agreed

83

Major Meek.

'At great personal danger he crawled out to find them – or what was left of them. They'd all been killed. But that action of Meek's was typical of him, because when I say "great personal danger" I really mean it. The machine-gun fire was spraying over the ruins like film rain, whining and ricocheting in every direction. Curiously enough it did very little damage, apart from minor snicks. The bother was it kept us pinned to the ground, just like the others had been the day before. And to add to our discomfort the weather clouded over and it started to rain in torrents. That had one good point – we were able to collect enough water in our battle-bowlers to slake our thirst. I noticed Sergeant Blake had produced a stout piece of brown paper and had made a broad funnel down into his water bottle. He was still wearing his steel helmet. Maybe that was why he was a sergeant.

'Anyone who as much as showed a finger was met with a devastating hail of fire, and we had nothing much to reply with. "Let 'em waste it!" shouted back Meek, who remained forward in the gatehouse ruins. "If they come out at us there's enough of us to eat 'em at close quarters!"

'After what seemed an eternity of scorching fire, which was made more interesting by being larded with tracers and incendiaries, there was a sudden cessation, and a stick with a near-white handkerchief tied to it was pushed up over the parapet of the left-hand post up the road. We waited events – it wasn't a question of withholding fire, we just hadn't been firing. After a moment or two of silence, a German N.C.O. clambered up into the road and strode to within shouting distance of us, stood stiffly to attention, and addressed us in German. Meek called me and Sergeant Blake forward. "Don't tell me *they* are surrendering!" he grinned as the speech ended with an abrupt *Heil Hitler!* "Well – what is it, Lingard?"

'"They are commanding us, in the name of the German High Command, to surrender immediately," I translated. "Otherwise they will eliminate us with their very efficient Spandau machine-guns."'

The Commander (Crime) sat back in his chair. There was a lupine grin on his face. 'I just can't wait to hear what Major Meek's reply was,' he said.

'Major Meek considered the matter carefully,' continued Lingard, 'and then said, "Tell them, in the most offensive German you know, just what they can do with their very efficient machine-guns in relation to their unmentionable High Command. Anything else to add to that, Sergeant Blake?"

'The sergeant sucked his teeth thoughtfully. "You could ask if any of 'em were ever lucky enough to trace their fathers," he

85

suggested off-handedly.

'"Yes, add that, Lingard. That should rile them, and they'll waste even more ammo than before. Sergeant, warn everyone to take cover."

'Blake complied with the order, and I yelled back the reply to the emissary, who clicked his heels and marched stiffly back to his post to report.

'Some of the masonry from the main factory had crashed through into one of the tunnels, and a number of the men made themselves scarce under the lee of the jagged tunnel roof. It was just as well they did, because the fire that suddenly opened up again was all hell let loose, in spite of the fact that none of us was visible and they were obviously firing blindly. It went on intensively with no sign of letting up – where they got the ammunition from I just don't know. First one gun, and then the other, then both of them.

'After what seemed an interminable period, Meek came to a decision. "Is the Piat still with us?" he asked. The sergeant thought it was. "Then in the next lull, call it forward here. And the Bren."

'In due course, a couple of men, with the Piat and its two remaining bombs, crawled out to us. Their observer had been killed when the gatehouse went up. One of the men was of partly Dutch extraction – his name was Strookman, they called him "Rip". The other was a Cockney, whose name, strangely enough, *was* Dutch; they called him "Dutchy".

'When the Bren came up, Meek checked the magazine. It was only half full. The spare mag was empty. "I want a full magazine," he said to the sergeant. "Get everybody to throw a few rounds over into the kitty. Recharge the magazine for me – space out the tracers." When this was done, Meek slapped it in position on the weapon, and laid it on a convenient ledge. "I want the Piat over in that corner. You've only two bombs left, and that means only one bomb for each machine-gun nest. Estimate the range very carefully. When I give the command, I want you to fire one bomb at the left-hand target – which is apparently the Command Post – and then as quickly as possible, the second one at the right-hand target. If you chaps get bang on each time, it will help me considerably, and I'll remember you for the rest of my days. If you don't, it probably won't matter anyway." Blake asked him what he intended to do with the Bren. "I'm going along to winkle 'em out," was the brief reply.'

Lingard paused reflectively and his eyes swam mistily into the past. They came back into the present with a jerk as the Commander's eye flickered over to the clock on the wall.

'I've almost finished, sir,' he said hastily.

'You have?' The Commander managed to convey surprise and doubt that this could possibly be the case. 'Don't let me hurry you,' he said affably. 'I haven't to be at the Home Office till six o'clock.'

It was already dangerously near six o'clock. Lingard hurried on.

'Major Meek filled his pipe, lit it to his satisfaction, and then picked up the Bren. He pulled back the cocking handle. Looking through a wrecked doorway, he sized up the quickest way through the rubble to the road. Blake asked him what was going to be the drill. "As soon as the first bomb has been delivered – dead on target, I hope – I shall be on my way up the road. I hope that the second one will be equally on the spot, and that both posts will be stunned for a bit, or at least made a little cautious. By that time I trust I shall be near enough to have a crack at them myself. It's getting too uncomfortable here in all this wet and mess, there's no future in it. Not that there's any future in anything else, so far as I can see." A sudden bitterness entered his voice which to me seemed alien to his character. Sergeant Blake grinned "You'll get no promotion this side of the ocean..."

'"You'll get no promotion the other side of the ocean, either," grunted Meek. "Mark my words, if and when you get back to

Civvy Street after all this, every one of the good jobs will be taken by those who scrambled into reserved occupations, the conscientious objectors and the cherry pickers, who've seen nothing of all this stink and filth. If there's no quick easy cash for me within a year or two by the normal methods, then I'm going to get what I want in life by abnormal methods.'"

The Commander looked interested. 'Abnormal methods,' he repeated. 'Just what did he mean by that. What was his particular line of business?'

'I never got to know, sir. Though, strangely enough, Meek himself brought up the question of private occupations.'

'Brought up the question?' The Commander cocked his head to one side. 'Now why should he do that?' he asked.

Lingard shrugged his shoulders. 'Oh, so far as I remember, it was done casually enough. He seemed very bitter about the way he thought things might go when we got back home – almost masochistically bitter. I think he would have been really annoyed if he'd suddenly been told he was going to be promoted to managing director when he left the forces. Seemed to have a bee in his bonnet about it. Not that it mattered much then what any of us were or would be – I think we all secretly thought we'd had it. The chances of getting out of that shambles alive were very remote. As Sergeant Blake aptly remarked, the whole operation was the biggest box-up since the Flood. Anyway, the little group of us fell to talking about our jobs. I imagine Meek got us thinking along those lines to give us determination to get out of the mess we were in, alive. I can remember their occupations quite well.'

'What was so special about them that they should stick in your mind for so long?'

'They were only special in the light of a remark of Meek's,' said Lingard slowly. 'I often used to think about it, but you know how it is – gradually the whole thing faded into something quite nebulous.' He racked his brain for a moment. 'Meek had passed some remark such as "War is a great leveller–"'

'Indeed it is,' agreed the Commander, 'especially to those who ended up as a number on a headstone.'

'–and he went on to say that although he was then in command of them, when the uniforms were finally stripped off there would probably be revealed the secretary of an oil company, the estate agent owning half of Park Lane, the prosperous bank manager, and he himself would turn out to be a bus conductor, and he would discover to his horror that his batman was the Duke of Loamshire. The uniforms levelled everybody out into carefully calculated grades, and everybody knew just by looking at the sign language on them the precise lengths to which the wearer could go and how much he was being paid for it. That was when they started to talk about the jobs they hoped to go back to.

'Strookman said he was in the diamond trade in a Hatton Garden firm. He'd spent part of his life in Holland and part in England, and he'd worked his way right through the business on both sides of the Channel. The war had given him a taste of the Continent again, and his ambition was to get back to Amsterdam where his father was.

'The unpretentious Cockney, Dutch, said he was quite happy selling plants and fertilizers from his stall in one of the London markets – Petticoat Lane, or some such place.

'Blake's hope was to open up a café in the heart of the City, where he'd observed that the eating facilities for the gentlemen of Throgmorton Street were comparatively few, and he aimed to provide quick, clean, cheap meals. He wasn't counting on an era of staff canteens and luncheon vouchers. Before the war he had worked for Lumm's, the safe makers–'

'Lumm & Co!' interposed the Commander. 'That was a good old family business, if ever there was one! Been at it for over a hundred years, I should say. Why did he want to leave them – I would have thought they treated their staff pretty well.'

'The Lumm brothers, both very aged, were killed by a V2, and I believe the firm went into liquidation towards the end of the war.'

'Ah, I remember now, they were bought up by Rempert's Safes, and I seem to remember talk of a consequent reduction in staff. Well, go on with your story, what happened then?'

'Meek said "What a glorious set-up for roguery! We must get together after the war. With the inside knowledge I have we could very soon be living in luxury for the rest of our lives. What about you, Lingard?" I said to him "If it's roguery you're contemplating, you can count me out – I'm a copper, and it'll be my job to bring you in." He looked at me sharply. I can see him now as he seemed to size me up. And then the tension in him suddenly ebbed away. "Don't worry," he said, relaxing, "I probably shan't reach the end of the road in front of us, let alone the one to Civvy Street! Anyway, if I become a successful business man I shan't worry the law!"

'I asked him what his particular line was, and I think he was about to tell me when both M.G.s along the road started up on us again. "Remind me to tell you all about it when I come back," he grinned. "I'm going to put a stop to this nonsense first. Ready, Dutch?" Dutch took a firm grip on the Piat, and took careful aim. "Ready, sir."

'Meek waited till the next lull in the firing. 'Now!' he said, and with a quick "Cheerio!" was out across the rubble on to the road. The Piat went off with a roar in my ears. The bomb-strike appeared to me to be slightly short of the target, and that brought a withering blast of profanity from Sergeant Blake. 'If you don't score with the next one, Dutchy, I'll come over and strangle you with my own bare hands! And don't knock off the O.C. – he's got the Bren and most of our ammo!'

'The Major actually paused to ram his pipe more firmly between his teeth, and then with the Bren against his hip, he walked steadily up the road towards the gun-posts, withholding his fire.

'The left-hand post was momentarily quietened and possibly a little stunned by the bursting Piat bomb, but as Meek reached about a third of the way along the road, the other post opened up on him. Once again Dutchy took careful aim and fired. This time there was a direct hit on the right-hand emplacement, and I remember ducking automatically as the tail-fin of the bomb hurtled back directly at us in a perfect reverse trajectory, in the manner peculiar to Piat bombs. It was now the turn of the right-hand post to be silenced, and still Meek strode relentlessly on without firing a shot. Suddenly the left-hand post woke up and chattered away at him. How they missed him I just don't know, but miss him they did. They must have been all fingers and thumbs.

'If ever a man walked into a fiery furnace, it was Major Peter Meek. The tracers told just how near they were to him, and at any moment we expected him to be cut to ribbons. They talk of the Miracle of Dunkirk, but to me, this was the miracle of the war. As the hot lead spattered round him, still he walked steadily on, his pipe jutting out sideways at an angle, a gesture of defiance. He reached more than half-way to his objectives before he fired a couple of short bursts either side to discourage them. Then suddenly he faltered, and half spun round. We thought he'd had it. But pulling himself together, he covered the last bit of the journey blazing away like a maniac. I think he'd been winged and stung into fury. He sprayed the Bren from side to side like a garden hose. Trotting the last few yards, he clambered to the top of the pit on the right and wiped out the crew; and then, as if protected by all the gods, magic, voodoos and armour in the world, he staggered across the road to the other pit. A stick grenade came flying towards him, but with the lightning precision of one about to die, he grabbed it in mid-air in his left hand, and lobbed it back. It was a mad thing to do – he knew it would be fused for something under four seconds. But it came off, and it burst over the top of the emplacement. He staggered jerkily up on to the parapet, and fired burst after burst down into the pit. I saw a man break cover and run frantically in a wide arc towards a clump of trees on the brow of the incline. With a bellow of rage, Meek was after him, blazing away like a hellhound from the bottomless pit. And then the whole horizon went up in a series of shattering roars.'

'And that was the last you saw of Major Meek,' said the Commander, with an air of finality.

'No, sir. I saw him again today.'

'Ah! Your ghost! I wondered when you were coming to the point. Where did you see him?'

'I'd been along to the Tyburn & New York's building in Fetter Lane – the insurance company – making an inquiry in connexion with a Missing Person, to wit, Fenner, the bigamist – thought we had a lead – and I'd just left the place when I saw Meek buying a paper.'

'Well, well! What did he have to say? It must have been interesting after all these years.'

Lingard looked uncomfortable. 'He entered the building, and by the time I chased into the entrance hall after him, he'd vanished.'

The Commander chuckled. 'Perhaps it was a ghost, after all!' he commented. 'What's your angle?'

'All these unsolved major burglaries of recent years–'

The Commander got up suddenly and reached for his hat.

'That reminds me! I really must be on my way – I've got to answer some questions on the very subject over at the Home Office. And all these robberies with violence. The "cat" is the only answer to that one – hot and strong.' (The Commander, Crime, came from a long line of military gentlemen who knew what discipline was, who knew the Army in the days when it was wise to salute anything that moved and whitewash anything else that didn't.) 'I fancy I'll also be asked about the loss of the van Meyer diamonds in that fire at Reigate. He's quite a big boy, is van Meyer. Did you see the report? One wing of his mansion was completely gutted.'

'I saw something in the evening paper about the diamonds. I can't help feeling that if this unpleasantly-wealthy little man was foolish enough to leave his jewellery about in a wing that gets burned down, then he's just asking for it. But where do we come in? Surely they'll find them in the debris – diamonds don't burn!'

'True. But these were intelligent diamonds. They were in a safe, and they got so
hot inside that they unlocked the door and
got away.'

'Oh, they're missing from a safe. I didn't
know that. What caused the fire?'

'The theory at present is that the burglar
took the diamonds and then set fire to the
place to obliterate his tracks. The local
people thought we might be interested. You
see, the fire took place last night, and it was
not until this afternoon that the debris was
cool enough to clear to get to the safe. And
I fear I shall now have to answer why wc
were not sitting on top of it to stop the
diamonds escaping.'

Lingard looked thoughtful. 'There could
be an alternative theory,' he said slowly. 'I
shouldn't say this, perhaps, but maybe the
diamonds were never in the safe in the first
place.'

'You are quite right, you shouldn't say
that,' agreed the Commander. 'So why do
you say it?'

'I was reading recently on the City page
that van Meyer was going through a rough
patch with some of his ventures, and that
made me quite happy, because I think he's a
scoundrel of the first order. I wouldn't put it
past him to rig the whole affair. I bet the
diamonds and the mansion are more than
adequately insured.'

'I advise you not to think on those lines outside this room, Lingard. All we know at present is that diamonds which were alleged to be in a safe are no longer there. And we have no reason to believe that he had anything to do with the fire. In a couple of months' time, if we are privileged to look at the insurance companies' Loss Adjuster's report, we shall probably see a paragraph to the effect that 'a fire occurred, cause of which remains unknown'. What were you going to say about unsolved burglaries when I interrupted you?'

'I was thinking of Strookman, with his intimate knowledge of the diamond industry. And of Blake—'

'With his sandwich-bar, trying to undermine the confidence of the Bank of England Staff Canteen?'

'No, sir. With his years of experience at Lumm's Safes, Ltd. Coupled with Major Meek's talk of "inside knowledge" and the fact that I've just seen him go into the chief office of the Tyburn & New York Insurance Company.'

The Commander looked at him shrewdly. 'You mean that if he worked there he might be in a position to obtain inside knowledge regarding say, burglar alarms, types of safes and where they were – to say nothing of what was in 'em! And all manner of other interesting information.' The Great One turned it over in his mind for a moment. 'He's left it a long time before he's started operations, hasn't he?' he asked critically.

'There have been a lot of unsolved burglaries over the past seven or eight years,' countered Lingard.

'I can't help feeling from what you've told me of him that by now he'll be some big business executive, leading the blameless life that all big business executives lead – did you say something? – and even if he hasn't achieved that position, he won't be eating his heart out with frustration, he'll be doing something outside as well, to satisfy his ego.'

'That's what I'm worrying about,' said Lingard.

'My dear Lingard,' said the Commander. 'Hundreds of thousands of men came back from the war feeling frustrated. After five or six years of more or less doing what they liked in spite of war discipline, it naturally took a time for them to settle down to the humdrum way of life again. And yet ninety-nine per cent of them did. In time.'

'And the other one per cent, sir?'

'Ah! There you have me. I'll ask you something. Where in the scheme of things does the Cockney, Dutch, selling his plants and fertilizers from a stall in a street market fit in? And could not Major Meek have been going into the Tyburn & New York building to take out a motor policy, or to cancel his life insurance? And correct me if I'm wrong, but isn't there a bank on the ground floor of that building? Couldn't he have been going into the bank to cash a cheque?'

'Not at that hour, sir.'

'Well, then, he could be working in the bank and not the insurance company, and then where's his access to special information?'

Lingard looked slightly uncomfortable. 'I must admit it's all a bit thin, sir,' he said reluctantly.

The Commander fiddled with his hat. 'Tomorrow, make some discreet inquiries at the insurance company and the bank, and see if he's employed at either of those places. Then you can set your mind at rest and get on with the job of catching thieves. You need only report to me if you get some positive information.'

'Yes, sir,' said Lingard, pushing his temper back where it belonged – under the layer of skin the Commander had penetrated.

'D'you know the character I find most interesting?' continued the Great One. 'What about this batman fellow – Hammersley? – you've told me nothing about him yet, and yet he must have been very close to Meek. What did *he* do for a living?'

'I don't know, sir. When we were discussing occupations it didn't get round to him either. You see, Meek did most of the talking, and I suppose he knew all about his batman without further questions.'

'I wonder if we could trace him?' mused the Commander. 'Army Records? Telephone Directory? Criminal Records, even. Yes, try C.R.O. It's a long shot, anyway. If all these people are hanging together now, there may be something in your hunch after all. Would you know Hammersley if you saw him again?'

Lingard ran a finger round his collar and frowned thoughtfully. 'I don't really know, sir,' he said doubtfully. 'From what I remember of him he was a mild, self-effacing little man – the sort you just don't see to start with. He might have changed a bit since those days.'

'Yes, he may not be so self-effacing,' said the other helpfully. 'And perhaps it wasn't Meek you saw this afternoon anyway.'

'Oh, it was Major Meek, right enough,' replied Lingard. 'He was an impressive character, and I never forget a face when once it has registered. Hammersley's different – he never really registered. All I have is a hazy blur, but it might clarify if I saw him again.'

'Find him,' said the Commander briefly, 'just for me. Tell me – with all Major Meek's background of aggressiveness, would he engage in robbery with violence?'

'I would say no,' said Lingard, without hesitation. 'I can no more imagine him hit-ting old ladies with iron bars, or aged night-watchmen with broken bottles, than – than–'

'Working as a clerk in an insurance company?'

'Your point, sir. I rather imagine he would want to pay back these hoodlums in their own coin and give them a good thrashing.'

'A man after my own heart,' reflected the Commander; he caught Lingard's eye, 'always assuming he's not responsible for all these burglaries,' he added hastily. 'You know, I can never understand why these throw-backs should be put in prisons-without-bars for long cosy periods, and treated as psychiatric cases at the everlasting expense of the community.'

'Something to do with not putting the clock back,' grunted the Superintendent cynically.

'*They* haven't hesitated to put it back,' growled the other. 'I would treat them like the scum most of them are – give them short sentences and flog 'em every day. I would not consult the long-haired politicians who theorize on the subject of the poor hard-done-by criminal, I would consult the injured person and his or her relatives. Oh, I know the poor prison officials are likely to be brutalized through administering the punishment; I would therefore take it out of their hands, and ask for volunteers from the relatives. I've a feeling they wouldn't mind being brutalized. However, this time I really am on my way – I had no idea you were going to talk for so long. I must confess your story has interested me. Your seeing Major Meek today was quite a coincidence.'

'Yes, sir, although I think there's usually a reason for everything. By and large, I don't believe in coincidences – just like you don't believe in ghosts.'

'Well, you've convinced me there *must* be ghosts,' grinned the Commander.

'Perhaps you can convince me there are coincidences, sir.'

'Perhaps I can,' said the Commander, making for the door. 'The safe from which the van Meyer diamonds vanished was a Lumm safe...'

6

A Bag of Mutations

At ten o'clock the following morning, the adjusters' preliminary report on the van Meyer fire was placed before Simon by Mr Moran, who had recovered from his severe chill. He, like a number of the departmental heads at the T. & N.Y., was an import from America, and for a man who had just been ill he looked exceedingly fit and well. This was not astonishing, because he spent so much time getting that way. However, he always liked to get back in harness by Thursday or Friday so that he could clear up any odds and ends and really relax and enjoy his week-end with a clear conscience.

'The G.M. has marked this report, Good,' he said briskly. 'He wants a note of our position under the Global Reinsurance Treaty. Right away.'

'Yes, he had a word with me about it, yesterday,' said Simon woodenly.

'Then you know all about it,' said Mr Moran, with a flicker of annoyance at having missed this opportunity of contact with the G.M. Reports on the efficiency of the American staff went back to New York quarterly. 'It seems I'm wasting my time.'

'You know best, Mr Moran,' smiled Simon in such a pleasant way that even Moran found it difficult to take offence, although he tried hard, and although Jim Laker saw fit to blow his nose violently.

'Let me have a typed note as soon as possible,' he said, turning abruptly into his room. Mr Moran was no fool. He was well aware of the friction that existed between the English and American staff, and it was perhaps only natural that the rubs were there, if only because of the different standards of living. That aspect, however, wasn't his concern, one got the best one could out of life, it was win or lose. Since his G.I. days he'd had a yearning for travel. He'd applied in New York for a post in Tokyo. There, he felt, was a vast and easy field for furtherance of the business, and scope for improving his own status. American money was opening up industrial Japan, and that meant insurance coverage in a dozen different directions. The Japanese companies were competing fiercely for it, but an American would always give to an American, and Mr Moran felt he was that American. To his chagrin they sent him to London for three years instead, to gain more experience in the underwriting field. And he was fed up to the back teeth with London, and he'd be glad to get out of it. He grinned to himself as he looked at the mail. No wonder Jane Seymour thought him a bit of a grouch, and had her own pet nickname for him which he wasn't supposed to know!

Simon Good studied the adjusters' report. Although it was primarily a Fire loss report, and a rushed one at that, mention was made of the fact that all the evidence pointed to the loss of the van Meyer diamonds as being the result of burglary or housebreaking, during the course of which the fire arose; the seat of the trouble appeared to be in the vicinity of the forced safe, which was of Lumm design but of fairly recent installation by Rempert's, the firm which had taken them over. The expert advice of the Fire Avoidance Association had been sought, and their investigators were making a detailed examination. The local Fire Brigade Chief and the police seemed to be extremely interested in certain facts which so far they were reluctant to disclose. The report was essentially brief and concluded with an estimate of the probable Fire loss, which was considerable. This gross figure, however, was not the ultimate one the G.M. was interested in – his particular anxiety was the *net* loss the company would suffer after taking into account the reinsurances they had made on the particular risk. In this case the figure was an easy one to arrive at, as the loss fell within the terms and limits of the Treaty to which the G.M. had referred, and there were no complications of outside covers with other companies or Lloyd's.

Simon Good quickly worked out the loss position, according to the information in the house, on a sheet of foolscap, and took it over to the typist. 'Jane, my lotus flower,' he said affably, 'here's a note that Mr Moran wants quickly for the G.M.'

'And pray what sort of a mood is His Moronic Majesty in this morning?' she asked.

'Full of the milk of human kindness,' affirmed Simon. 'The only trouble is that it's gone sour. It's not what he says, it's the way he says it. And I'm in no mood to cross swords with him this morning. I had a bit of a thick night last night.'

'It's about time you did your duty, got married and settled down, Mr Good,' said Jane primly, as she inserted a sheet of quarto paper in her machine.

'I haven't met Miss Right, yet, sweetheart,' said Simon regretfully.

'I can well believe that. Who were you with last night? Miss Behave?'

'If you must know, I spent last night in my modest bachelor establishment – and I use the word "modest" advisedly – studying Personal Accident Insurance and ironing my shirt.'

'It probably needed it. One carbon copy enough, Mr Good?'

'If you're using a new sheet of carbon paper – yes. But if you're going to use those dirty, dog-eared, moth-eaten scraps of carbon you save especially for my work – do three, and I'll pick the best.'

An apt rejoinder was stifled at birth by the appearance of Mr Moran in the doorway of his room. He was rubbing his hands to restore the circulation, for the morning was very cold and the insulation of the new building left much to be desired. 'Strewth, why was it that the central heating never worked in these refrigerated English blocks! He must indent for one of those modern electric space-heaters.

'Bother!' said Jane under her breath. 'Here comes His Moronic. It's cold enough in the room without him coming over to lower the temperature. What's he doing with the thermometer – trying to break it?'

Moran was irritably tapping the base of the wall thermometer, glaring at it with concentrated venom.

Young Jim Laker passed with some papers. 'He's trying to intimidate it,' he muttered.

Moran bustled over with an air of noisy efficiency. 'Is she doing that note, Good?'

'*She* is,' said Miss Seymour with emphasis.

'As quickly as you can – the General Manager's waiting for it.' Mr Moran's hide was very thick. A few minutes later, the duly initialled note in hand, he hurried importantly from the room.

'He's buzzing about like a blue-nosed fly this morning,' growled Pemberthy. 'Anyone would think the whole fabric of the company was about to collapse because he's had a couple of days off with a cold. Simon – a little while back I thought I heard you say you'd spent last night studying Accident Insurance. I realized, of course, it must have been a trick of the acoustics.'

'Your hearing is not at fault, Pemberthy,' said Simon Good with considerable dignity. 'One can never learn too much. What I've learned about Personal Accident business in the last twenty-four hours would fill the record book at the Old Bailey. You are much younger than I, and if you want to get on here I suggest you study hard and take the examinations. And remain celibate.'

'Celibate!'

'Yes, then there'll be plenty of opportunities for progressive well-paid overseas jobs – see the world, Canada, South America, Tristan da Cunha–'

'But why celibate?'

'It's pretty obvious, isn't it? Whole attention to the job. You want to taste the fruits of success, don't you?'

'Yes – but I want to taste the fruits of marriage, too.'

'Can't have both, old boy, can't have both. At least, you're not supposed to. Perhaps you can if you go to Cunha. I wouldn't really know. I've only been to Brussels, Paris, and Chowringee Road, Calcutta.'

'You're celibate with umpteen exams but where's it got you?'

'You'd be surprised,' said Simon.

And Pemberthy would indeed have been surprised if he'd known precisely where Simon Good's knowledge of insurance had got him. It certainly wasn't being used for the furtherance of that great invisible export built up over centuries on a mere 'promise to pay'.

'If I had your qualifications, Simon, I'd be out like a shot.'

'Your advice to others is always generous,'

agreed Simon, 'and quite useless.'

'Well, it's a wonder to me you're so satisfied with your position here,' said Pemberthy, disgruntled a little.

'Satisfied? Who said I'm satisfied? Who's been bearing false witness? Nobody's ever satisfied, no matter what job they've got, from the chairman down to the cleaners. We can all do the next job up so much better than the present bloke – until we have to try, and then we realize our shortcomings. But I tell you this, my dear Pem, in all modesty, one of these days I'm going places.'

And perhaps even Simon Good would have been surprised if he could have foreseen just where he was going.

The telephone rang on Simon's desk. 'Good here,' he announced, picking up the receiver. He listened for a few moments. 'I'll come and see you,' he said, replacing the handset. 'If anyone wants me, I've gone to the Shares Department to fix in some dates for overtime.' He made for the door.

Simon Good was not averse to doing overtime for any department that cared for his services during the periods of crisis which arose from time to time. For example, in the spring there was the rush for Motor policies; there was the solid slog in the vast Accounts Department for two months before the end of the financial year; there were the half-yearly dividends – the Interim and the Final – which were the bane of the Shares Department; there were the little spurts of business brought in by highly specialized advertising in a dozen small departments, all of which required extra help for a time to add punch to each campaign. Overtime rates were quite generous, the tea allowance adequate, the work not too onerous. Simon Good worked hard, always welcomed the extra money at the end of it. It is to be regretted that whilst he worked hard, it was not always for the benefit of the company. Fifty-one per cent of his effort was usually for the benefit of Simon Good, his mind busily analysing systems, noting the snags already known to the particular department, trying to find the unknown ones, docketing snippets of information about clients and their property, pigeon-holing names, learning and dissecting all the time, no piece of information being too small provided it was interesting. For example, he discovered that whilst the special ink used for inscribing the claims cheques could not be removed by a chemical eradicator (this was in accordance with the label on the bottle) a good clean job could be made with an ordinary soft pencil rubber without damaging the paper or the printed wavy background.

It was ironical that most of such information was obtained at considerable expense to his employers.

'You've just missed your friend, Mr Good,' said Jim Laker when Simon returned to the department some ten minutes later.

'Which one? I'm a lone wolf, and yet I have so many friends.'

'The one who comes in very occasionally, who's interested in gardening. You know – you order his bulbs for him in the "Lane". What's his name – Blake?'

'Why didn't you ask him to wait? You knew where I was.'

'I told him you wouldn't be long, but he was in a tearing hurry. He left a parcel on your desk, and said will you do the necessary for him.'

Simon examined the package. It was a large, well-filled, stout brown-paper bag, narrow in girth in relation to its height, with a cut-out grip reinforced with cardboard.

'He said they're'– Jim hesitated. '–mutations, I think. I believe they're bulbs, though.'

Simon laughed heartily. 'If they're mutations, they certainly *are* bulbs,' he proclaimed. 'Do you know what a mutation is, Jim?'

Jim Laker looked very young and very innocent. 'Yes, any two from three,' he said, and his eyes were wider than a cherub's.

'You're very near,' commented Simon encouragingly. 'A mutation, though, is any

112

one from *two*. You've got a garden, Jim. Has it ever struck you how or why you've got all those different varieties of tulips and daffodils in the spring?'

'Yes, we bought them,' said Jim simply.

'Fathead! I mean, do you realize how it came about there are so many different varieties?'

'The growers cross-breed them, I suppose.'

'How delightfully simple. D'you know how long it takes to cross-breed bulbs so that the mother bulb will produce bulbs that in turn will produce bulbs that won't revert to the species of either of the grandparent bulbs?'

'I haven't a clue, Mr Good. I really hadn't thought about it.'

'It takes years and years to get a genuine mutation. Until the variety is well established there's always a chance it will revert. Rather like lupins and hydrangeas tending to go back to their original blue if you leave them alone long enough. So when, one day, you wake up and find a true mutation in your bulb plot, guard it with your life. You'll earn anything from fifty to a hundred guineas a bulb for the first few bulbs of the new variety. Of course, it has to be an attractive variety. If the one you breed buries its head in the earth and has its roots in the air, it won't command a high price.

But if you've got an eye-catcher, you'll be in the money. For the next few years, as the variety gradually becomes known, you still won't find the price quoted in the catalogues. You'll read all about them, you'll see beautiful plates in glorious technicolour, but you won't see the price.'

'So that a bagful like that would be worth a tidy penny.'

'You've said it, Jim. Mutations! No, these are to go back for exchange – out of that last lot I ordered. Mr Blake buys large quantities of unsorted bulbs on the understanding that any rough stuff goes back. I suppose I should really do it for him today, but I've arranged to meet someone at lunch-time.' Simon hesitated. 'Would you like to do me a favour and take them back for me?'

Jim Laker was an obliging lad. 'Yes, I don't mind, Mr Good. I'm not doing anything particular in the lunch-hour. But there are several bulb stalls in the "Lane" – which one is it?'

'You've got a point there, Jim. For heaven's sake go to the right one, or else you'll be thrown under the stall with the blighted bulbs. The merchant you want is the one who dresses up like a Dutchman, complete with clogs, and says *ja* and *mjnheer*. He was probably born in Mile End Road. He's quite a decent chap, though, and he'll take them back without any trouble. Tell him I sent you.' Simon Good's eyes twinkled. 'Tell him they're mutations – only keep a straight face.'

'O.K., Mr Good. I'll shove 'em in my locker till I go out. What do I get in exchange – money or more bulbs?'

'Leave it to Dutchy. He knows the form. And thanks, Jim – I'll do the same for you one day.'

7

Principles without Practice

At eleven o'clock precisely, Superintendent Lingard was shown into the presence of the Secretary of the Tyburn & New York Insurance Co., Ltd. That gentleman, a Mr Earnshaw Withers by name, had been promoted by way of the Legal Department, where he had been in charge of American Contracts. The experience thus gained, together with a wide knowledge of British insurance company law, befitted him for his present unenviable job as secretary to a company which had tentacles in most parts of the world, a company subjected to a certain amount of direction from America. His voice was firm and decisive, and one was conscious of a keen, analytical brain which moved with the precision of an electronic computer to an irrefutable answer. As Lingard shook hands for the second time within two days he felt that behind those shrewd eyes the cogs were already beginning to mesh.

'Back again, Superintendent Lingard! Who is it this time?'

'I'm endeavouring to trace a man named Meek, sir. I was in the Army with him. I thought I saw him coming into this building last night just after I'd left, but by the time I'd got through the doors he'd vanished, presumably in one of the lifts. I decided not to worry you again then – at what must be a very busy time of the day for you – and so here I am this morning, at probably what is, if I did but know, an even more inconvenient moment.'

Withers made deprecating noises which somehow conveyed that that was precisely the position. 'Meek, you say?'

'Yes. Peter Meek. He was a company commander then. Major Meek.'

'If it's not asking too much, what do you want him for? Business or pleasure?'

'At the moment, pleasure.'

'H'm!' Withers reflected for a moment, as he always did before committing himself. 'We have no Meek in this building,' he said. 'In fact, we have nobody of that name in the whole organization. I'll confirm that.' He dialled a number on the internal telephone.

'Mr Withers here. Check that we have no Peter Meek employed anywhere in the company's service. I'll wait.' There was a pause whilst the locked card index in the Personnel Department was being opened up and consulted. The telephone crackled again, and Mr Earnshaw Withers permitted a frosty flicker of self-satisfaction to disturb his features – for one brief instant. 'I'm sorry, Superintendent, we cannot help you. The only Meek we can trace is a Hiram Meek who once worked in our San Francisco office. He died twelve years ago, a pensioner aged eighty-two. Not your man, I fancy!'

'Indeed not!' smiled Lingard. 'I'm sorry to have troubled you.'

'Have you inquired at the bank on the ground floor?'

'I have, sir.'

'There are, of course, a few other tenants in the block – we don't occupy the whole building. I'll ask the Property Department to supply you with a list.'

'That would be most helpful,' said Lingard, 'and then I'll leave you to your work – which could be, I suppose, paying for the burglaries committed by the burglars *we* hope to catch!'

'And if the burglar happens to catch fire to the premises we have to pay out for both the burglary *and* the fire!'

'An expensive business to be in, sir.'

117

'Yes, but after all, it is our business. And we do discharge our side of it.'

'Meaning that we don't?' commented Lingard pleasantly.

'That is for you to decide, Superintendent,' replied Mr Earnshaw Withers. The smile was there, but so was the sting. 'We have figures to support our contentions – our loss payments run into millions of pounds sterling, annually. But I expect you have statistics which give you equal satisfaction.'

Superintendent Lingard nodded equably. 'Quite so, sir, quite so.'

'With figures, one can prove almost anything,' said Withers offhandedly. 'It's the presentation that counts. I'll get you your list,' he said abruptly, pressing a button for a messenger who entered almost immediately. 'Ask the Property Department for a list of the tenants in this building – I want it quickly so as not to waste the Superintendent's time.'

Lingard affected not to notice the oblique shaft. 'I take it, sir,' he asked, as the man left the room, 'that your reference to a simultaneous fire and burglary was prompted by the van Meyer incident?'

'Yes, I did have that in mind. Are you in any way connected with the inquiries, Superintendent?'

'Not directly. I know of certain investigations taking place. Is the Tyburn & New

York involved?'

'To a considerable extent, I'm afraid!'

'Let's hope the police discharge their duties efficiently this time and catch the culprit. And I hope you've sufficient money in the kitty to keep up your vital statistics.'

Superintendent Lingard could be pleasantly nasty at times.

'I can assure you we have,' said Withers huffily.

Lingard hesitated and then took the plunge. 'It occurs to me, sir, that insurers have a vast amount of private information at their disposal. In general, do you think it beyond the bounds of possibility that some person might be using part of this knowledge to his own advantage?'

'You mean apropos the spate of unsolved burglaries we've had of late?'

'I did mean something like that,' smiled Lingard, 'although for the record there hasn't been a spate of *unsolved* burglaries. Burglaries, yes, but eighty per cent of the serious ones are cleared up. And even the serious unsolved ones – which frankly do worry us – are beginning to take on a very definite pattern. We appear to be coming unstuck about once every five or six months, and there's a certain precision about them which puts them all in the same category.'

'Well, of course, we do have a lot of confidential information of a certain kind in the house,' agreed Withers doubtfully, 'but I would hesitate to say that much of it was very useful from the criminal point of view. We might know how old an actress really is, or whether somebody's property is mortgaged and how much for, or even the rate of gross profit on their business, all sorts of little titbits – but what does it add up to? Of course, during the war, insurance companies supplied the War Office with much really valuable information – from the point of view of running a war – plans, reports, and photographs of all manner of risks in enemy territory, oil installations from Bremen to Trieste, factory complexes from the Ruhr to Tokyo – right down to the last detail of the number of floors and what they were made of. That was intrinsic information, Superintendent, which helped Intelligence to build up a picture for the bombers and for the ultimate invasion of Europe. Some of our insurance street plans have to be seen to be believed. Give me an address in Birmingham or Buenos Aires, and I'll tell you all about it in a very short time.'

'Now that sounds like real information!' said Lingard enthusiastically. 'Rather like what we could tell you about quite a lot of the inhabitants. Now, sir, you've answered me in general. In particular, and entirely off the record, would it be altogether too preposterous to suppose that some such knowledge was being used by somebody in this building?'

'Peter Meek?' came the swift inquiry.

Lingard laughed back into the upturned inquisitive eyes.

'Good Lord, no!' he said easily and untruthfully. 'He's the last person to be involved in such – goings on. No – I mean by someone who would have access to papers in the normal course of work – say a filing-clerk, who could read up a file and find out all about the burglar alarms that were installed in a building, the type and the vulnerable points, and so on.'

Withers pursed his lips doubtfully.

'It would be extremely unlikely, Superintendent. For one thing, all the current files are kept in the particular departments concerned, and that would mean it would have to be somebody who was in a position to wander round those departments, who was *persona grata* – say, a messenger, for example. Even so, however well known such a person might be, he couldn't poke around the files without exciting comment. I suppose someone on the housekeeping or maintenance-staff could do it after office hours, but even then they'd have to be very careful, and quite frankly I can't visualize a master mind amongst the whole bunch of them.'

'It needn't be a question of somebody being *persona grata* in *all* departments,' pointed out Lingard, 'it need affect only one department – your Burglary Department, for instance – do you call it the "Burglary" Department? I wouldn't know, of course; I don't even know if you *have* a separate department for the business.'

'Oh, yes, we call it the Burglary Department, right enough,' said Withers absently. 'On the face of it, Superintendent, there could be something in what you suggest, but if you're going to town on it, there are several other fields in which an unscrupulous person could be interested. For example, Cash-in-transit insurance. We have a certain amount of information there – in fact, in some cases we lay down the method by which cash shall be sent or collected. But in any event, even if the details were obtained by somebody in the office, the actual crime remains to be put into commission, and I still can't see any of the staff here being a master criminal – it just isn't feasible.'

'It need only be the obtaining of the information that is being done at this end,' pointed out the Superintendent, 'the details could be passed on to people who are prepared to execute the crime. You confide that the Tyburn & New York is heavily involved in the van Meyer fire and burglary. The burglar had certain knowledge which might have been obtainable from the files of an insurance company. I wondered if it could have come from here. It's a long shot, and I wouldn't have asked you if you hadn't told me your company was interested in the first place.'

'*Told* you – as I remember it, you *asked* me!' said Withers shrewdly.

'Oh, did I?' said Lingard vaguely. 'Maybe I did – the whole thing was perhaps triggered off by your mentioning a hypothetical fire and burglary claim.' He skated over the thin ice hurriedly, knowing that at any moment the list he was waiting for would arrive and the interview would be over. 'You see, whoever broke into the wing of the van Meyer mansion – I tell you this in confidence as an interested party – had precise knowledge of the burglar-alarm system in operation. The alarm was coupled direct to the local police, and they should have received a call even if it was set off accidentally. No such call was received, yet the place was entered. As regards the safe, the Yard experts feel the job was tackled by someone who knew what he'd be up against, who would have carried it out very smoothly but for one small fact – but for which fact there might not have been a fire. However, that is to a certain extent conjecture. You see, though, why I ask whether your Burglary Department is above suspicion.'

'Indeed, I do,' agreed Withers. 'You have

posed a very interesting situation, but I think I can demonstrate why our Burglary Department is blameless. You have kindly put your side of the picture to me, and before I can show you our side of it, I shall have to give you a little of the background to the way we run our insurance business.'

'I hope it will not waste too much of your valuable time,' said Lingard, knowing he was on a safe bet if he could induce Mr Earnshaw Withers to mount what was obviously a favourite hobby-horse.

'Not at all,' said that worthy, half-way up the straight. 'There are various ways in which we, as insurers, can be interested in a risk. The first is where the business comes direct to us via one of our world-wide branches or agencies, and we deal with the whole thing from A to Z. We know all there is to know about the insured and the risk, all about the moral and physical hazards involved. We call this "Direct" business. If we bite off rather more than we would care to lose for a particular class of risk, we effect what we call "reinsurance" – in popular parlance, we lay some off. Thus if the amount at risk were £100,000 and we were prepared to lose only £20,000, we effect reinsurance to the extent of £80,000. That brings us to another way in which we get business – by reinsuring other companies who feel they are holding too much on a risk.'

'Rather like bookmaking,' said Lingard indiscreetly.

'Dear me, no!' exclaimed Mr Withers, horrified. 'The similarity between contracts of insurance and wagers exists only in the minds of the uninitiated. You must get out your Moriarty, Superintendent, and study the references to the Gambling Acts. However, if we reinsure another company by what we call a "facultative guarantee", we initial a slip showing brief particulars of the risk, and that binds us to follow their fortunes. This business is generally known as "Issued Guarantee" business. Are you with me so far?'

'Just alongside of you, sir, no more. It strikes me if I were running the business I'd sooner be writing Issued Guarantees than doing Direct business.'

'Why?'

'Surely the acquisition costs would be heavier in running Direct business than in merely sitting back and waiting for the Issued Guarantees to roll in.'

Mr Withers's eyes twinkled. 'Superintendent, you do yourself an injustice – you are way ahead of me! I must hasten to explain the snag. Because of the very fact you've just mentioned, the commission on Issued Guarantee business is considerably higher than that allowed on Direct business.'

Lingard thought that one out for a moment. 'In that case,' he pursued, 'wouldn't it be better to reinsure all your risks one hundred per cent, and make a handsome profit with no risk attaching? Pay, say, twenty-five per cent commission for the business in the first place, and then collect thirty-five per cent for getting rid of it!'

'I should hate to be on the wrong side of you, Superintendent, you're just like a – I was going to say ferret, only you might not consider that altogether polite. Once again there are snags. The eligibility of a risk is judged partly by the amount the ceding company is keeping for its own account – their "retention" – and you could imagine what a good impression would be conveyed if the whole risk was being got rid of! Generally speaking, the less the ceding company retains the more difficult it is to effect reinsurance, because reinsurers usually accept so many times the ceding company's limit. The Tyburn & New York's policy, for example, might be to accept up to five "lines", as we call it. Thus if the offering company is retaining, say, £20,000, we would be prepared to accept five lines – £100,000. On the other hand, if they retained only £20, we would accept only £100 by way of reinsurance, and that wouldn't be much help to them! Are you still with me?'

'I've dropped behind a little now, but I think I get the general drift. What happens with claims? Does each company have to settle its own share with the insured?'

'Oh, no! The insured looks for indemnity only to the company with whom he took out his policy. Even if all the other companies didn't pay up, he couldn't be less concerned, he has no contract with them.'

'I see.' Lingard looked thoughtful for a moment. 'But where does all this link up with our burglary case?'

'Ah!' Withers pursed his lips. 'You've been an apt pupil, Superintendent – does any fundamental difference strike you as between "Direct" business and "Issued Guarantee" business?'

Lingard dwelt on that for a little. 'Well, it seems you might have more details and knowledge of your own direct case than one offered to you by another company as a *fait accompli* on a slip of paper.'

'Excellent, excellent!' exclaimed Withers, rubbing his hands. 'You've hit the nail right on the head! Whereas with a direct case we have to make up our minds as to the insurability or otherwise of a risk, with a reinsurance we assume the ceding company has already made all the relevant inquiries, and we judge our acceptance almost solely by what we read into the other company's retention, the rate they have charged, and our own knowledge and experience of the class of risk. Beyond that, we have no special information at our disposal unless we make a point of asking the ceding company for it.'

Lingard sighed. 'I know what you're going to tell me, sir, I can smell it a mile off. You're interested in the van Meyer diamonds only by way of guarantee to another company, and as such your Burglary Department are not in possession of any special details of the burglar alarms and so on as they would be if it were your own direct case.'

'Superintendent, if I had my way I'd make you an honorary Fellow of the Chartered Insurance Institute.'

'You say, sir, that you may ask another company for extra information if necessary. Do you ever do so?'

'Very rarely. We rely in varying degrees on the name of the company offering the risk.'

'Does that mean some aren't so honest as others?'

'No, it means that we know what to expect some companies to offer. They'd be keeping it themselves if it was any good.'

There was a tap at the door, and Mr Moran put his head round. He withdrew immediately he saw the secretary had a visitor.

'Mr Moran!' called Withers. 'You're just the man we want.'

Moran slid into the room, and Withers made no introductions. 'I want a snap answer,' he fired. 'How often do you ask another company for a plan and report in connexion with a guarantee acceptance?'

'Very rarely, sir – in fact, I don't think I can recall the last occasion.'

'You don't find it necessary to help you assess the risk?'

'It isn't the practice, sir. We can usually make up our minds from the information on the slip. If we don't like the look of an offer immediately, we turn it down right away. If we have any doubts, we might, on occasion, ask for more details over the telephone, but if we're so doubtful as to want to borrow plans and reports, we'd sooner rely on our underwriting sense and decline it. In any event, sir, our acceptances by guarantee are usually modest *because* of paucity of details. Of course, in a Profits reinsurance, it is useful to see, if possible, an Interruption Report indicating how long say a factory is likely to be out of commission if the power-house were blown up. I'll have a word with Mr Good, he fixes up quite a lot of the guarantee acceptances.'

'That won't be necessary,' replied Withers, waving the other away. 'Thank you. You see the position, Superintendent?' he went on, as the door closed behind Moran. 'That was the head of our Guarantee & Reinsurance Department, and you heard what he had to say. I purposely didn't mention the burglary angle, but I can assure you he would be even less likely to seek special information from another company in respect of a burglary acceptance because the amounts involved by guarantee are, as Mr Moran said, very modest – by insurance standards, that is. Look, Superintendent, I have tried to teach you a little of my business, and you appear to have absorbed it very rapidly. I therefore hesitate to make a suggestion for fear you would think I were trying to teach you a little of yours.'

'I'm always open to suggestions, sir, and I'm sure one of yours would only be helpful and not frivolous.'

'Well, if you really believe this – hunch of yours that someone is using private inform-ation, why not circularize all the insurance companies – I could also put you in touch with somebody at Lloyd's – and ask them confidentially if they have been involved in any, or all, of the unsolved burglaries that you tell me are now taking on a pattern. If there's anything in what you think, then somewhere along the line there must be a common factor which the replies will reveal.'

'Such as one particular insurance com-pany suffering loss in respect of each bur-glary?' suggested Lingard admiringly.

'Something like that,' smiled Withers. 'You see, even if only one company is involved, the pattern of the unsolved burglaries wouldn't necessarily strike them amongst all their other claims – particularly if, as you suggest,

130

there is a five to six months' time-lag.'

'An inquiry like this would set them thinking!' exclaimed Lingard. 'I must hasten to point out that this is purely my own personal, unofficial hunch – I'll have to get the Commander's blessing before I can proceed on such a wide scale of inquiry.'

The messenger slipped back into the room and discreetly placed a typewritten list before the secretary. Whisking up a few papers from the 'Out' tray, he left as silently as a bird.

'Your list,' commented Withers, glancing briefly at it before handing it over. 'Now, Superintendent, as soon as you let us have a note of your major unsolved burglary cases, we'll be only too happy to supply you with our answers. And I'm sure everyone else will. And if you draw a graph from the replies, you'll probably be surprised at what you find.'

Lingard rose and shook hands.

'You make it sound like an exercise in calculus,' he smiled. 'I think mathematics must be your strong point, sir.'

'It is,' agreed Mr Earnshaw Withers modestly. 'You can prove almost anything mathematically.'

Superintendent Lingard smiled happily. 'Yes, but it's the presentation that counts,' he said.

Simon Good was totting up the initialled

amounts on a reinsurance slip to find out how much more cover was required on a tea factory in Assam, when the house-telephone on his desk interrupted the cast. With a cluck of annoyance he stretched out for the handset.

'Good, here.'

A soft, very feminine voice came over the wires.

'Simon, the police have been here this morning. They are inquiring for a Peter Meek. I thought you'd like to know.'

Simon Good almost stopped breathing, so still was he.

'How did you come by this information?' he asked at length.

'I was in the Personnel Department when an inquiry came through from Mr Withers. And somebody remarked that a police super-intendent had been shown into him a few minutes previously. I know nothing beyond that – obviously *I* couldn't start making inquiries.'

Simon Good took a grip on himself. 'Thanks for letting me know,' he said very quietly.

There was a brief, fluttering pause.

'Take care of yourself, Simon.'

The line went dead.

Superintendent Lingard made systematic calls on the tenants in the building, ticking off his list as he did so. It was about a quarter to one when he finished at the ground-floor level, having found one Mr Meek who so perfectly fitted the name – he was a bald little man with a wispy moustache, and sad, faded eyes which peered hesitantly over cheap pince-nez – that one would have been surprised if he was anything else but.

Lingard looked out through the plate-glass doors into Fetter Lane. Many people were on the move, the first shift of the lunch-hour was on its way back, and in a few minutes the one o'clock crowd would be pouring out of the building. He made a quick recce of the ground-floor exits. To the rear of the block was a large secondary way out, leading to a labyrinth of bomb-sites and ancient premises in the process of being mopped up by modern planning.

If Peter Meek worked in the building, it was a toss-up which way out he would normally use for lunch, always assuming he lunched at one o'clock and that he didn't patronize a staff canteen on the premises. People are largely creatures of habit, rather like ants with their inexplicable set runs to and from the queen ant's abode. Lingard had seen his quarry at the front entrance once, so the front entrance it would be again. At least, the chances seemed that way. They *seemed*.

He left the building, bought a paper from Old Fred, and took up an unobtrusive

position on the opposite side of the road...
Simon Good also could be unobtrusive.
He left the building by the other exit.

8

Off the Record

Mr Hammersley stood doubtfully outside
the Public Record Office in Chancery Lane,
and studied one of the notices at the main
gateway. He read the top portion twice. It
ran:

PUBLIC RECORD OFFICE

THE MUSEUM OF
THIS OFFICE IS OPEN
DAILY FROM
1.0 TO 4.0 P.M.
EXCEPT SATURDAYS
OR DAYS ON WHICH
THE OFFICE
IS CLOSED

A small plaque, hanging on one of the huge
wrought-iron gates and tastefully executed
in scumble, cream paint and varnish, and
reading *Museum Open*, left him in no doubt,

although he was still slightly over-awed at the hugeness of the building in front of him. The presence in the archway of a large policeman and a peak-capped official in no way allayed the impression he had of a better-class jail.

It is a curious thing that it seems to require quite a lot of courage to enter the Public Record Office, alone, for the very first time. People turn up there daily, full of eagerness, having heard vaguely of the blot on Will Shakespeare's Will, only to turn away in doubt and sorrow when faced with the actual psychology of having to get into the building. We'll come another day, they seem to be saying as they make their way round to the Seven Stars in Carey Street.

The clock in Chancery Lane Post Office had said one-fifteen. Hammersley always liked to be on parade before time. Taking the plunge, he nodded affably to the policeman, walked through the wicket gate, and as instructed by Simon Good, followed his nose and the arrow up a few steps into the building. He was just thinking, as so many people had thought before him, that he was getting away with it all too easily, when he came to a bend in the corridor, was courteously stopped by an attendant, directed to a desk and requested to sign the record of visitors.

He wondered if Simon Good had already arrived, and he glanced rapidly at the names before him. The record, however, was not in book form, but in single sheets, previous pages having been set aside in a folder, leaving only half a dozen names for him to look at. Neither Simon Good nor Peter Meek figured amongst them, although that didn't prove he wasn't already there. He might turn out to be Ezekiel Klaufmann, of 839, The Barbecue, Massachusetts.

Hammersley picked up the pen, and also like many others before him who had been relieved to find the procedure really quite simple after all, signed his name with an air of importance that was completely unwarranted.

At the top of the few steps leading down into the Museum he paused in admiration. He appreciated well-appointed things, and the simple magnificence of this chamber, with its well-arranged modem showcases, met with his complete approval. He caught the eye of an attendant.

'I would like to see the showcase relating to the Great Charter, if you please,' he said, with a certain quiet dignity.

The helpful attendant (at the Record Office Museum, the attendants really do their best to make any visit worth while) pointed out the case on the far side of the room. 'You are interested in the roots of freedom, sir?' he ventured smilingly.

'I am,' replied Mr Hammersley with fervour. 'Very much so, in the very tap-root itself! You see, I've always enjoyed a measure of freedom myself, but, alas, I've seen the other side of the picture, too. I get almost claustrophobic when I think of confinement.'

'So do a lot of people,' grinned the other cheekily. He suddenly wondered if the visitor was referring to prison, if the Museum's treasures were safe, and the grin went from his face.

'I was referring to a little place near Fall-ingbostel in Germany,' said Hammersley, reading the change of countenance. 'I was there many years ago, in the Army. My O.C. insisted on taking me. You may have heard of the place – Belsen. I didn't sleep properly for a long while after.'

The attendant made sympathetic noises, and Mr Hammersley made his way over to the Magna Carta showcase, glancing round at the handful of visitors to confirm that Simon Good had not yet arrived. Having a few minutes in hand, he wandered round the display cases to get a general idea of the place. He very quickly observed that here indeed was a wealth of entertainment that all the detergents in creation couldn't pro-vide on television. A map drawn by Major George Washington, which was now holding the rapt, almost reverent attention of an American and his wife. A letter from Marie Antoinette. The writings and signatures of kings and queens, inventors, authors and scientists through the ages. One of the few documents signed by Jane Grey during her short nominal reign of thirteen days – a Bill of Queen Jane for the issue of Letters Patent appointing Edward Bernarde to be Sheriff of Wiltshire. The Domesday Book. And a thousand and one other items of interest.

The place called for a long visit on a wet or cold afternoon, and this Hammersley decided to do. He drifted back to the Magna Carta case. He was rather intrigued by the bottom portion of the Indenture, with its wavy top line where it had been cut through the signatures; the indented counterpart, probably authenticated by the Great Seal, and presumably given to the barons, being missing. He idly speculated what the top portion would be worth, if only someone could find it.

'Too late,' said Simon Good softly, at his side.

Hammersley didn't look round. 'Too late for what?' he asked, looking at the reflection in the glass of the case.

'I've already thought of it.'

'I wish you wouldn't talk in riddles,' muttered Mr Hammersley irritably. 'Thought of what?'

'Thought of finding the top half of that document. But I don't know enough about it to know what it's supposed to look like.'

Mr Hammersley was startled. 'You must be clairvoyant!' he exclaimed.

'Possibly,' agreed the other modestly. 'But I think the real answer is that I know you rather better than you think I do. Always bear that in mind in your dealings with me. It will avoid a lot of unpleasantness.'

'If nobody *knows* what the top half looks like, perhaps we could – um – *find* it,' said Charles Hammersley hopefully.

'Don't be a clot, Charlie. What did you think of the notice outside? How did it strike you?'

'Notice? Oh, it seemed perfectly straight-forward to me.'

'Yes, I suppose anything with a slight twist in it would. A number of people I know find it a wee bit confusing – even amusing – at first, although I must admit there's nothing really wrong with it.'

'Some people are easily confused and easily amused. It takes more than that to amuse me.'

'Yes, I expect you take a lot of amusing. I feel you would be happier if you had a regular job.'

'Perhaps you're right,' agreed Hammersley, with no immediate prospect in view.

'I've got you one,' said Simon simply.

The Magna Carta case swam before Mr Hammersley's eyes in a misty blur. 'A job?' he gulped in alarm. Freedom was in the balance. 'What do you mean – *work?*'

'Work. And keep your voice down.'

'But I don't want work – I've got other things to think about. What sort of a job?'

'On the housekeeping staff of a large insurance company.'

'Which one?' Although Mr Hammersley had no intention of taking any job of work, he found himself perforce asking questions.

'The Tyburn & New York.'

Hammersley's knees wobbled a bit and seemed to have no strength.

'But I simply can't get a job there!' he said in anguish.

'Why not? It's a first-class company.'

'I know. But they're already keeping me!'

'Are they?' Simon Good was seemingly surprised.

'Yes, they're paying me full benefits for my shoulder – one of my Oxford Street accidents. I can scarcely expect them to give me a job as well! Especially while I'm incapacitated – it would be like biting the hand that feeds you. It – it wouldn't be fair!'

Simon Good's face, contorted in a ghoulish grin, projected itself back at Hammersley from the plate glass. 'Nevertheless, if you were on the housekeeping staff of the Tyburn & New York, you would have access to certain keys, and that would mean access to certain information. And that would be very useful to me.'

Hammersley looked thoughtful for a moment. 'Would I have to do menial work – cleaning, scrubbing, and so on?'

'Undoubtedly, but the wages are good, and the work would amount to no more than when you were my batman. And this particular job calls for batman-like qualities – that's why it's still vacant even after they've tried half a dozen applicants. Part of the job,' explained Simon Good carefully, 'is to be factotum to the General Manager of the company – a certain Mr Jullien Fane. You would have to do odd jobs at his house at Dorking, and there you would pick up quite a lot of useful information for me. With the good references you doubtless possess, the job is yours.'

'The only references I have are my Army ones, and they're a bit ancient now. Needless to say, they were of the very highest order.'

'I would remind you that I wrote them,' pointed out Simon. 'It was one of the last jobs I did before I was blown up, such was my devotion to duty.'

'I was forgetting,' apologized Hammersley.

'Never forget people who are so fond of you that they are prepared to lie on your behalf,' said Mr Good. 'If it's merely a question of references that's holding you up, I'll send you two or three different sets tomorrow.'

'It's not entirely a question of references,' said Mr Hammersley. 'I wouldn't be able to do the work. The fact is' – he hesitated, and then the words came tumbling out – 'I've fractured my wrist.'

'You've what?' exclaimed Simon incredulously.

'Fractured my wrist.' Hammersley pushed back the sleeve of his heavy overcoat, and displayed the bandaged wrist. 'It's only a slight one, fortunately, but very painful.'

'Excellent!' said Simon Good enthusiastically. 'Of course, you'll claim partial disablement benefit for it, won't you. It'll make a nice change from your shoulder.'

'It's no laughing matter,' expostulated Mr Hammersley.

'Certainly not,' agreed Simon. 'Anything that affects our income is serious.

'*Our* income?'

'Yes, yours and mine. I don't expect to take all of it – we're in this together, remember? Which company do you intend to claim from?'

'Well, I don't really know. I'm in a bit of a fix. There were no witnesses, and I've never had to make a genuine claim before.'

'How did it happen?'

'As I was going home yesterday after seeing you, I was thinking of – of things, and I slipped off the kerb and put out my hand to save myself. I fell on my wrist, and that was that.'

'You worry too much,' said Simon. 'Have

you got the list I asked for? Slip it over, discreetly, and I'll advise you the best company. It would be too ironic if they thought the first genuine claim you made was fraudulent. How long is it likely to be before it mends?'

'They said at the hospital some weeks.'

'Oh, you went to hospital?'

'Yes, the local doctor sent me to have it X-rayed.'

'Well, I'm afraid that's snookered the idea of working for the Tyburn & New York Insurance Company. A pity, I had great hopes of getting all sorts of private titbits from you. Never mind, perhaps the job will still be open when your wrist is better. I'll study this list of yours and let you know when and where you can have your next accident. I'll be able to give you invaluable advice.'

There had been a question on Hammersley's tongue for some time, and out it came. 'Where do you work, anyway, Mr Good?'

'You wouldn't be any happier if you knew, Charlie. Be a good boy and get well. I'll let you know how to make payment to me. Now I must be about my lawful occasions.'

'You have those as well?' asked Mr Hammersley, faintly surprised.

Simon regarded him with a sorrowful eye. 'There are times when you pass remarks that are unworthy of our great friendship. I'm only trying to help you. But for me you would be languishing in jail waiting for the

143

tumbril to bear you to the Old Bailey. Let us part on a happy note. And give me a few minutes start – I'd prefer you not to follow me.'

Good drifted casually towards the exit, and Hammersley's eyes gleamed. This was the moment he was waiting for. With luck he might be able to tail the other and find out what he did for a living and where he lived – this information might form a basis for retaliation. He waited till Good left the chamber and then, counting ten, followed quickly in his wake.

He was dismayed to find Simon Good talking to an attendant just round the corner.

'Ah, this is the gentleman!' said Mr Good. 'He tells me he's very interested in the Domesday Book. Is it possible to trace his family in it for him? He's a Kentish man. Or a man of Kent. I'm not sure which. He comes from a little place that was called Hammers in Anglo-Saxon times. His ancestors were blacksmiths. The one holding the tenure when the Domesday Book was being compiled was known as "the Hammer". The Hammer of Hammers. You've heard of Abinger Hammer? Well, he was one of the Surrey branch of the family – always on the binge. However. When the Hammer retired from active life – of course, there were no pensions in those days – he laid down his hammer on the anvil, and the hamlet became known as "Hammers-lay-

Anvil". Heaven knows what they call it now, but that's how he got his name, so he tells me. Of course, over the years they dropped the Anvil, and the "lay" became shortened as in Hammers*ley*. I think he'd be very grateful if you could find out all about it in the Domesday Book for him, and possibly give him a photostat copy of the page – I believe you do do that, don't you? And when you've done that, if you've got time, he'd love to see the traditional iron-bound chest linked with the Domesday Book – wouldn't you, sir?'

'Yes,' said Mr Hammersley weakly.

'I thought you would,' burbled Simon. 'As they say in Lincoln's Inn – *'Volenti non fit injuria'* – don't you agree?'

'Ha!' said the attendant. 'This way, sir. I'll show you the box first – it's just round here...'

9

New Name for an Old Tulip

Leatherwick Way, that cramped, narrow overspill which swings back from its parent, Leather Lane, towards Hatton Garden, lies a few minutes' walk to the north of the Head Office of the Tyburn & New York Insurance

Company, and is the site of one of London's busiest lunch-hour markets. Clerks and typists while away part of their feeding time listening to the spiel and searching for bargains. The majority of the traders have been long established, and carry on the businesses of their forebears. They have a reputation for honest trading and are independent to a degree. Money is refunded without question to any dissatisfied customer.

There are also, as one would imagine in the hurly-burly of the open market, traders who suddenly appear with a wonderful line in a suitcase and then vanish into the limbo of another sentence. If one is attracted by a bargain offered by one of these gentlemen, it is advisable to snap it up quickly before it and the gentleman are themselves snapped up by a Market Inspector accompanied by a policeman. Frequently these traders without licence employ look-outs, and on receipt of a signal from them their disappearance – sometimes in the middle of a sale – surpasses the Indian rope trick for sheer magic.

It was into this atmosphere of hectoring and good-natured repartee that Superintendent Lingard wandered after an abortive half an hour's vigil in Fetter Lane. At one stall he was offered toothbrushes and bath cubes at ridiculous prices, and at another was invited to try on a pair of shoes on the 'concrete carpet' at the rear of the stall – these and many similar offers he turned down with friendly firmness. He drifted past the chemical factory with its curious odours, along into the heady, sweet-smelling atmosphere of the tobacco works, keeping a weather eye open on all the plant and bulb stalls, at the same time turning over in his mind all that Mr Earnshaw Withers had told him.

Retracing his steps just short of Clerkenwell Road he turned left into the hotch-potch of Leatherwick Way, which was generally accepted as being part of the 'Lane', and listened for a minute or two to a very well-dressed gentleman who was extolling the virtues of a new scientific system for winning football pools. This gentleman had a fat wad of registered envelopes which had contained gratuities from grateful clients, and the magnificent American car, parked half in the gutter, half on the pavement, added a nice touch of veracity to all that was being said.

More toothbrushes – it seemed the traders had cornered the market in toothbrushes! – fruit, china, tools, electrical goods, bankrupt stock, the lot. More bulbs–

Superintendent Lingard stood stock still, to the intense irritation of two labourers following close behind who expressed themselves forcibly in Anglo-Saxon. There, over on the left, were two stalls side by side, laden with bulbs, mainly daffodil and tulip. One stall appeared to be devoted to carefully segregated and named topsize bulbs, each tipped-up display box sporting a gaily coloured picture of the variety. The other stall, stacked with daffodil and narcissi bulbs had fewer varieties, and they were, even to the lay eye, ungraded. Both stalls were flanked by large wide-meshed sacks of bulbs with the Dutch labels of origin still attached. Three men were serving as fast as they could go, and Lingard had a fleeting thought of the amount of money people were prepared to spend on their gardens. A boy was constantly replenishing and topping up the boxes from a lorry parked in a near-by cul-de-sac. The three men were dressed in picturesque Dutch attire, correct to the last detail from cap to clogs. The thing that had brought the Superintendent up with a jolt was the oiled-cloth banner stretched high across the two stalls, a banner painted in blue and black and gold, which read:

DUTCHY
For Bulbs – Every Bulb Guaranteed.
Biggest Bulbs – Lowest Prices.

Gauging by the crowd, the business certainly had plenty of goodwill. The turnover was incredible. Each man had a zippered pocket in front of his costume into which pound and ten-shilling notes were thrust with amazing rapidity. Lingard worked his way to the front of the crowd with quickening interest, subjecting each of the three salesmen to a quick scrutiny. He was conscious of a feeling of deflation. None of them resembled the mental image of the man he once knew, although the man behind the stall of ungraded bulbs, whom he took to be the boss, was about the right age.

He rescrutinized them carefully. There was only one salesman on the 'topsize' stall, and he was in front serving a constant stream of customers with bulbs that were already bagged-up in dozens. Customers buying several bagfuls could help themselves to a large brown-paper bag from the side to accommodate their purchases. An order of six dozen or more warranted a free carrier bag. Lingard watched fascinated. This man was obviously too young.

At the neighbouring stall the two other men were working hard selling the ungraded bulbs. There would be a short period of spiel from the man at the back, followed by frantic bagging-up of bulbs and taking in the half-crowns hand-over-fist. These bulbs were not being sold by the dozen, but by the bagful, and were good value for money. To sell bulbs at that price meant that turnover was of prime importance, and to achieve a high turnover in a 'lunch-hour' market lasting approximately from midday to two o'clock meant plenty of hard work. The man in front of this stall was likewise too young to have been in the war, and it was to the spieler behind that Lingard directed his attention.

As he had already noted, the age was about right, the build – apart from a certain stoutness which may have come with the years or the costume – was approximately what it should be, but the face seemed altogether *too* different to be the face of the man he had once briefly known, the man he still held in his memory as a grimy, hollow-eyed Cockney with only one Piat bomb, grinning in reply to the blistering threats of Sergeant Blake. Of course, time worked curious wonders on some people, but Lingard was reluctantly compelled to conclude that this man also was not the Dutchy he once knew. The name and the trade and the market stall was one of those coincidences the Commander had been talking about. Of course, business could be flourishing to such an extent that perhaps Dutchy himself was at home with his feet up, whilst his minions did the work. Could be. Lingard edged nearer so that he could read the address inscribed in small lettering at the bottom of the oiled flysheet. It was, however, only the address of the sign-writer. There was a lull in the sales, and the spieler started again.

'If you people want topsize bulbs then Jan over there will serve you at prices that'll make you ashamed to take the stuff away – that so, Jan?'

Jan paused in the middle of serving a customer, looked up, and grinned a wide, toothy grin. '*Ja!*' he said, 'dot is so!'

'But if it's quantity you want, I'll give you the biggest bargain you ever did see in your life, and I know this, you'll be back for more, not only this year but next year, too. There's a gentleman there who's a regular customer, and another there – how many years have you been buying off me? I'm not out to catch you people – believe me, I could if I wanted – it's your regular custom I want, so I can live in luxury not only next year but the year after, as well. So why should I want to catch you for half a crown, eh?' This was the point which always delighted the crowd, when the zippered-pocket was pulled open and two fistfuls of treasury notes were produced and waved temptingly at them, only to be thrust back contemptuously into the kangaroo pouch in front. 'I don't have to beg for your custom – you come to me. And why? You know why. Because I give you the best half-crown's worth you've ever had in your life. Because I deal with you fair and square. Because if you're dissatisfied I'll give you your money back or change your bulbs if you think you've been done. Because if you can get 'em any cheaper anywhere else, I'll give fifty quid to any charity you like to name. Money, don't talk to me about money! I've got enough money to last me for the rest of my life – if I die tonight!' The crowd grinned dutifully. 'You gentlemen want quantity and quality. It's no good buying a load of tripe just because it's cheap – next spring it's flowers you want, not a lot of spring greens. I don't buy one crate of bulbs and keep 'em in a shop for months waiting for the mugs to come in to buy 'em at seven and six a dozen. I buy several *tons* at a time direct from the growers in Holland. And I can buy 'em that way at the right price for two reasons. One is that these bulbs you see here are unsorted, just as they come from the ground. If you want 'em sorted, you can get 'em from Jan, but you have to pay for 'em. And why? Because the growers have graded 'em and cleaned 'em. How come those tulips over there look so nice and shiny? I'll tell you. They wash 'em and dry 'em and trim 'em, and treat 'em with linseed oil and give 'em a gentle polish by machinery. And you pay for all that. Granted you get a good bulb, you're entitled to. The second reason is that I know you're prepared to take a chance and buy two or three times as many for the same money. And I'll show you what sort of a chance you're taking.'

He groped in the box which served as a till, and produced a well-worn jack-knife. 'Pass me a bulb, sir – any one you like.'

A man stepped forward and picked a bulb

at random.

'Ah, Golden Harvest! You've picked a winner there, sir. Golden Harvest. Here's a coloured picture of it. Look at that wonderful golden centre. When they were first bred they were marketed at two guineas a bulb. Not a sackful. Not a dozen. One bulb. Look at the quality of this one you've just handed me. Firm as a rock, hard as iron.' The jack-knife sliced expertly down through the middle of the bulb, just off-centre. 'Look at that – clean as a whistle, white as milk, not a trace of black blight.' The point of the knife got busy again, easing up the very heart of the bulb, the delicate miniature flower with its pale yellow tip. 'And there you see, gentlemen, the flower itself, all the way from Holland, waiting to come up in your garden. You can see for yourselves, you're buying *flowers*, not a load of rubbish only fit for the compost heap. I said flowers, gentlemen, and I mean flowers, even if you only buy one bulb.' The knife quartered the bulb. 'Look, there you see two "eyes", and each "eye" is a flower. Pass that one round, gentlemen, and have a look at it. And I'll cut up a few more to show you what you're buying.'

The jack-knife flicked through half a dozen more specimens, and these also were passed round for examination. Lingard got hold of one and turned it over in his hand with interest. Whoever Dutchy was, he seemed to be carrying on a genuine business, selling good quality stuff – not that the Superintendent knew a great deal about gardening. The spieler continued from the back of the stall.

'Now, ladies and gentlemen, I'm going to give you the greatest half-crown's worth you've ever had in your life. Two giant Alfred's – you won't get those at less than a bob each in the Strand – a handful of Cheerfulness, a few Pride of Haarlem, some mixed narcissus, and four or five Golden Harvest – there's ten guineas' worth alone – on top. Half a dollar. Two to three dozen bulbs, at least fifty head of bloom, half a dollar. And if you're dissatisfied with any of 'em, bring 'em back and change 'em! I'll be frank with you – some of 'em aren't quite up to standard; I've told you, they're unsorted. At this ridiculous price, you're doing the sorting. Don't be afraid to come back with 'em, I've been here long enough for you to know how I do my trading. Half a dollar, guv'nor – or should I say *"Mijnheer"*?'

The sale was on with a vengeance. There was no question of begging for customers, the bags couldn't be crammed full fast enough. Occasionally a buyer would probe in his bagful, produce a doubtful-looking bulb and hold it out diffidently. It would be grabbed from him by fingers that automatically tested its firmness, sometimes the knife snicked down it for examination, but every time the customer was invited, without question, to help himself to a replacement and the reject was tossed under the stall. It struck the Superintendent that better stuff was being thrown away than was sold at a good many shops.

After a few minutes of high-pressure exchange of money and merchandise, there was a brief lull and Lingard noticed a pleasant-faced young man with a shock of hair pushing his way forward. In his hand he held a large brown-paper bag which he thrust over at the spieler.

'Hey! What are you trying to do, young man, sell us some? We buy ours direct from Holland!'

There was a stir of interest, and the crowd craned forward to watch what promised to be a good situation.

'They're from Mr Good,' explained the young man.

'Mr Good? Mr–? Ah, Mr Good! The gentleman who orders them from me by the hundredweight?'

'Well, I know he orders a lot – he gets them for a friend. He says these are mutations.'

Jim Laker's face was very solemn. The man behind the stall grinned broadly.

'Mutations? I bet they are! He will have his little joke!' He poked round in the top of the bag with a stubby forefinger. 'The gentleman these came back from orders his bulbs from me by the hundredweight – don't ask me why, he's probably got a big window-box.' He reached over for a blue-backed order book and thumbed back through the carbon copies. 'There you are – five hundredweight!' Folding back the cover, he exhibited a smudgy carboned page, in a nicely-timed arc, to the crowd. It was nicely timed in that everyone could see but nobody could read. 'That's the way he buys 'em. And now he's got a bagful of mutations! Blimey, if they was he wouldn't be giving 'em back to me! In case you don't know, they'd be the first of a new variety. What are these going to be – a world shaker like Golden Harvest? What's he going to call 'em? Dutchy's Duds?'

The crowd tittered.

'No, just one better than Golden Harvest,' said Jim solemnly. 'Diamond Harvest, I shouldn't wonder.'

The other blinked once or twice rapidly and then slapped his thigh. 'The young gentleman has a sense of humour, too.' He crimped up the bag by the corners and threw it alongside the till. 'What can I give him in exchange? At the ridiculous price he paid for five hundredweight it works out I owe him about three pence ha'penny, and that would be insulting him. Still, that's the way you buy your bulbs from Dutchy – if you're dissatisfied with one, or fifty, bring 'em back. Jan!' he called, 'give the young man three dozen mixed topsize tulips and daffs – they're paid for.'

The sale proceeded at an increasing tempo till quite suddenly the crowd, in the words of Omar, melted like snow upon the desert's dusty face. This puzzled Lingard for a moment, till he realized the lunch-hour was at an end, and even now the stall-holders were beginning to pack up their wares, kicking all the left-over cartons and rubbish into the gutter to facilitate the work of the street cleaners.

The Superintendent lit a cigarette, taking the opportunity to have a closer look at the man he thought might be Dutchy. No. There was a certain overall likeness, but beyond that it didn't go. Lingard pushed his hands deep down in his greatcoat pockets, and casually watched the clearance of the stalls. The road sweepers were soon on the job, and the rubbish was shovelled expertly into their low carts. There was a certain camaraderie with the stall-holders, who assisted where they could in disposing of cartons and boxes. And the peculiar part about it all was that Superintendent Lingard found himself curiously disturbed. He couldn't put a finger on it, but disturbed he was. Something bothered him subconsciously, something had half-registered, and was nagging vaguely yet insistently at him like the first approach of toothache when you try to tell yourself it isn't. He went over in his mind all he'd seen and heard in the market, all he'd seen and heard at Dutchy's. Something hadn't jelled somewhere or the other – was it in something he'd seen, or in something he'd heard?

He watched Dutchy & Co. pack their remaining stock on to their lorry in the cul-de-sac, saw the man he took to be the boss pick up the blue order book and a pile of brown-paper bags, together with the till and a filled brown-paper bag beside it, saw him stroll over and place it all in the driver's cab. Finally the oiled-cloth banner was taken down, carefully rolled up and put on the back of the lorry. All very ordinary and straightforward. The boy brought out some steaming cups of tea from a near-by café, and when these were consumed they all climbed up on to the lorry and drove slowly away towards Hatton Garden.

Lingard threw his cigarette end in the gutter and walked back to Holborn, deep in thought.

Although he didn't know it, two things had upset his subconscious equilibrium, one he'd heard, and one he'd seen, neither of which had wholly registered. The first, the one he'd heard, was when Jim Laker had mentioned Mr Good. Whilst the name hadn't exactly struck a chord, it had at least started off a vague uneasy twanging which died before the Superintendent could place it. For a split second he knew that he had heard that name somewhere before, that day. Had he not been concentrating so hard on Peter Meek, it might have dawned on him that he had heard it not a couple of hours previously in the secretary's room at the Tyburn & New York's office in Fetter Lane. Even so, he couldn't have been expected to know that Jim Laker was referring to the same Mr Good, or that Mr Good was Peter Meek. But it might have started the machinery creaking, especially if his brain had registered what his *eye had seen.*

The irritating thing was that he knew his brain had let him down. His eyes had superficially seen the second point which should have registered, something which was so obvious that although he'd seen it he hadn't noted it. Which was a pity, because it was the one thing that really mattered.

And that was that the bag of bulbs which Jim Laker had returned had not been tossed under the stall like all the other rejects, but had been thrown carelessly, but nevertheless carefully, beside the till, still in the bag. None of these had been slit up with a jack-knife. And whereas the others were by now being swept up by the street cleaners, this bag had been transferred with the till to the lorry-driver's cab.

The van Meyer diamonds were on the first

stage of their journey to Holland...

At five-thirty sharp, Simon Good left the office and made his way to Temple Station, where he caught a train to Richmond. Thence he made his way to his modest bachelor establishment overlooking the river.

10

Axes to Grind

Almost opposite St. Dunstan-in-the-West, Fleet Street, is a teashop, and from Monday to Friday, from 8.30 a.m. or thereabouts, there gathers for morning coffee the rank and file of the local banking and insurance worlds to thrash out all that their respective executives have failed to do the previous day. As in the days of Mr Lloyd's Coffee House, many far-reaching decisions are made there daily, and fortunately for both professions nobody takes any notice of them. In spite of all that, however, much general information passes hands between the staffs of friendly companies, there is much good-natured ribbing of rival ones, and the grapevine truly lives up to the best Fleet Street traditions. New appointments, revised salary scales, impending bonuses, all are known down in that basement in Fleet Street well before the official announcement is made, and at times it seems rather a pity to have to make the announcement at all.

Simon Good went down the stairs into the welcome warmth, bought a coffee, and joined a table in an alcove where a handful of T. & N. Y. men were already sitting in a cloud of blue smoke, contentedly pulling everything and everybody to pieces.

'In spite of all you're saying,' Pemberthy was holding forth, 'I still think old Jullien is all right. I had a spot of private trouble recently, and not only was he very sympathetic but he rendered practical assistance.'

'You've got to take 'em as you find 'em,' agreed Rumbold, sucking noisily at his pipe. Rumbold was the Registrar of the Shares Department, young, alert and, with an eye to the future, studying automation. 'He's not without his own troubles.'

'We've all got troubles!' snorted old Bob Marden at the end of the table, with feeling. He slapped his milk-and-dash down with a clatter.

'Don't start him off, for heaven's sake!' said Freddy Hall, 'else we'll never get to the office this morning. We know you've got troubles, Bob — so have I, so's my bookmaker, so's my tailor, so what? Look at old Simon here — looks like death warmed up —

I expect he's got trouble, too.'

'I'm just a little tired, that's all,' said Mr Good, with dignity. 'I was up late last night.'

Pemberthy clicked his tongue offensively.

'Studying Personal Accident Insurance, I suppose?'

'Your supposition is incorrect. I'm decorating my kitchen, if you must know. It's all right for you chaps living at home with all mod. con., but for fellows like me, living in desolate isolation, life becomes a lonely battle.'

'Why don't you apply for a District Visitor?' suggested Freddy Hall helpfully.

'Or do what Jane Seymour's always suggesting – get married,' added Pemberthy.

'Marriage is not necessarily the answer to loneliness,' put in Bob Marden, ready as always to start off on a completely new tack. 'Look at the head of your department, Simon – what's his name? Moran? – there he is, married, with his wife in New York.'

'Well, that's an exigency of the service, as we used to say,' said Simon reasonably. 'Just bad luck. Must be happening all over the place. That's why it's preferable to send single blokes on these overseas jobs. No complications.'

'Complications!' growled old Marden. 'Huh! Look at Moran!'

'What about Moran?'

Bob Marden remained silent for a moment. 'Nothing,' he said shortly, and picked up his

162

mug again.

'What's that supposed to mean?'

'Forget it,' grunted the other.

Freddy Hall glanced shrewdly at Marden. Freddy was a Claims Inspector, and under his mantle of carefree vagueness he had a facility for reading people's minds; this was often disconcerting for people he was interviewing. He proceeded to throw a little more fuel on to the fire. 'You know, I would say our Jullien's a lonely man, too,' he said casually, and Bob Marden glowered at him malevolently.

'Lonely!' ejaculated Pemberthy in some surprise. 'What, with that young American actress wife of his? Is his eyesight bad or something?'

'You haven't been with us very long, Pemberthy,' growled Marden, 'so perhaps you haven't heard. That marriage is all washed up. He's old enough to be her father. A few kids about the place might have saved it. Now, by all accounts, they seem to go their own ways.'

There was indeed no future in the Fanes' childless marriage. There had been much head-shaking when it had first been rumoured. Dominique Fane, daughter of a wealthy South American industrialist, had, for some reason or another, fallen hook, line and sinker for Jullien during a six-month stay in England, and nobody was more surprised and flattered than he. It was one of those things that are continually happening, either as a result of capriciousness on the part of Cupid, or a sheer bad shot. Things went well at first, Dominique loved the beautiful English house and grounds at Dorking, there was a round of parties and celebrations, and as it was voiced abroad she was an actress, demands on her services at local fêtes and church bazaars kept her too busy to notice that their interests were really poles apart. The first disquieting note had crept in when she decided to hold one of her noisy parties on the same evening that Jullien had invited several managers along to mull over quietly, away from the atmosphere of the City, several points of future policy. She remained adamant, and Jullien never forgave her. The rift had gradually widened into an irreparable breach since that day, although both put on a bold front of marital bliss when the occasion demanded, a front which fooled most people but not all.

Rumbold tapped out his pipe and made to get up. 'Won't be needing you much more on dividend-bashing, Simon,' he said. 'The electronic age is with us to stay. They're doing it in America untouched by human hand, as they say. I'm off to a lecture about it this morning, so if you want to write yourself out a few dividends before it's too late – I've often thought I'd like to do so myself! – make the most of it!'

'I will do just that,' promised Mr Good, and something clicked...

'I remember Moran and Dominique were as thick as thieves at the Staff Barbecue at Dorking last July,' said Pemberthy.

'How did all this get round to our Jullien, anyway?' asked Simon Good curiously.

'It all started because I happened to mention I saw him with Quenny Mansfield,' said Freddy. 'At least, I think it was Jullien.'

'What's peculiar about that?' said Simon. 'She's his private secretary, isn't she?'

'This was in Shepherd Market at three o'clock in the afternoon,' grunted Freddy. 'And he didn't look as if he was going shopping. And she didn't look as if she was going to take down shorthand.'

'I see what you mean,' nodded Simon Good thoughtfully. 'But isn't Quenny Mansfield supposed to be friendly with Mrs Fane?'

'Maybe. But is Mrs Fane friendly with Quenny Mansfield?'

'Ah, like that, is it? Your guess is better than mine, I don't know enough about the wench. I was speaking to her the other afternoon outside the G.M.'s room – she seems a nice enough girl – quite capable of keeping him at bay if necessary, I should think.'

'If *necessary!*' rumbled Bob Marden, swilling the remains of a knob of sugar round in the bottom of his mug. 'Jullien Fane may have been a true Christian in his time, but he's certainly developed an Old Testament outlook towards wives and concubines!'

'Well, that was what I was wondering,' said Freddy Hall.

Simon leaned over and prodded him in the waistcoat. 'And what precisely were you doing in Shepherd Market at three o'clock in the afternoon?' he asked.

'It's time we got going, we're late already!' said Freddy, showing a sudden desire to get to work. This desire was not normally there…

When Simon Good entered the room, Mr Moran was standing outside his box comparing his wrist-watch with the clock on the wall.

'Cold morning, Mr Moran,' said Simon casually. 'Having trouble with your watch?'

'The watch, and the clock, keep perfect time,' was the icy rejoinder. Moran swung back to his desk with no further word.

Simon hung up his hat and settled down to deal with some of the many problems which arose from day to day, not all of them the office's. Jim Laker sidled up with a file of papers.

'Your friend Mr Blake has been on the phone,' he said *sotto voce*. 'I told him you hadn't arrived, and he said to ask you if you'd done the necessary with the bulbs. Of course, I was able to give him the answer to that one – I told him I'd taken them back to Dutchy myself, and had got three dozen of the very best in exchange. I thought he'd be pleased.'

'Wasn't he?' asked Simon.

'Well – he sort of went quiet,' said Jim, puzzled. 'He didn't *say* he wasn't pleased – on the other hand, he didn't say he was. And then he said something which seemed a bit queer to me. He said if you hadn't already taken them home, *I* could have them for my trouble. That seemed crazy to me, after all the bother he'd been to to get them exchanged.'

'He is crazy,' declared Simon Good with feeling. 'Who otherwise would buy five hundredweight of bulbs? He likes to get value for money, and can't bear to be diddled, even if it does mean giving away a few bulbs after he's asserted his rights. You'd better take them before he changes his mind – they're on the shelf there. And remind me to get him re-certified and put back in the asylum before the police arrest him for toting a tort, or fathering a felony ... or something.'

'Miss Seymour. Take a letter.'
'Yes, Mr Moran.'
'To Monsieur Marsat. *Agence de la Caisse du Monde*, Paris. Dear Sir. Following my

recent visit to Paris, I have pleasure in informing you that draft translation of the Special Reinsurance Treaty (terms of which you will recall we discussed in detail) is in course of preparation, and will be forwarded to you shortly for approval. Paragraph. I have to thank you for your generous hospitality, and hope soon to be able to reciprocate. Yours truly, etc. Do an extra copy for the Continental Department.'

'Shall I make the tea first?'

'Tea?' Moran sighed. It was a constant battle nowadays. He mustered all the grace he could. 'I think I'd prefer the letter, Miss Seymour, if it wouldn't upset your routine too much.'

'I was only thinking of you, Mr Moran, I thought you might like a cup. I'm in no hurry.'

'Thank you. On your way back, ask Mr Good to see me...'

'This has just come down from the American Department, Mr Good,' explained Moran, waving a cablegram. 'It's a new pipeline linking Texas and Wisconsin, and we're already on risk for three million dollars. They've accepted it locally for prestige purposes, and we'll have to reinsure it heavily and quickly. The Foreign Manager says keep a hundred and fifty thousand dollars net, so we want nineteen lines cover. It includes every peril under the sun, including earthquake, seaquake, rain of volcanic ash, impact, and loss from falling aerial devices. Heaven knows why they want all that cover in Texas – they're either nervous or somebody's thrown the book at them. But remember, until you get the cover, every single peril is a possibility for eleven hundred miles. I want you to go to our likeliest reinsurers and exercise your – well-known charm' – the sneer didn't quite break the surface – 'and keep in touch by phone. Decide what you can cope with, and Pemberthy and I will try and place the balance by phone. Get moving on it, and don't fall asleep in your tracks.'

Simon Good took the cable, to which was pinned a note hastily scribbled by the American Department, and made his way back to his desk.

'What's His Moronic beefing about now?' asked Pemberthy. 'Look at the pompous way he's bustling out of the room. I suppose he's going round to the Gent's for a smoke. Clot!'

'There's work to do, Pem, and your fair name was dragged into it – you've gone quite pale, are you all right?'

'That jumped-up-jack annoys me, Simon. *We* do the devilling, he gets the kudos.'

''Twas always so my Red Knight. He annoys me, too, but he's not the only one. I'll have to acquire this company, and fire the lot.'

'Yes, I know, old boy – win the Pools and emigrate to the South of France. We all do it, regularly, once a week – usually on Thursday when we nip down to Fleet Street Post Office to kiss the envelope good-bye. Join the Happy Family. Blimey, by Saturday you know you're only shaking hands with yourself. Still, I suppose we make the Pools promoters happy – there's always two ways of looking at these things.'

Simon Good looked very thoughtful. 'I wonder how you go about it?' he mused, beating a tattoo with thumb and middle finger on the low, shiny desk. The spoon started to rattle in his saucer.

'I've got quite a good block perm – four by five by six, a hundred and twenty lines at twopence a line,' said Pemberthy. 'Only costs a pound a week. Trouble is I seem to perm the homes instead of the draws.'

'I mean how would you set about acquiring a company of this size?' said Mr Good patiently.

'Get control of the shares, I suppose. Long job. Requires money. Can I have some more sugar, Jane?'

'No,' said Jane.

'Let's get down to earning our bread and butter,' suggested Simon rationally. 'It's getting on for twelve o'clock and we've got to place nearly a million pounds before the setting of the sun. The pipeline has probably been wrecked by falling moon-rockets by now. Why His Moronic Lowness always picks on me to do all the traipsing round the City while you sit on your backside with the telephone, I just don't know,' he grumbled. 'I'm as tired as the tail-end of a week in Paris. I suppose I'm studying too hard in the evenings.'

'Why don't you marry her, Mr Good?' suggested Jane.

'This seems to be an obsession with you, sweetheart,' said Simon. 'When will you get it into that beautiful, but chuckle head of yours that I'm living a life of monastic seclusion, not polygamic seduction. Marriage is not my line of country. Have you finished that memo yet?'

'I haven't started it.'

'It's immoral what they pay you.'

'I always say why buy a book when you can get one out of the library,' said Pemberthy solemnly, and was pleased to see Jane Seymour rise to the bait indignantly. 'Anyway, you can't expect any girl to want to tie herself up with an impecunious insurance official. And you've got to face it, Simon, you are impecunious.'

'Am I?'

'You are. You'd be making twice as much if you were working on your own account, instead of for a lot of "takeover"-mad stockholders who don't want to know you unless their dividend warrant doesn't turn up. And then it's your blood they want!'

'You're a bit of a Red, Pem, aren't you? Why don't you clear out if you don't like it here? On your own admission you'd be making twice as much somewhere else.'

'I said *you* would. You've got brains.'

'Yes, you're right there,' agreed Simon pleasantly, 'and there are so few of us left. Business on my own account – sounds good,' he mused. 'One thing, if ever I acquire this company, I'll fire you for a start – I know too much about you. You want too much money for too little work.'

'Brother, the day you acquire this company, I'll resign of my own free will.'

'Please remember that,' said Simon coldly.

'I'm safe for a while, anyway,' grinned Pemberthy. 'Meantime you'd better start buying up all the shares you can.'

'Yes, I'll have to think about it. I suppose you couldn't lend me a couple of quid till pay-day? I happen to be temporarily embarrassed–'

'Not the hope of a fly in an Otway-pit, old boy!'

'What about you, Harry?'

'You've got about as much chance of getting two pounds out of me as I have of getting back the last two.'

'I'll remember that remark,' said Simon

Good with dignity.

'Remember the two quid you owe me – that's all I ask,' said Harry.

'And you, Jane? My dearest Jane! What about you?'

'Don't you read the Sunday papers, Mr Goode? It's illegal to live on a woman's immoral earnings.'

Simon Good sighed, and reached out for some reinsurance slips... His brain was really very active.

11

Explosive Report

At precisely that moment the Commander (Crime) pressed a button which brought Superintendent Lingard smartly to his presence. With years of experience it was possible to assess the urgency of the matter, or the degree of irritability of the Commander, by careful, if automatic, attunement to the sound emitted at the receiving end.

'Glad to catch you in, Lingard,' said the Commander briskly. 'I thought you'd be out looking for this Peter Meek and his band of middle-aged warriors you suggest are plundering the countryside.'

'I wasn't successful in tracing him at the insurance company,' confessed the Superintendent.

'I realize that,' said the Commander. 'I told you not to report to me unless you had some positive information. If you had found him and had not informed me that would have been dereliction of duty, and I can't associate that with you, Lingard.' (It was irritability, today, thought Lingard, not urgency.) 'I've just had a report from the Safes and Explosives experts on the safe that the van Meyer diamonds disappeared from. Thought you'd like to hear about it. Sit down for a minute. Here is the specification of the safe: Fire-and/or-thief-resisting–'

'Cor!' breathed Lingard.

'I beg your pardon?'

'Just clearing my throat, sir,' hastened the Superintendent. 'A tickle.'

'Oh! Fire-and-thief-resisting, five-inch-thick laminated twelve corner (edge) bent construction, but without anti-explosion bolts. As you know, the latest safes have anti-explosion bolts which only move back and forth by the normal use of the key; any attempt to destroy the main bolts or the lock by explosives causes the dowel connecting-rods to fall away, leaving the anti-explosion bolts in position. Of course, that puts paid to the safe, because the only way you can now open it is to cut it open. But it's achieved its purpose and saved your valuables. In fact, you can't even get at 'em yourself! You have to get an expert in to cut through the anti-explosion bolts. However, van Meyer's safe was of Lumm design, one that had been taken into stock by Rempert's when they took over Lumm's. Now Rempert's recently brought out a modification on a par with an anti-explosion bolt, for use with a Lumm safe, and they circularized their customers suggesting they took advantage of the extra precaution which could be fitted at a nominal charge. This modification was added to van Meyer's safe a few weeks ago. It will be interesting to find out if the insurance company was advised of the fact.'

Lingard raised a polite eyebrow. 'I don't quite get the point, sir.'

'I haven't come to it, yet,' said the Commander. 'Now, it appears to the experts from the positioning of the bolts that whoever opened the safe had no difficulty at all on the purely Lumm part of it. Up to that point it was almost as if it had been opened by a key, or by someone who knew all about Lumm safes. The snag was the Rempert modification, which judging from the series of exploratory drillings on the safe door, was a totally unexpected feature to the cracksman or -men. This Rempert device was evidently blown to smithereens by a pretty hefty charge of polar-ammon gelignite. It must

175

have taken quite a time to prepare the charge, and as you know with this paste-form explosive, the prolonged exposure to it must have given whoever did it an almighty headache. Now don't look at me like that, Lingard, I can read you like a book. You're thinking "The old man is nuts! He's going to suggest that I've only got to look for a cracksman with a nasty headache and we've solved the mystery". We thought at first, of course, that the burglar set fire to the place to hide his tracks. It may be, however, that the theory I mentioned to you yesterday morning was correct and that it was the unexpected and comparatively hurried use of the explosive that brought about the fire.

'The point I want to stress is this. The job looks as though it was done by a man who knew all about Lumm safes but not about the Rempert modification. That could mean someone who once worked for Lumm's but who was not absorbed by the Rempert take-over, and who thus has no knowledge of the extra safety precautions now used by that firm. In other words, it could mean some-one like this man Blake you were telling me about who suffered by Lumm's liquidation and wasn't taken on by Rempert's. Altern-atively it could mean someone who could easily have dealt with the safety device if he had known about it beforehand, but whose intelligence corps had let him down – an intelligence corps like this ghost of yours, Major Meek – always assuming he's still alive, is in the insurance industry, and is not earthy dust scattered somewhere in Europe. So you see why I'm wondering if the insurers had been advised of the improvement to the van Meyer safe. If they *had* been, and Meek was in cahoots with Blake, then Blake would have known how to tackle the job, which I understand is really quite simple to a peterman if he knows what he's up against. But whoever did the job apparently *didn't* know, so perhaps he wasn't working with a man like your ghost, or perhaps your ghost didn't know anyway, because his company hadn't been advised of the improvement in the risk by the insured. You may wonder, Lingard, why I am suddenly interested in that hunch of yours. I'll tell you. I've had the tabulators working overtime, and it transpires that in addition to certain characteristics of which I think you are fully aware and which are beginning to form a pattern, it emerges that of the thirteen largest unsolved burglaries over the past five years involving safes, eleven of them relate to a Lumm safe of the Blake era. You know how it is, somebody buys a safe in 1890, and it's passed on from father to son till the end of time. Everyone overlooks the fact that the modern home drill outfit complete with tungsten-carbide-tipped drill

177

will have the back off it before the owner gets back from the local. You tell me the Tyburn & New York know nothing about Peter Meek?'

'That is so, sir.'

'He could be working there under an assumed name?'

'Could be,' agreed Superintendent Lingard, 'but the snag then arises that although the Tyburn & New York insures van Meyer's mansion against fire, they don't directly insure the diamonds; they are only interested by what they term "guarantee" to another company, and they therefore haven't the detailed information about the actual risk that they would have if it were their own case.'

The Commander looked crestfallen. 'That seems to let Meek out,' he growled.

'The secretary of the company made quite a good suggestion though,' said Lingard. 'He said we ought to circularize the insurance companies and Lloyd's asking if they have been involved directly in any of our larger unsolved burglaries. He's a bit of a mathematician, and feels convinced that if there's anything in my idea, a common factor will be revealed. For example, one particular company may be involved more than any other one. That could mean that our man, if such a man exists, works there. It occurs to me that it could even produce Meek.'

178

'H'm!' The Commander thought about it for a moment. 'A good idea, Lingard. Go ahead with it. I don't suppose it will produce your ghost, but it might produce some sort of a rabbit. When you write the companies why not ask them if they employ Meek – it will save time. You will write, I suppose, not put men out on inquiry?'

'Oh, yes. There are rather a lot of companies, far more than I ever anticipated.'

'How many?'

'Two hundred or so.'

'Formidable! To say nothing of all the brokers and agents in the business. They, too, have private information, you know. And what about all the underwriters at Lloyd's? They're in syndicates, I understand. I wonder how many syndicates there are?'

Lingard felt the warmth of his own enthusiasm dropping mercurially. 'I think we'd better start with the companies, sir,' he said somewhat dispiritedly.

'I agree,' said the Great One. 'But don't lose your enthusiasm. It's your hunch, you know! Write a "private and confidential" letter to the secretary of each company.'

Lingard looked doubtful. 'Even that might be opened in the normal course of business by an underling, sir, and the news would soon be all over the City that we were looking for Meek. I was hoping to keep that as quiet as possible.'

'You can't expect to circularize two hundred companies and keep *anything* quiet, Lingard. I know what we'll do. Knock me up a draft personal letter to be addressed to the general manager of each company. Ask for the information to be kept strictly private. I'll sign the letters myself. I only hope something comes out of it all, else you'll be back on that beat you were telling me about the other evening. Whilst we're on the job we may as well go the whole hog. Strookman, the man of Dutch extraction who fought with us during the war, with a background of the diamond business, who wanted to get back to Amsterdam – get Interpol to put us in the picture – I assume he actually got back to Holland after the war. Try and find Blake, and see if all his profits are coming from his Espresso bar, or if he even has an Espresso bar. Let's have some action all round. Hammersley – was that his name? – the batman? Has he turned up yet?'

Lingard was overwhelmed at the Commander's burst of energy over what a couple of days before he was regarding as a pipe dream. 'Well – I've hardly–'

'He will,' declared the Great One, 'if there's anything in your hypothesis. Let's look all these gentlemen up and see what they're doing. But find out discreetly so they're unaware of the interest we're taking in them. We may get the right answer by the wrong method. If, after all, they're on the level, then, my dear Lingard, I'll give you time off to have a beautiful reunion. One more point. The man Dutch.'

'I almost thought I'd run him to earth yesterday, sir, in Leatherwick Way.'

'With his fertilizers and bulbs?'

'Yes, sir. There was a firm trading as "Dutchy", and one of the salesmen – I took him to be the boss – could almost have fitted the bill, right age, right build, but his features were not as I recalled them, even after making allowances.'

'Probably not. You see the Services gave Dutch a fresh start in life.' (Lingard raised an inquiring eyebrow.) 'I lunched yesterday with a friend of mine in Army Records,' went on the Commander. 'I asked him if he could dig up anything for us about these men. It's not easy at this late stage, of course, to dig up much of interest about the majority of ex-service personnel, but he said he'd do what he could. He passed on one small point of interest about Dutch over the telephone this morning, and I advise you to go back to Leatherwick Way and have another look at him. Unobtrusively, of course, because if these men are conspiring together, they are probably doing so quite happily – because they've overlooked your existence in the scheme of things, and they couldn't possibly know you had such a long memory, anyway. Dutch was seriously burned by a flame-thrower near Bremen in the last stages of the war. He was fitted up with a new face by the plastic surgeons at Shaftesbury Military Hospital...'

12

Shocks and Shares

Simon Good observed that he was alone in the room, except for a typist busily engaged in the far corner. He reached for the telephone and asked for a number.

'Swithin & Matthews, Ltd,' said a brisk female voice.

'Mr Soames, please.'

'Who is calling?'

'Mr Good.'

'Hold the line, please. You're through.'

'Hullo, Bob, Simon here.'

'Why, you old son-of-a-gun! Long time, no hear. What can I do for you?'

'I want to buy some more stock.'

'That is what Swithin & Matthews are here for. Your wish is our whatnot. What is it this time?'

'Insurance stock.' Simon lowered his voice. 'Tyburn & New York.'

'They're at a hundred and six.'

'I want some.'

'How many?'

As many as you can get without causing the price to harden. Say twenty thousand pounds' worth for the time being.'

A whistle came over the line, causing Simon Good to wince.

'What's so good about them, Simon?'

'I just want them, that's all. Don't worry about settlement day, you'll get my money.'

'In your name?'

'No. The same old holding company – Roag's Syndicate.'

'It'll take some time to do it quietly.'

'Time isn't of the essence. Keep plugging away until I tell you to stop. It's absolutely essential that you really are discreet.'

'You can rely on Swithin & Matthews, Simon. We actually coined the word.'

'Both Swithin and Matthews are dead,' said Simon darkly. 'It's Soames and his jobbers that I worry about...'

Quenella Mansfield came away from Jullien Fane's room deep in thought. Glancing up, she caught sight of Simon Good approaching, hat in hand, and she sought to avoid him.

'Good morning, Miss Mansfield,' he said intrusively.

'Hello, Mr Good,' she said, veering slightly

to pass him.

Simon side-stepped in the same direction and collision was inevitable. 'I beg your pardon – will you have this one with me, or shall we sit it out?'

'I have no time for games, Mr Good.'

'No?' Simon Good considered this reply and appeared to doubt the truth of it. 'Were your ears burning at nine o'clock this morning?'

'Should they have been? Or are you trying to sell me a fire policy?'

'It wouldn't be a bad idea, for the amount of fire you play with.'

Miss Mansfield gazed at him coldly. 'Meaning?'

'A little bird told me you're getting thick with our Jullien.'

'A little bird? You're sure it wasn't a little wolf? You men ought to have something better to do than scandal-monger down in the basement of a coffee shop.'

'True, true. And by all accounts it seems our Jullien has found that something better.'

'Mr Good. Although it's none of your business – or anyone else's for that matter – I'll have you to understand I'm just good friends with the Fanes, and nothing more.'

'Excellent, excellent. You sound as if you meant it. It shows you what adequate rehearsal will do, even if you have no faith in what you're saying. But I'm only giving you a slant on what people are thinking – and hinting.'

'The people you mix with must be scurrilous vermin. In point of fact, the Fanes have only today invited me to a week-end party.'

'The Fanes plural, or just Jullien Fane?'

Quenella Mansfield hesitated. 'I don't see that it matters to you. The invitation is in the form of a printed card. It's going to be a party, not a tête-à-tête, if that's what you think, and Mrs Fane will be there. I don't know if I shall be going, anyway.'

'You'll be there,' declared Mr Good. 'Run along and enjoy yourself. When's he picking you up?'

'Don't be cynical.'

'I'm not. You're only young once.'

'Don't remind me! Anyway, I haven't a thing to wear.'

'I don't suppose he'll mind that.'

'I think you'd better go about your business, Mr Good, and let me go about mine.'

'Yes, but you should go about yours a little more circumspectly, or else before you can say *caveat emptor* some nasty blackmailer will up and start to blackmail – no, not you – our Jullien.'

'Who, for instance?'

Mr Good regarded her gravely.

'You, for instance?' he suggested.

'Me? Why me?'

'I think you know he'd pay almost anything

to avoid being hoisted through the Divorce Court by Mrs Fane. But I suggest, Miss Mansfield, that you really be more discreet.'

'How do you mean, more discreet?'

'Miss Mansfield. More discreet means more discreet. Yesterday Mr Fane had a business appointment in the City at two-thirty. You had time off for a dental appointment near Charing Cross at two-forty-five. At three o'clock someone in this building saw you together in Mayfair. By now everyone is telling everyone else the story with all its lurid implications. Confidentially, of course – you know the sort of thing. "Between you and me, don't pass it on, I know I can rely on you." You see, they could all believe Mr Fane had a meeting at two-thirty in the City. They could all believe you had a dental appointment at Charing Cross at two-forty-five. But what they can't believe is that the two appointments should bring you both together in Curzon Street at three o'clock. Now perhaps you'll see why I say you should be more discreet.'

Quenella Mansfield digested this for a moment. 'Were we actually seen together in Curzon Street?' she asked.

'No. My informant tells me Shepherd Market.'

'H'm! What was he, or she, doing there at three o'clock?'

'If it's any consolation to you, I asked

precisely the same question. And the reply was most unsatisfactory. And now, if you'll excuse me, I really must get out to the City. You've detained me long enough already.'

Simon Good moved away with an assumed loftiness.

Superintendent Lingard took the Commander's hint and made his way once more to Leatherwick Way with a view to appraising Dutchy's bulb stalls again. Deciding that later in the lunch-hour, when the market was crowded, would be a safer bet, he came to a halt near the Tyburn & New York building in Fetter Lane. In a few minutes the first wave of starving typists and clerks would be on their way out to assuage their hunger in the lingerie shops and amongst the bargains of 'the Lane'. This was a good opportunity to watch for Peter Meek again – the man was becoming an obsession, confound him! – because with an hour to waste he would catch both the twelve o'clock and one o'clock waves. And so he merged himself in a suitable part of the background to the passing show, unobserved by anyone. Except Old Fred, whose tired ancient eyes reacted to any part of the backcloth that shouldn't be there. For example, even though Lingard's trained eye took in a short, plumpish, round-faced gentleman with glasses, idling with a newspaper in a doorway across the

187

road, he paid no particular attention to him because quite a number came up for air between shifts from various printing works in the vicinity. Old Fred, however, had catalogued Mr Hammersley as a new bit of scenery, and he wondered if he was a plain-clothes man too, for both appeared to be watching the entrance to the Tyburn & New York building in a highly casual manner. Both were unlucky in their objectives, because by now Simon Good was on his way to the heart of the City to place reinsurances on a pipeline in Texas.

That evening found both Superintendent Lingard and Mr Hammersley lurking in the shadows in Fetter Lane, again watching the stream of exhausted clerks and typists hurrying home with surprising verve to their fires and television sets. Although visibility was poor, their presence at different vantage points was once again noted by Old Fred. And once again they were unlucky, because their quarry had started several nights' overtime in the Shares Department, and instead of going down to a teashop in Fleet Street, had accepted the invitation of the Addressograph girls to join them in tea and cakes. Mr Good had an ulterior motive in doing this, as he particularly wanted to master, without appearing to do so, the method of operating the machines. This work was an integral part of the process of 'getting out the dividend', and for what he had in mind he wanted to be able to get out a dividend on his own account.

For the next few evenings of overtime, therefore, Mr Good concentrated on familiarizing himself with the intricate foolproof system obtaining in the Shares Department, brushing up what he'd already absorbed during previous dividend periods, searching all the while for the loophole he knew must exist.

The patient Superintendent Lingard could afford no more lunch-hour vigils owing to pressure of other work. Unfortunately the job of watching could not be delegated, as he was the only one who knew what he was looking for. Therefore, for several days he focused his efforts on an evening watch from about five o'clock to seven. In any event, he felt less likely to be observed in the gathering gloom than at midday. But even the patient Superintendent became impatient at the lack of results and decided to break off this cold routine sentry-go at the worst end of the day. Perhaps Mr Withers's graph would produce results in the warm!

Mr Hammersley continued to watch at both noon and night; being a man of comparative leisure he had more time at his disposal.

On the very evening that Lingard's

impatience reached its height and he had decided the vigil was a farce, he rounded a corner from the rear of the Tyburn & New York block just in time to see, in the nimbus of light cast from the vestibule of the building, the round-faced gentleman he had accepted as part of the scene whip a newspaper from his overcoat pocket and peer hurriedly into the middle pages. What he expected to see in it so far from the direct light was a little obscure, but what attracted Lingard's attention was that as the newspaper was withdrawn from the pocket, something white, like an envelope, ski-ed out into the roadway. His first reaction was to call 'You've dropped something!' but before he could act on his impulse, the round-faced gentleman with glasses thrust the paper back into his pocket and rushed off down Fetter Lane apparently in the wake of another man who was fast disappearing in the evening mist.

The Superintendent hurried forward and found a small envelope – evidently an opened letter – almost in the opposite gutter. Grabbing it up, he called after the plumpish gentleman who by now was also being swallowed up in the gloom. As he didn't stop, either not having heard or being too intent on his own bit of tailing, Lingard decided to call it a day so far as his own work was concerned, and to try to catch the other before it was too late. He broke into a gentle trot.

Old Fred, still at his post, never ceased to marvel at the incredible antics of all the puppets in his daily scene, and he often wondered who or what pulled their strings...

Lingard, still holding the letter between thumb and forefinger, found himself at the entrance to a narrow alley on the left, down which both men had apparently disappeared. At this point he was in a quandary, for the alley opened out into an assortment of passages liberally larded with quaint little public houses. Eventually he found himself in Fleet Street, near the *Daily Telegraph* offices, having lost all trace of the round-faced gentleman – with glasses but without letter.

Turning westwards, he made his way towards the Strand, idly flapping the envelope about as he wondered what to do with it. Crossing over Aldwych into the blaze of animated light from the electric signs on the corner of Wellington Street, he casually glanced at the address, canting the envelope to get the doubtful benefit of the neon lights. He stood stock still and gaped, peering thunderstruck at the name 'Charles Hammersley, Esq.' which leapt out at him with more eye-dazzling brilliance than all the electric signs put together. He was suddenly conscious of a driver of a large car speaking to him somewhat curtly.

'The quickest way to Charing Cross

Hospital, sir, is right where you're standing.'
The Superintendent got the point.

Meanwhile, Mr Hammersley successfully trailed Simon Good to his modest bachelor establishment at Richmond. It was situated in a rather dark tree-lined road near the river, but this Mr Hammersley did not mind, as it afforded him plenty of cover. The house lights were already on when Mr Good arrived; about half an hour later an elderly and portly woman, presumably a species of housekeeper, left the house and toddled up the road.

Although it was chilly, Mr Hammersley decided to wait for a while. He was rather interested in Simon Good's mode of living. At first blush, it seemed very ordinary, for at half past nine the front door opened and Mr Good placed a milk bottle on the step. Shortly afterwards, the ground-floor lights went out, and the upstairs' ones came on, in what presumably was a bedroom. A wireless programme could be heard through the open window. Simon Good evidently liked good music and fresh air. At ten-fifteen the bedroom lights went out and the music stopped. This little corner of Richmond became very quiet. Mr Good evidently liked plenty of sleep too.

It was all very straightforward and innocuous, and Mr Hammersley looked forward to making further investigations in the immediate future, because he just couldn't believe it. There was plenty of time. That was one thing about being a 'Factor' with a fractured wrist, you always had plenty of time. The great thing was to avoid getting even more of it from the judge.

13

Moral Hazard

Jullien Fane was sitting grimly at his desk when Quenella took him a neatly-typed note he had dictated a few minutes previously. The angry glint in his eye didn't fade as she walked over to him, the corners of his mouth remained hard and uncompromising as he re-read what was obviously a personal letter set before him on his unblemished blotting pad. When at length he did look up, there was no soft smile of welcome.

He took the page of typescript from her and laid it aside with scarcely a glance. She waited attentively, noting the full play of the worry and indecision in his eyes, saw puzzlement and anger and frustration all skeetering along a modulation of baffled impotence. The usual lurking, half-veiled invitation in his eye was conspicuously absent.

'Something serious has happened,' he said worriedly. 'I'm in a spot.'

She noted with faint contempt the use of the pronoun. Something had happened to upset the equanimity of the great Jullien Fane. That was all that mattered. Anything which ruffled him had to be trodden underfoot immediately. It was of paramount importance that everything in his life ran smoothly, right down to his ten o'clock dose of indigestion powder.

'I'm sorry to hear that,' she said soothingly. 'Is there anything I can do?'

He kept one eye on the half-open door. 'You're already involved,' he said grimly.

'Already involved? I'm afraid I don't–? What do you mean?'

'Read that,' said Jullien Fane. He pushed the letter over.

'"Dear Mr Fane",' she began.

'Not out loud! Read it to yourself,' he rapped irritably.

The letter, which was typed, continued:

'I am very much impressed by what I hear of all the good works you do in connexion with local charities in Surrey and with charities of a world-wide nature emanating from the City of London.

'Some people might carpingly suggest that everything you do in that connexion is

194

ostentatious (and I think we must face it, it is) but I take the broader view that much good is nevertheless done with all the contributions you donate in furtherance of your self-esteem.

'What touches me deeply is the fact that you make all local subscriptions in your dear wife's name. This may be to boost *her* reputation. Or it may be because such subscriptions come out of a joint banking account at Dorking which consists largely of her money – I just don't know.

'I am also impressed by the cheerful readiness with which you vote large sums of your *company*'s money to whatever might be the then current disaster fund in the City.

'I feel, therefore, that if only you used some of your own wealth for a change you would enjoy a self-righteousness beyond your wildest dreams.

'I am therefore inviting you to patronize yet another worthy cause. Me.

'There will be a reversal of procedure as there will be no call for ostentation, the whole thing will be done very quietly. Doubtless you will prefer it that way, for £8,000 is quite a lot of money, and perhaps it would be difficult to explain it away to Mrs Fane.

'To avoid unnecessary embarrassment to all concerned including me, I have therefore devised a "Method" – one hears such a lot about methods nowadays, does one not? –

195

and this is it: on your forthcoming visit to the Hague – a business trip, of course – you will express your usual desire to spend a week-end in Amsterdam. Once in that picturesque city, you will put yourself in funds to the extent of about £13,000 in guilders. You will do well not to waste any of it on Liselle, who resides not in the de Walletjes quarter as one might suppose, but in an expensive apart-ment near the Juliana Park. You are aware of this, of course, as you pay most of the bills. Having obtained your supply of guilders – you observe you will be spared having to answer any awkward questions this side of the North Sea, you merely draw on funds salted away in Holland – you will then proceed to a jeweller I shall name, and buy unset diamonds which I could resell for £8,000. The jeweller, who will be in a small way of business, will have to make his profit on the deal; he will probably charge you about £13,000. Your heart will sing when you see the joy you have brought him.

'These diamonds will be placed in a tobacco pouch which I shall send you later. You will then proceed to a travel agency I shall also name, and book a boat trip along the charming waterways of Amsterdam, using your correct name. You will insist on being on one of the agency's own launches. The seating on the launch will mostly be under cover, but you will prefer to travel in the open portion of the vessel in the stern. At this stage you may be ostentatious to facilitate identification. You will smoke your pipe, and in your hand you will have the tobacco pouch containing the diamonds. You will be approached by a friendly fellow-traveller who will remark upon the excellent quality of your tobacco. He will have identified the pouch. You will be flattered and will offer him a fill. He will take your pouch, and slip it momentarily into his pocket whilst he cleans his pipe. You will be handed back another pouch, and what looked like being a great and beautiful friendship will wilt and more or less die. By all means then seek consolation in Liselle.

'My fingerprints aren't on this letter, I used some excellent rubber gloves advertised on the television.

'The typewriter, although efficient, is a very old one, and virtually untraceable.

'Although your proposed visit to Holland is not for a month or so, you will receive no further instructions other than the names and addresses of the jeweller and the travel agency.

'I enclose a couple of negatives of photographs taken in the Juliana Park on your last business trip. They are only small ones from a very ordinary camera, but they seem quite sharp and should enlarge well. They are of you and Liselle happily discussing – business? Mrs Fane will be delighted to see them. She will be relieved to know she need have no qualms for your welfare when you are away from home, to be sure you are in good hands. Come to think of it, one of the photographs shows that Liselle is in good hands too. I'm sorry I haven't sent you proofs, I only have proofs done of the more interesting photographs in my possession. One has to economize as much as possible, everything is so expensive these days.

'I also enclose an enlargement (positive, this time) of yourself and your secretary, Miss Quenella Mansfield, happily discussing – business? – over a coffee outside a café in Shepherd Market, W. It is an interesting photograph, I think, because two news-bills outside the newsagent's (one saying Bank Rate Down, and the other, Russian Delegate Assassinated) pinpoint the day; a clock over a neighbouring shop pinpoints the hour; and a street-sign near the clock pinpoints the place. Mrs Fane would be amused trying to pinpoint what you should have been doing.

'I'm afraid I have digressed so much that I have left no room for my signature; in fact, barely room for Yours faithfully.'

Quenella Mansfield looked up as she came to the end of the letter, and reached over for the photograph.

Jullien Fane cocked an eye at the door.

'Please close the door before you pass comment,' he said.

She did as directed and came back to his desk. 'As you say, a spot,' she commented, frowning. 'It's quite a good photograph.'

'What am I to do?'

'Go to the police,' she said without hesitation.

To give Jullien Fane his due, this had been his own immediate reaction to the letter, but an obstinate streak made it difficult for him to accept advice however much it coincided with his own ideas on the subject.

'The police? What good would that do?'

'You're being blackmailed. It's going to cost you at least thirteen thousand pounds. They might be able to catch the blackmailer and put him away.'

'They'll do nothing unless I'm prepared to lay a charge, and be dragged through the courts.'

'Your name won't appear – you'd be known as Mr "X".'

'My dear Quenella, the judge would merely direct that during the trial I must be referred to as Mr "X", and that the Press should refer to me likewise. But whatever he directs won't necessarily prevent someone from recognizing me and passing the glad news round. And there'd be no direction to call me Mr "X" in the Divorce Court. It's put me in a devilish spot.'

'And where do you think it's put me?' asked Quenella.

Jullien Fane nearly blurted out 'Oh, it's different in your case, it doesn't matter so much!' but called back in time. He said instead, in quite considerate tones, 'Oh yes, I agree, my dear, it's done you no good, either. What can we do?'

'The only alternative is to pay,' said Quenella.

'It's a lot of money,' said the other, chewing on his lower lip.

'If this letter's anything to go by, you can afford it.'

'It's still a lot of money.'

'Quite, but whoever's gone to such lengths to dig up this information means business, and if you don't want to go to the police, the only alternative is to pay.'

'There's no guarantee it'll stop with one payment,' growled Fane. 'Besides, it's the principle of the thing.'

'Oh, yes, there's the principle of it. Who is Liselle?' asked Quenella bleakly.

'Liselle?' said Fane, vaguely. 'She's – eh?' His jaw swung up grimly. 'There's no need to go into that now,' he grunted.

'Who is Liselle?' insisted Quenella.

'I told you about her, didn't I?'

'No. Who is she?'

'She's – just a good friend in Amsterdam, that's all. And it's about as uncomplicated as our *affaire*.'

'Would you say ours is uncomplicated?'

'It could have been more complicated, Quenella.'

'Yes, it wasn't for want of trying on your part, was it? And why "could have been"? Do I detect a slight change of tense?'

'We'll have to see considerably less of each other,' said Jullien Fane.

'I suppose you say that to all your women,' she chided, 'in time. Very well, then. We'll see less of each other, if you imagine it will help. Personally, I think you'll have to pay.'

'We'll see about that,' said Mr Fane. 'I'm not going to Holland for nearly two months yet, and something might turn up in the meantime.' He was grasping at straws, and knew it, but any trouble which is two months ahead is not really so bad, there's always hope. 'I'd hate to see him get away with thirteen thousand pounds of my money.'

Quenella Mansfield laid the letter and photograph down before him. 'I shouldn't be too certain it's a "him",' she remarked coolly. 'It could be a "her". Liselle, for instance. Or – even Mrs Fane – *sir*.'

She swung round and left the room. He didn't call her back, he was too occupied with the unpleasant train of thought she had planted in his mind. In any event, he found her presence altogether too disturbing…

14

Fair Shares for All

Simon Good gleaned a considerable amount of interesting information over several periods of overtime in the Shares Department, and this he carefully reviewed with an idea of turning it to his own account. He discovered, for example, that some people, although the recipients of dividend warrants for sizable sums of money, were very lax about paying them into the bank, that others who for some reason or another had not received their warrant, raised no immediate hue and cry but waited first to see if it turned up, and then dropped a casual inquiry by postcard a couple of months later; certain banks with instructions to credit their customer's account with the half-yearly dividend would, in the absence of a warrant, probably not discover the omission till the end of the month when the accounts were balanced, and even then, before doing anything about it would first raise the matter with their client in case there had been any alteration of instructions; and, incredible though it may seem, it appeared that certain warrants which were dispatched regularly to stockholders resident abroad never were claimed, and no complaints regarding them were ever received by the company. Thus the Stock Account at the company's bank was never cleared and always had an outstanding balance. This to Simon Good seemed a pity.

One facet of the complicated system in the Shares Department was that there was always readily available a list of the most important stockholders, and Mr Good studied this carefully and discreetly until he found what he wanted. A stockholder who rejoiced in the name of John Heathersedge Smith, who lived near Yeovil, Somerset, and who hoped shortly to rejoice in a net dividend of £5,184 provided the previous dividend was maintained and provided Simon Good didn't deprive him of it.

The Stock Registers which the company by law was bound to keep and which could be inspected by the general public, faithfully recorded all the stockholders' names, addresses, purchases and sales of stock, and the actual dividends paid from time to time, a loose-leaf page being devoted to each individual or corporate body. Simon Good consulted the page headed 'Smith, John Heathersedge' and from it divined that Mr Smith's dividend was paid to the credit of his account at the Carbis Bay branch of the Newquay & District Bank.

The information contained in the somewhat cumbersome Stock Registers was transposed for handy reference to a card index system. These cards showed not only abridged particulars of the fluctuations of the holdings, but also, against each dividend payment, the actual number of the warrant issued. When the warrant was finally cleared by the company's bankers and returned rubber-stamped 'Paid' and perforated with the date of payment, the relative card was referred to and the warrant number ticked in blue pencil. Thus it could be quickly ascertained by picking out those unticked how many were still outstanding. The sum of these should, of course, agree with the outstanding balance of the company's Stock Account.

From his careful, if surreptitious, study of Mr J.H. Smith's record card, Simon Good turned his *sub rosa* investigations to the batch of cards relating to the Newquay & District Bank, Ltd. There was a card relating to each branch of each bank, and recorded thereon were the names of the stockholders whose dividends were to be credited to an account at that particular bank. On the card relating to the Carbis Bay branch, Mr J.H. Smith's name was the only one. Now the Newquay & District Bank appeared to have branches all over Cornwall, at Penzance, Truro, Bodmin, Helston, Redruth, St Ives, to name but a few places. Simon Good examined them all, and found what he was looking for at the neighbouring branch at St Ives. This branch card reflected two stockholders, one in the name of Mrs E. Truscott and the other, the Botallick Hotel, Ltd.

The germ of an idea was beginning to fructify. By now, Simon Good felt he could, if left alone, produce a new plate on the Addressograph machine. He took careful note of where the spare plates were kept, and at an opportune moment appropriated a few. He observed where the blank record cards (both stockholders' and banks') came from, together with the new sheets for the loose-leaf stock registers, and noted that the cupboards were not locked. Blank dividend warrants, however, were kept in a special safe. During the course of the preparation of the warrants for payment, quite a number were, for one reason or another, spoilt. One evening, Simon Good made an error on one of the warrants he was filling in, and therefore went to the safe (which during office hours was usually kept open with the key dangling) to procure a blank for one of the Addressograph girls to reprint the stockholder's name and address on the top half, and the address of the bank and account to be credited on the bottom portion. He watched her very closely as she found the relative two plates, fixed them in the machine, and carried out the operation. In removing the blank form (impressed with an Inland Revenue stamp) from the safe, he unaccountably took three, two of which never reached the Addressograph room.

His attention was also turned to where the previous dividend warrants – cleared and returned by the banks – were kept in neat bundles secured by rubber bands. At a suitable opportunity, he ferreted out the one applicable to John Heathersedge Smith, and slipped it in his wallet. The 'Paid' stamp and the perforated date would require a little careful thought at his modest bachelor establishment at Richmond.

There came a stage in the preparation of a dividend when there were literally many thousands of warrants spread about in orderly disorder on specially erected trestle tables, and during this period the suite of rooms comprising the Shares Department was kept securely locked overnight. Even the cleaners had to forgo the pleasure of knocking over the inkwells and flicking dusters in most improbable places. Once again, the keys were left dangling during the day, and it required no great skill to remove them one evening, on the way out to the cloakroom for a wash, to take a set of impressions with a couple of cakes of the company's soap.

Practically all that remained now was to find a suitable accomplice, and unless Simon

Good was very much mistaken, this was going to turn out to be Mr Hammersley…

Although Mr Hammersley was satisfied with his investigations concerning Simon Good, he was, at the same time, dissatisfied, for whilst he had drawn quite a nice picture of that gentleman from various local sources at Richmond, the overall canvas was one of such saint-like piety that the only place to hang it was in a cathedral.

Simon Good was apparently a man of regular habits. The milk bottle would go out at some time between 9 and 10 p.m., followed by the downstairs' lights, there would be an hour or so of radio and presumably reading in bed, general lights out, and then silence, whilst Mr Good presumably slept like a babe. The plump, elderly lady came at seven in the morning, and so far as Mr Hammersley could judge, prepared his breakfast, tidied up, did a bit of shopping, had the afternoon off and returned in time to prepare his evening meal. Nobody else appeared to live there, there were no cats, no dogs, and apart from occasional tradesmen who dealt entirely with the motherly lady, no visitors. At the week-end, Simon Good just wasn't there, although Charles Hammersley never saw the going of him. Not that he ever saw the going of him, even in the evenings.

On this particular one, for example, whilst

Hammersley waited outside in the cold for 'lights out', Simon Good was actually on his way to Mayfair. His method of procedure after putting out the milk bottle (which action covered a quick glance along the road at the front) would have intrigued Mr Hammersley no end.

Before ascending to the upper regions, Mr Good first looked at the dials on the electricity meter under the stairs, and made a swift mental calculation. Then he went through the kitchen to the back door and made sure it was *un*bolted. Switching off the lights downstairs, he made his way up to the bedroom and adjoinings, and dressed rather than *un*dressed. Whilst he did this he switched on a small radio connected to the mains, and sang and whistled in unison with the top ten. He had the air of one who anticipates a very pleasant late supper party.

Although he liked fresh air, he apparently liked warmth too, for he switched on a bar of the electric fire in the wall. At length, when a glance in the long wardrobe mirror told him he had reached the height of sartorial elegance, he looked at his watch, and switched on another bar of the fire. Taking a final quick look round he left the room, leaving the lights and fire on, gently closing the door and making his way downstairs without switching on the landing lights or those below. With the stealth of a cat he left the house by the kitchen door, and made his way down the gentle slope of the garden to a gate leading directly on to the gloomy towpath. Five or six minutes' brisk walk brought him to a lock-up garage in a lane at the foot of some gardens.

Simon Good was soon speeding to the West End in his beautiful cream and crimson Jaguar...

Eventually reaching Curzon Street, he turned off into Shepherd Market, and turning right once again, nosed his way along the narrow confines of Shepherdess Walk, an ancient, cobbled mews now consisting mainly of miniature luxury flats over lock-up garages. Where bomb damage had been suffered, tiny houses had sprung up, with doors of reeded glass and wrought iron, with jardinieres and evergreens, with gaily painted windows – in all, inviting, secretive, exclusive, the lot. All this was not apparent at that moment, Shepherdess Walk was ill-lit, and there was a trace of fog in the air.

A car was already parked in front of the midget house Simon Good was making for – in spite of the 'No Parking' request – and this brought a mild expletive to his lips as he inched in behind it. He switched off the ignition, checked the doors, and was about to slide out, when a light sprang into being under the porch, the door opened and

209

Jullien Fane stepped out into the gloom. Simon Good froze.

Fane got into his car and started the engine. Powerful headlights leapt the length of Shepherdess Walk, and Mr Good was very pleased they were reaching away from him.

'Good night!' called out Fane somewhat sharply, as he pulled away up the mews.

'Good night, Jullien,' said Quenella Mansfield softly, and watched the car turn left at the top of the mews. She turned to go in.

'Wait for me!' said Simon.

Quenella spun round quickly, a soft light of welcome in her eye. 'Simon! What are you doing here tonight?'

'More to the point, what's *he* doing?'

'Oh, it's his way of seeing less of me!'

'Well, let me in, woman! Then you'll be able to see more of me. I don't pay for this expensive establishment for fun!'

'No?' Her eyebrows were humorously interrogative. You mean you've come to propose *marriage*?' She bestowed a light kiss on his cheek, and taking his arm, drew him into the discreetly lighted hall with its brightly coloured doors and horizontally striped wallpaper. He gave her an affectionate squeeze.

'Quenella, my dear, I've told you before, I'm not the marrying sort. I'd only bring you trouble and unhappiness.'

'Trouble, but not necessarily unhappiness,' she breathed.

'Trouble *and* unhappiness,' he reiterated firmly.

She gazed at him rather sadly for a moment. 'You'd sooner be an outlaw than an in-law, Simon.'

'Nicely phrased, but not altogether true, Quenny.' He steered her gently into the cosy drawing-room, where a log fire crackled cheerily, and the lighting was subdued. 'If ever I married anyone, it would have to be you. But in practice it just wouldn't work out. No, you take your cut from Jullien Fane, and forget all about me – *and* him. He'll do you no good, either. How is the old trout, anyway? Rising? Or will he fight like a lion?'

'No, he'll pay up like a lamb,' said Quenella confidently. 'I suggested he went to the police, and that, psychologically, was enough to make him jump violently in the opposite direction.'

Which showed just how wrong a woman's intuition could be, for Jullien Fane had already made up his mind to call at New Scotland Yard and put the facts before them.

Quenella moved over to the corner cocktail cabinet. 'What's it going to be, Simon, long or short?'

'I'll join you in a wee Drambuie, light of my life. Is there anything good on the moronic vision box?'

'That's what I like about you, Simon, your unfailing optimism. Let's have some records.'

211

They were soon quietly enjoying Liza Lehmann's setting of 'Omar Khayyam', and one would say, to watch them sitting close together on the settee, that here indeed was true companionship.

Quenella put out her hand and touched him gently. 'Couldn't it always be like this, Simon?' she murmured.

'It wouldn't last, Quenny, nothing ever does. It would end with you having to visit me once a month at Wormwood Scrubs. No, as soon as we've made friend Fane pay through the nose for trying to fool around with you on the quiet, I advise you to move on, and find someone to look after you who won't be a constant source of trouble to you.'

'You're no trouble to me, Simon.'

'Not now, no. But what of the future? I've got a horrible feeling the proverbial web is tightening around me, and that there's no escape. Call it a premonition, if you like.'

'It's this music,' decided Quenella. 'It comes too much from the soul, it's exciting, yet it's depressive. Let's put on something that's more lively and not quite so fatalistic as dear old Omar.' She moved over to the record player and put on some hits from current musicals. 'I'll make a few sandwiches, there's some chicken and ham in the larder.'

'I'll tell you this, Quenny, I'd sooner be in here with a ham sandwich than outside in the fog with cold feet. It was quite thick in patches coming up from Richmond.'

It was indeed unpleasant out in the wispy fog, and at Richmond it had thickened considerably, much to Mr Hammersley's annoyance. The damp river air seeped through to his bones as he kept his lonely vigil outside Mr Good's modest bachelor establishment. But Charles Hammersley was nothing if not patient. He had set himself the task of finding out all he could about the man who sought to hold him to ransom, and until that man actually went to sleep, there was no saying but what he might suddenly leave the house on some nefarious venture, the knowledge of which would give him, Hammersley, the whip hand. It was just his bad luck that Simon Good had apparently chosen such an infernally bleak night to keep awake longer than usual, for the lights did not go out till twenty past eleven. Presumably Mr Good intended then to go to sleep, for the radio stopped at the same time. There was, of course, nothing left in the meter to keep either amenity going...

By this time Mr Hammersley was very cold and miserable indeed.

Superintendent Lingard, also watching and waiting, and also very patient, was almost inclined to feel sorry for him.

The great majority of the replies coming into Superintendent Lingard's office from the insurance companies, in response to his circular letter, were in the nature of *nil* returns, and could therefore be discarded immediately. The Superintendent was only interested in the remaining hard core, which, if things went according to plan, was to produce a common factor which would solve a baker's dozen of burglary files not yet closed. As soon as the final replies were received and analysed, therefore, the sergeant dealing with the matter brought him the results of his labours. Lingard's interest quickened.

'Well, Sergeant, two questions. First, in how many of the thirteen unsolved burglaries we listed were insurance companies involved?'

'Twelve, sir. But that doesn't necessarily mean there was no insurance for the thirteenth – it could have been done at Lloyd's.'

'Yes, yes,' said Lingard, irritated at this show of learning, 'but what about the twelve?'

'One concerned a Masterlok safe, and the insurance company refused to pay the claim owing to infringement of certain warranties under the policy. The remaining eleven all involved Lumm safes, as we know.'

'I can scarcely wait – let me have a look at your short-list – what's the common factor we're looking for? Which company shows up more than once?'

'None of 'em, sir, they're all different.'

'Eh?' Lingard blinked disbelievingly at the list. The Tyburn & New York's name didn't appear *once*, let alone duplicate itself. 'Mr Differential-Earnshaw-Calculus-Withers, and his many-hued common factor!' he snorted fiercely. 'Every single flipping company's different! And the one I want's not there at all!'

He consigned Mr Withers to an impossible fate.

15

Brandy for Anna...

Not very far from Amsterdam is the world-famed centre of flori-culture, Aalsmeer; and not very far from Aalsmeer are the sizeable communities of Veerdijk and Zaanbroek. Young Rip Strookman lived in a fine house in a village situated approximately equidistant from Veerdijk and Zaanbroek, and nothing pleased him better than to be able to stroll, on market day, round and about the stalls erected in the respective market squares, listening to the excited chatter and making an occasional purchase. He was known as 'young' Rip Strookman to distinguish him from old man Strookman, although even

Strookman the younger had been old enough to participate actively in the Second World War, and by now was no *poulet*.

The markets of the neighbouring communities were held on different days, and this afforded many people the opportunity of visiting their friends in the next village, buying any goods which caught their eye, and generally making a day of it. Indeed, given a bright day, the whole proceedings were usually invested with an air of carnival.

There was a time when old man Strookman loved to stroll around the markets too, but now his bones were getting tired, and he was quite content to live surrounded by his books and music in Amsterdam. It was left, therefore, to Rip Strookman to support local industry and trade, and to exude the radiant *bonhomie*, for which the Strookmans were noted, to all and sundry. Rip took great delight in giving little presents to those less fortunate than himself, and would distribute many of his purchases to the old, the sick, and the needy. His quiet generosity was legend. What his work was nobody quite knew, and they were too polite to inquire. His father's business had been the diamond trade, and it was generally assumed that enough had been made in the past to keep them both in moderate comfort in the present, although it was rumoured that the younger Strookman had an interest in a travel agency in Amsterdam. Whatever his occupation, however, young Rip was a friend of the people, and they were glad he had returned after the war to live in Holland.

Occasionally he would make a purchase in the market for himself, and who would deny him this little pleasure? The fine house in which he lived had a very beautiful walled garden. The flower-beds were always exquisite, for young Strookman had a passion for rare plants and bulbs, many of which he bought in the market at Veerdijk.

It was a curious thing that although his little world was right in the middle of the bulb-growing area of Holland, top-quality bulbs were neither plentiful nor cheap. One had to go to Amsterdam for these. It was rather like having to go to London for cheap Worthing tomatoes. There was one man in the cobbled Veerdijk market, however, who sold an infinite variety of topsize stuff at reasonable prices. He had forsaken the traditional Dutch costume for that of a Cockney Pearly King, and was affectionately known as 'the little Londenaar'. He sold quite a number of English bulbs, for to some customers the finest goods always come from somewhere else.

One crisp morning, the 'English Specials' which Strookman had been inquiring after for some time had arrived, and for quite a modest sum he obtained a nicely filled

217

carrier bag of assorted strains.

He did not distribute these between old Mother van Rijn and old Father Meekeren. He took them home for himself, as pleased as a schoolboy with a bag of sweets, smiling goodwill and doffing his hat courteously to such of the local folk who knew him and respected him. It was indeed a pleasure, in this age of nuclear fission, to know that such a homely and well-loved man still existed.

Such indeed was the picture that Interpol presented to Scotland Yard after careful inquiry. Had there been some mistake? Was it some other Strookman, had the details got crossed? If all their inquiries pointed to such examples of blameless piety, then Interpol could assuredly shut up shop.

The bulk of the bulbs sold by Dutchy of Leatherwick Way came from Veerdijk, and probably so had the 'English Specials' for which Mijnheer Strookman had waited so eagerly. He, too, thought that Diamond Harvest was a very good name for them, but not for the same innocent reason advanced by young Jim Laker.

On reaching his fine house he passed through the beautiful wrought-iron gate set in the high garden wall, and made his way up the gravel path to the front door. The high wall not only sheltered the gardens from the keen winds which swept across from the reclaimed land to the east, but also afforded a certain amount of privacy. For so popular a young man, Rip Strookman had few visitors.

The glass-panelled outer door was opened by an ancient male servant who had served the family so long that he was almost a relation. He smiled a tolerant welcome.

'The market again, Mijnheer Rip? More bulbs?' There was a faint trace of complacent disapproval in the inquiry.

'Yes, Willem, more bulbs. And please do not be so critical, for I have brought you back some of your favourite tobacco.'

'Then all is forgiven,' chuckled the old man delightedly.

'To say nothing of a small bottle of brandy for your beloved Anna – how is she, if one might inquire?'

The old eyes clouded momentarily. 'Her rheumatism, you understand, Mijnheer Rip.'

'Then perhaps she had better not have the brandy,' said Rip slyly.

'The pain will go with the mere thought of having it,' said the old man hastily. 'Especially when she knows from you it comes. Shall I take those bulbs and put them in the potting shed?'

'No, Willem. They are a few "English Specials" for my very own cultivation.'

'So. From Lin-col-n-shire, *ja*? For which you have paid twice the price for half the results of a good Dutch bulb. The last lot came to nothing.'

'We must be patient,' smiled Rip equably. 'Here, take your tobacco, and tell Anna not to drink the brandy all at once!'

Clutching his bag of bulbs, Rip Strookman proceeded through the house and up several flights of stairs to his private workroom, which was always kept locked. It was in fact a converted attic, and no expense had been spared in the conversion. The floors and walls and roof had been insulated with fibre glass, which kept it warm in winter and cool in summer, and kept sounds out so as not to disturb Mijnheer Strookman at work, and, more important, kept sounds *in* so that nobody knew what he was working at.

The workroom was fitted up with all manner of home workshop equipment, to say nothing of the professional tools of trade of an expert diamond worker. Nevertheless, it was a homely place, with much litter and shavings which would have made his insurers strike him off their books if they only knew.

Often he would spend hours fashioning intricate working models and toys for the poor children of the village. He would spend much time tending the scores of miniature cacti lined up on the sill beyond his long workbench, which was set against the dormer window in the roof. Today he carefully locked the door, tipped out his bulbs on to the bench, and then, sweeping another corner clear of rubbish, he spread out a square of baize.

He then reached out, not for any of the elaborate tools that surrounded him, but for an old army jack-knife which had seen good service. It was very sharp, and the blade was usually kept open. An army jack-knife thus is almost a tool in its own right, ranking with chisel and spokeshave. The one that Rip Strookman held was very similar to the one Dutchy held in Leatherwick Way, and Rip put it to a very similar purpose.

Selecting a bulb, he very carefully scraped the traces of earth from the base, for these bulbs were not the highly polished commercial variety, but more like the down-to-earth ones sold to visitors in Cornwall, England. Quartering the bulb, he jabbed about in the pieces, almost totally dissecting them. Then with an impatient grunt, he swept the fragments aside and selected another bulb. This one had rather more mud caked round it, especially at the roots. He scraped it clean, and probed gently in at the base. A little plug of dried earth dropped out. Eagerly he quartered the bulb, just off-centre, and explored gently with the knife tip in the largest portion. He was not seeking the tiny embryo daffodil, although he never ceased to marvel when he saw that wonder of nature.

He came up against something hard. With mounting excitement, pulse running high, he eased the glittering object out on to the piece of baize.

Taking the bulbs one by one, he repeated the process. With some he drew blank, with others came the jackpot. Soon he had a little pile of stones before him. He spread them out into orderly lines and counted them, and knew that all had arrived safely. Reaching up and pulling down a powerful bench light capable of being manipulated, he played it over the glittering ranks to give an added light to the now thin daylight. He drew a deep breath. Yes, the van Meyer diamonds were truly wonderful. It was a pity their shape would have to be altered, their value would be considerably reduced...

16

Appreciation of the Situation

One evening, Mr Hammersley, whose thirst for knowledge began to exceed his caution, was tiptoeing up Mr Good's front garden path with a view to peering through the interesting cracks of light showing through the downstairs' curtains, when the front door suddenly opened and Simon Good said 'Welcome to my humble home, Charlie, I've been expecting you.'

Hammersley turned to flee into the night, but a hand shot out and grabbed him in a grip of steel.

'Come on in,' said Simon Good gently. 'Don't be frightened. You know me, I shan't eat you – much.'

Hammersley found himself being steered into the house, and his knees suddenly turned to jelly, for at that moment all the lights went out.

'Why, you're trembling, Charlie, it's not as cold as all that! Let us shut the door and get out of the draught. Have you a shilling for the meter? Then we can have a measure of light.'

Hammersley hurriedly felt in his pocket for the requisite coin, running his nail along the milled edge. He thrust it into the other's hand in the dark.

'Half a sec!' said Simon Good, fumbling for the slot. 'Let there be light!' The knob grated, the coin dropped, the lights came on. 'And there was light! You've arrived just in time. Now we're at it, have you any more shillings? I'm right out of them.'

Hammersley produced two more, which Good placed in the meter without offering anything in exchange.

'You'd only be insulted,' he explained

223

cheerfully. 'Now we can have the fire going for a bit. Two bars, I think. In here.' He guided Hammersley into a comfortless front room, which, whilst containing all the conventional articles of furniture, had an unlived aura about it that gave Hammersley the shudders. Simon switched on the electric fire.

'That's better!' he declared. 'Expensive, but why worry about expense when comfort is at stake? After all, you can't take your money with you, can you?'

'I certainly can't take mine,' agreed Mr Hammersley. 'Do you always wait for someone to call before you put a shilling in the slot?'

'Not always. But I like to get as many genuine coins in the box as possible?'

'Genuine coins? Surely it's not much use putting in counterfeit coins? I mean, once they're in the meter, they're in, and they're in until they're taken out.'

'Very profound.'

'Well, surely if you're putting in counterfeit shillings they must find them, and then you're for it.'

'Not the way I do it. Think, Hammersley, think. What sort of a coin would you use that as soon as it had done its job of clocking up some electricity, would then vanish?'

'Some sort of a conjuror's coin that will operate the meter and then won't be there when the collector calls?'

'Yes. Should be right up your street, Charles, after all the years you've had living on your wits.'

'I'm afraid this one eludes me. What is required is a dud coin that leaves no trace, one that evaporates into thin air.'

'My dear Charles, you've got it! Congratulations! And I thought you wouldn't solve it!'

'But I still haven't got it,' confessed Hammersley.

'You haven't?' Simon Good was disappointed.

'Unless it's some sort of psychic phenomena shrouded in ectoplasm.'

'Eh? My, my, you're certainly getting back the use of those long words, Hammersley. It wasn't so long ago when you couldn't remember "posthumously"'. Would you like a drink?'

'I would!' declared Mr Hammersley emphatically.

'Tea or cocoa?'

'Er–'

'Something stronger?'

'Please.'

'There's some beer in the kitchen. Come with me and I'll show you my ectoplasmic coins at the same time.'

The kitchen was austerely utilitarian in the modern idiom, and, like the front room, lacked warmth. This struck Hammersley as being somewhat odd, for the Meek of the old days enjoyed his creature comforts – as had Hammersley in his own modest way.

'You really need someone to look after you, Mr Meek. Far be it from me to pass comment, but this place of yours is about as cheerful as a council igloo.'

'I get by,' said Simon Good. 'But please! – remember my name – *Good*.' He extracted a couple of bottles of beer from a cupboard and put them on the table. 'Grab a brace of glasses, Charlie – over there on the dresser. I'm always telling people how monastically I live, and nobody ever believes me, but you can see for yourself how true it is. Before we go back to the other room, have a look here in the fridge.'

Yanking the refrigerator door open, he pulled out a frosty tray. For a moment Hammersley gazed without comprehension at the rows of small frozen discs.

'My "mad" money,' explained Simon Good with a flourish. 'I was waiting for that set to freeze when fortunately you arrived. You see, the operative word *is* 'evaporate'. These ice coins will operate the meter, and then – *voilà!* – in a short time they melt, and what little moisture there is trickles over the other coins and dries out.'

'Very ingenious,' agreed Hammersley doubtfully, 'but there must still be a day of reckoning when the man who empties the meter finds there is a difference between the electricity consumed and the money paid.'

'I only use these in an emergency,' said Simon, 'although I must have used more than I intended this last quarter. Normally there's enough money in the meter to adjust the difference – I merely don't get so much of the overcharge returned – but the good lady who does for me says the Electricity Board inspector came along today to check up the meter. He was not pleased. He's arranged to have it changed tomorrow, as it seems to be working out wrong for the Board. I really must be more careful in future.'

'It seems there's no fiddle you haven't thought of,' said Hammersley, 'no matter for what trivial an amount. I should have thought you'd have had your electricity on a quarterly contract to save all this nonsense.'

'There is a reason, my dear Charles. It's cheaper than having a time-switch installed.'

'A time-switch? I'm afraid I don't follow.'

'You're not supposed to. Let's go into the other room.' They were soon settled either side of the electric fire. 'Did you say you'd brought me some money?'

'I didn't.'

'But you have? My expenses are heavy. The beer–'

'There's some cash in the post.'

'And talking of cash, how is your wrist?'

Hammersley felt his bandaged wrist carefully. 'It seems to be getting better.'

'A pity. Doesn't look like being a long claim then. Now tell me, how did you find out where I lived?'

'I followed you from your office.'

'My office? So Old Fred was right. And how did you find out I worked there? Where was I careless? What did I do wrong? Where did my reasoning fall down?'

'It was not so much your reasoning falling down as mine adding up. I put two and two together and hit the jackpot.'

'And what was your reasoning? I'm always interested in other people's mental processes.'

'In the first place you seemed to know a lot about my Personal Accident claims, and therefore you could have been connected with any one of the many insurance companies who contribute to my welfare. Knowing you as I know you now, it seemed obvious you wouldn't wait to use the information against me, but would turn it to immediate account. Hence it had to be one of the two companies I was currently claiming from, the Grampian Park Fire & Accident Insurance Company, and the Tyburn & New York. Working from that assumption, where would such general information be available, or from where could one instigate discreet inquiries? Where else than at a Head Office?

And where was the Head Office of the Grampian Park? Edinburgh. And the Tyburn & New York? Fetter Lane. I then reflected that you arranged to meet me, first in the Temple, and then in the Record Office – each a mere stone's throw from Fetter Lane. And then to cap it all you tried to get me to go after a job at the Tyburn & New York. Well, Mr Good,' said Hammersley, spreading his hands expressively, 'I ask you! The Tyburn & New York won. It seemed fairly obvious you had some connexion with that company. Perhaps if I waited outside long enough I might find out.' Hammersley gave a self-satisfied smirk. 'And find out I did. I got rather fed up with waiting in the cold, so I inquired after you in the front office, and they obligingly told me where you worked. By the way, I think that Aviation advertisement of yours is in rather bad taste.'

'Which one is that?'

'The one which depicts a business executive stepping up into a plane with a young lady who seems a little too – everything – to be his wife.'

'What's wrong with that?'

'It's the wording. It says "Flying to Paris this week-end? Cover that baggage with a 'Tyburn' Aviation Policy". Could be mis-construed.'

'I'll inform the management,' promised Simon Good.

'Thank you. It was of course comparatively easy to trail you home having once found out where you worked,' went on Hammersley, 'especially as you didn't appear to know you were being followed.'

'And what do you propose to do with all this information now you've got it?'

'I really don't know – yet. It will be useful.'

The temperature dropped perceptibly.

'That sounds almost threatening, my dear Charles.'

'Perhaps we could blackmail each other,' said Hammersley, blinking mildly through his spectacles.

Simon Good chuckled. 'I can see I'll have to make you a full partner, Charlie. I was going to suggest it anyway. Open up the beer and let's drink to it – the partnership, I mean, not the blackmail. Can you manage?'

Hammersley got busy with the bottles and glasses.

'I feel you are in need of a holiday, my dear Charles,' said Simon Good at length.

'Getting rid of your new partner rather quickly, aren't you, Mr Good?'

'Not at all. Any partner of mine is an active partner, even the sleeping ones. This is going to be a job of work. A nice holiday in Cornwall, with all expenses paid. You told me you weren't averse to earning a little money by almost any means short of violence, provided it didn't offend against your curious code of morals?'

'That is so. Heaven knows, I could do with it, if only to meet your blackmailing demands.'

'Please forget that aspect. My syndicate works for the good of all its partners. Even what little cash you've handed over to me so far has been invested on your – our – behalf.'

'It has?' ejaculated Mr Hammersley in surprise. 'In what?'

'Tyburn & New York stock.'

'Cor!'

'As you rightly say, cor! I take it that apart from your somewhat nebulous job of "factor" you have nothing else on your plate at the moment? You are, so to speak, resting?'

'I don't know about resting – I'm on edge all the time. Yes, I suppose you would say I'm at a loose end. A very remunerative income I had unfortunately folded up recently.'

'What was that?'

'A friend of mine, a bookmaker-cum-race-horse-owner was paying me to employ him.'

'Come again?' said Simon.

'Well, his bookmaking was really a side-line, a sort of hobby, although he made pots out of it. His chief income was from all sorts of illegal deals beyond the ken of simple folk like ourselves. Obviously he couldn't put these activities down on his income tax form, so I paid him fifteen hundred pounds a year as my clerk.'

'Fifteen hundred a year! *You* paid him?'

'Yes. It was like this. He was actually raking in about ten thousand pounds a year from his betting and various other deals, and his problem was how to avoid paying tax. So he got me to employ him at fifteen hundred a year; he paid tax on this. For my trouble I got an extra thousand. Thus he was in the habit of giving me two thousand five hundred pounds per annum in all. Got it?'

'I've got a glimmering of the implications. He makes ten thousand. He gives you two thousand five hundred, being a thousand for you, and fifteen hundred to "pay" his salary as your clerk. He pays tax on that fifteen hundred only, and thus has a bona fide front with the Inland Revenue. But he also has seven thousand five hundred tax free. Very clever,' commented Simon Good thoughtfully. 'To say nothing of the thousand *you* get tax free, too.'

'Yes. I used to toy with the idea of putting down the fifteen hundred he got as salary as an expense to my business, so as to get a little tax relief that way, but I never got round to it.'

'You're lucky to be alive, Hammersley. Why did the job fold up?'

Hammersley raised his eyes upwards, and Simon Good looked sympathetic.

'He's over the Other Side?' he suggested.

'No, he's inside. Over the wall. In the – er –

nick. Pity. Nice fellow. They caught up with him on a copper deal, nothing to do with tax, which was fortunate from my point of view.'

'So you are, virtually, resting?'

'If you are really investing money on my behalf, I am free to come into partnership with you.'

'Shall we say you've already been on probation, and let it go at that? You'll have to take my word about the investments – after all, during the dark days of long ago, I did hold on to the secret of your double-jointed circus act and you never even guessed I knew of it. I could have made things very unpleasant for you, you know.'

'I realize that now,' agreed Hammersley. 'What is it you want me to do?'

'I want you to go down to St Ives – do you know St Ives?'

'No – I've always wanted to go there, even as a boy,' said Hammersley. 'Something to do with the old jingle, I suppose.'

'Then you will be realizing an old ambition. I want you to install yourself at the Botallick Hotel, and pay a month in advance – I'll give you plenty of money, but don't waste it. You can tell the hotel manager confidentially that you won a football pool a year ago and that you've been travelling around ever since to dodge the hangers-on. For a man of your standing you'll need local funds, and you will therefore call on the manager of the branch

233

office of the Newquay & District Bank, and will explain the position to him, opening the account with one thousand pounds – don't look alarmed, I'll give it to you. (You see the amount of confidence I repose in you?) You will explain you have an eye on a house over in Carbis Bay (which is just round the point from St Ives), that it is likely to go up for private sale in about a month's time for four to five thousand pounds, but that the owner will want solid cash, and provided you have sufficient funds in the bank, will they be able to handle that amount of ready cash if you gave them, say, two or three days' notice. You will mention you have several share dividends becoming payable within the next week or so, one particularly large one being sufficient to cover the price of the house. If the bank feels it can cope with your requirements you will immediately write the companies concerned and give them mandates to pay the dividends direct to your account at that branch. You will, of course, be quite willing to pay what-ever bank charges are involved – within rea-son, that is – because you appreciate that the account, at least for the time being, will be of a temporary nature, and you're quite pre-pared to pay for having a handy local facility. Actually you don't want to live over at Carbis Bay yourself, you want the house for your spinster sisters, to get them away from the perpetual scroungers seeking to cash in on your good fortune. If only you could get them settled comfortably, you yourself would be quite happy to live in St Ives, and if you did, could you continue to bank with this branch which seems so handy? You could bring your business down from London – since winning your fortune you had virtually been turned into a limited company by the Pools' advisers – and what the Big Five Banks would lose, the Newquay & District would gain. Perhaps you ought to mention that the manager of the Botallick Hotel suggested you called on that particular bank, as he'd always been very pleased with the friendly atmosphere existing there. Perhaps you, too, could look forward to a long and happy association with the branch. It should not be too difficult for you to get the hotel manager to suggest the Newquay & District Bank, because it happens to be his own bank.'

'And what do I do then?' asked Hammersley.

'Enjoy a long and happy holiday.'

'I'll need it. What's the snag?'

'Snag? My dear Hammersley, you just put on the ritz as you've never put it on before.'

'And what about the bank, do I rob it?'

'No, you just pay in the odd small amount of cash once, or maybe twice a week.'

'And what about this house, do I buy it?'

'There isn't one, that I know of.'

'Supposing I'm asked about it?'

'If you were buying a snip up for private sale, would you tell everyone all about it?'

'What name do I use – my own?'

'No. John H. Smith.'

'Ordinary sort of a name.'

'You are, or appear to be, an ordinary sort of fellow.'

'Is there another John H. Smith?'

'Not at St Ives – so far as I know. The 'H' stands for Heathersedge.'

'I don't think that really answers my question,' said Mr Hammersley thoughtfully.

'Does it matter if there *is* another John Heathersedge Smith anywhere else?' asked Mr Good.

'If I've got to sign his name it does.'

'Listen. You open an account with a thousand pounds as John Heathersedge Smith. You pay money, which I shall give you, into that account. Other monies, over which you have no control whatsoever, will also be paid into it. All you have to do is, at the critical moment, to draw out enough money to buy a mythical house. What could be simpler?'

'Sounds easy enough,' agreed Hammersley. 'But this big money which is being paid in – where does that come from?'

'Does that matter either? You don't suppose it would get into John Smith's account at a particular bank in a particular town unless there were good reason for it getting there, do you? The bank will receive instructions in the form of a warrant to credit your account with a large sum. You don't handle the warrant, the bank receives it direct. All you have to do is to ask the cashier if there's enough for what you want and can you have it, and if he says yes, who are you to complain?'

'Who indeed?' murmured Hammersley. 'Do I go as I am?'

'No, I think a modicum of disguise is called for. A small moustache – a good quality theatrical one will do – your hair dyed, entirely new clothes, a sporting cap, and if you've got them, a different pair of glasses and an old ill-fitting denture that you can throw away at the end of the month.'

'Throw away?' said Hammersley, aghast.

'Yes. When you leave St Ives, you'll stop half-way and leave John Smith in Exeter or somewhere, and come back as Charles Hammersley.'

Hammersley's eyes gleamed with excitement. 'Sounds fun,' he said. 'What do I get out of it?

'A holiday, a thousand pounds – half in cash, half in investments – and experience.'

'Never mind the experience, the first two attract me enough. When do I start?'

'As soon as you feel confident you can carry it off.'

'Give me a couple of days,' said Mr Hammersley confidently. 'I am not without knowledge of the art of disguise.'

'The circus has its uses,' agreed Simon Good.

'Even my own mother wouldn't recognize me.'

'Very wise of her, I'm sure,' said Simon. 'Now I suppose you'll have to advise your doctors, and the insurance companies upon whom you are claiming, of your intention of taking a month's holiday – no need to tell them where. How many claims are you running now?'

'Three – including the genuine one.'

'I could almost see the halo shining then.'

'The first two are running into the stage where they'll only meet my standing charges, there's little or no profit attaching to them.'

'Write them off. Tell the companies a good holiday will put you on your feet again – they'll love you for your spirit and determination. Now whilst I think of it, Charles. The night you trailed me from Fetter Lane you dropped something from your coat pocket, possibly a letter. Do you know what it was?'

Hammersley glanced through the sundry bills and letters in his bulging wallet, and thought carefully for a moment. 'I wondered where it had got to,' he said at length. 'I think it must have been the letter you sent me – the one without a stamp.'

'Was it, by George!' said Simon Good.

'How did you find out I dropped it?'

'Old Fred – the newspaper man outside

the building – told me.'

'Did he pick it up?'

'No, someone else did. And whoever it was, chased after you with it down Fetter Lane. Didn't he catch you up?'

'No. Do you know who he was?'

'I wish I did. He's been asking Old Fred about me. He's almost got me worried. Do you want an old typewriter, Charles?'

'For nothing? Yes, please.'

'You're welcome to mine. I've got another one – a slightly newer model.'

'Wait a minute, though,' said Hammersley thoughtfully. 'If you've written other blackmailing letters on it, it would appear that I'm left up with the incriminating machine. Thank you all the same, but I've just remembered I've already got one.'

'Shrewd, my dear Charles, very shrewd. I like to see such perspicacity in my henchmen. I'll have to think of something else. I don't want you to waste all your spare time at St Ives. Before you go tonight I'll give you a batch of specimen policies covering everything from livestock to marine risks. I want you to study them carefully – as you must've done with Personal Accident insurance – and to let me know the possibilities, that is, the loopholes, if any. Policies are framed very carefully, backed by counsels' opinion, but you may be able to find something somewhere that we can use to our advantage. I've searched, but I haven't had any luck so far.'

'You certainly make your partners work for their money,' said Mr Hammersley.

'Nobody gets anything for nothing these days, my dear Charles. If you make a success of St Ives, I'll introduce you to the other partners, and that'll mean another holiday for you – in Brussels.'

'Your insurance adviser looks forward to it in keen anticipation, Mr Good. If the job comes off and I get my money, I'll see you get a drink.'

'Do you think you will be able to afford it?' said Simon Good with a trace of sarcasm.

'Oh, I shan't *pay* for it,' Hammersley hastened to explain. 'I'll wait for the right moment and show you how to get one for nothing...'

They fell to discussing the finer points of their project.

17

The Common Factor

'Did you find your common factor?' asked the Commander, with a twinkle in his eye.

'No, sir,' said Lingard with some feeling, 'I did not. As I mentioned in passing the other day, out of the thirteen unsolved burglaries we listed, insurance companies were interested in twelve; one involved a Masterlok safe – the insurance company denied liability owing to certain infringements by the insured; the remaining eleven, all involving Lumm safes, were insured by eleven different companies, and the Tyburn & New York was not amongst them.'

'And you've thought no more about it?'

'I wouldn't say that,' said Lingard, a shade aggrieved. 'It seemed like a case of where do we go from here, the answer being nowhere in particular.'

The Commander tut-tutted reprovingly. 'I'm surprised at you, Lingard. Your common factor is right under your nose.'

The other's face expressed bewilderment. 'But I don't see it, sir. No one company is duplicated.'

'Exactly, my dear Superintendent. *That* is your common factor – every single company on the short list is different from the others. It is the one thing they have in common.'

'Yes, that is so,' agreed Lingard thoughtfully, 'but where does that get us?'

'My dear Lingard, do I have to do all the thinking? I rather fancy you weren't really paying attention to what the secretary of the Tyburn & New York was saying. You heard the words, because you repeated them to me, but you didn't grasp the full significance of them.'

'Did you, sir?' asked Lingard daringly.

'Not until this morning, Superintendent. You see, we wrote to the various insurance companies asking them for the wrong thing – or at least, not asking them for enough. We asked if they were *directly* interested in the insurances relating to these robberies, and out of all the replies we got eleven different affirmatives. Now from what I gather there may have been other companies interested not *directly* but by way of *reinsurance* to the companies having the direct interest; in insurance parlance *their* answer should be "not a direct interest, but one by guarantee to another company", as indeed some of the companies have replied; I've taken the liberty of looking through a few of the replies your sergeant had discarded. Now there's your answer – find out from the eleven interested companies if they reinsured those particular cases with other companies, and if so, with whom. And if your hunch is correct, and someone *is* wrongfully using private information, then I'm willing to wager the true common factor will be somewhere in the reinsurers, and one company's name, like Abou Ben Adhem, will lead all the rest. Don't bother writing to this handful of companies, get some men out on the job and let me have the answer today.'

'I will indeed, sir. If you'll permit me to say

so, that was very shrewd of you. May I ask what started you thinking on those lines?'

'Jullien Fane.'

'Jullien Fane?' Lingard was puzzled. 'Who's he?'

'The General Manager of the Tyburn & New York. He came to see me this morning, and I took the opportunity of putting our problem to him. I explained that our answer didn't appear to be the one envisaged by the secretary of his company. Mr Fane very quickly perceived, of course, that we'd only worked out half the answer. I think he was rather interested in what the final answer would be.'

'But what was he doing here?' jerked Lingard inquisitively.

'He came to see me, Superintendent,' said the Commander gently.

'I beg your pardon, sir, of course,' mumbled Lingard in confusion. In the heat of the moment it appeared that all roads were leading back to the Tyburn & New York.

'Forget it, Superintendent, I quite understand your violent reactions at the very mention of "Tyburn & New York", and because of those very reactions I'm going to tell you why Mr Jullien Fane called here this morning. He's being blackmailed.'

'Wow!' exclaimed Lingard. 'Does he know by whom?'

'No. And the pay-off is to be in Amsterdam, not by bank notes, which we could mark, but by such an amount of unset diamonds as can be sold for the considerable net figure asked for. It's all laid on in this anonymous letter he's left with us for examination.' The Commander extracted from his drawer the letter Jullien Fane had received, and passed it over. 'Read that and tell me what you think of it.'

'Seems a nice sort of chap,' commented Lingard at length.

'The blackmailer?'

'I was thinking of Jullien Fane, if all that's suggested is true.'

'Between you and me, I'm inclined to agree with you. I almost feel the blackmailer is doing a good job of work. However, I'm glad it's going to blossom out in Amsterdam rather than here in London. I must hand it to Jullien Fane, though, he came right out in the open with his side of the story in a most forthright manner, which is more than most of 'em do.'

'This Quenella Mansfield looks a tasty dish,' said Lingard, slanting the photograph to get the best effect; out of the tail of his eye he caught the Commander's frosty look, and added hastily, 'What do you propose to do in the matter, sir?'

'Well, so far as the actual pay-off part of it is concerned I've told him we'll have to leave that to the Dutch police to deal with as they see fit, they're just as fond of black-mailers as we are. If they catch anyone in the act and that unfortunate individual happens to be a Dutch national, then of course they will have to bring him to book in Holland, and it might be better that way for Mr Fane if he can remain as Mr "X" in a Dutch court. If, on the other hand, the blackmailer turns out to be a British national, then there'll be other considerations, and we may have to extradite him.'

'Could be a "her", I suppose,' said Lin-gard. 'What about this girl Mansfield – his secretary? Is she all right – apart from her obvious qualifications?'

'Her immediate reaction when he showed her the letter was to advise him to go to the police. That seems to let her out, but we'll make a few discreet inquiries about her, nevertheless. There doesn't seem much we can do until Fane gets his final instructions as promised by the blackmailer. Then we'll have something for Interpol to get cracking with. That letter, by the way, was posted in Fleet Street – all right, all right, Super-intendent, I know – Fleet Street, Fetter Lane, Tyburn & New York, Peter Meek. All you've got to do is prove it. But I will give you one interesting bit of information if you promise not to get excited. The lab boys have had a look at this letter and envelope. They can't tell us much about it, except that the typewriter is, as the blackmailer says, a very old one. Envelope and paper – Woolworth's, Straker's, anybody's guess. Fingerprints, nil. But what will interest you is this – it's the same typewriter that typed that letter to Charles Hammersley, the one you picked up, the one that was signed "Simon Good".'

Superintendent Lingard stood there gaping and speechless. A wild helter-skelter of ifs and buts and ideas skidded round the periphery of his brain. 'All we've got to do is to find that typewriter!' he breathed at length.

'That's all,' agreed the Commander, gently. 'There are, of course, quite a lot of places to look.'

'Hammersley! Could it be Hammersley?'

'One letter was *to* him,' said the Commander, 'not from.'

'Of course! Foolish of me! In view of the typing, it sticks out a mile that this letter to Fane was from Simon Good – even though it wasn't signed by him. The one he wrote Hammersley, foolishly adding his signature, smacked of blackmail too.'

'Yes. As I see it, all that remains to be done is to find Good, prove he has a typewriter that will produce similar lettering to this, and – um – prove that nobody else could have used it.'

Lingard felt his sails flapping as the wind was being taken out of them. And then suddenly all the *ifs* and *buts* which were still skeetering round the periphery jostled together and rose up in a screeching starshell. A long way off he heard the voice of a guy whose name he couldn't remember saying to Mr Earnshaw Withers 'I'll have a word with Mr *Good*, he fixes up quite a lot of the guarantee acceptances', and as the starshell burst there came a picture of a young man in Leatherwick Way, at one of Dutchy's bulb stalls, handing back a bag of – yes, 'mutations' he'd called them – for exchange. From Mr *Good!* From a *friend* of Mr Good's! Lingard couldn't see what the connexion was, but that didn't matter particularly, it was all beginning to tie up. When was that now – the day after the van Meyer fire and robbery? Yes, that was it. The van Meyer robbery. The day after. There had been something that hadn't quite clicked that day in Leatherwick Way, something that had happened right there in front of him, something which had slid away as elusively as quicksilver. If he couldn't put his finger on it then, then there was no reason why he should be able to do so now. Another starshell screeched up but fizzled out, and there was no blaze of sudden illumination – he was almost there, but not quite. He was suddenly aware that the Commander was looking at him curiously.

'Are you all right, Superintendent? I thought you looked a bit queer for a moment. I don't know that you're in a fit state to hear what I have to tell you now, you might burst a blood-vessel. As a result of what the lab boys told me about the similarity of the typing, I got them to re-scrutinize the envelopes. Now, this envelope addressed to Hammersley. I think you remarked upon the great economy exercised by Mr Good over the matter of postage. It appears he was just as economical over his stationery. You will recollect a printed name had apparently been erased from the flap of the envelope. The infra-red process has brought up sufficient of the lettering to show that it was a Tyburn & New York envelope...'

The starshells screamed up again into the outer darkness, and Lingard clutched at the Commander's desk. 'Beautiful!' he breathed. 'I'll get some men round to those insurance companies in double quick time.'

'Yes, I should. And don't forget, it's Simon Good we're looking for now, not Peter Meek – unless Simon Good is your ghost of Peter Meek. We mustn't be too hasty and do any-thing to put our quarry on his guard – if he is our quarry! I don't suppose he has an inkling at the moment that the police are interested in him, and we want him to go on being like that for the time being. Have you traced the man Blake yet?'

'No, sir, but we do know he doesn't oper-ate any snack-bar within the City of London – the City police helped us on that one – so if he's still interested in sandwiches as well as safes, we'll have to look farther afield.'

'And Hammersley? What have you found out about him?'

'He seems to be a man of some means – he lives in an expensive block of flats at Mortlake. We haven't discovered what he *does* – he appears to be sick at the moment, judging from the number of doctors he visits.'

'Doctors?'

'Yes, the last day we were able to keep tabs on him he went to three doctors in different near-by districts, one after the other.'

'Perhaps he's not satisfied with the treatment he's getting,' suggested the Commander with a glint of humour. 'A lot of people complain about the National Health Service.'

'Or it may be something to do with his occupation,' said Lingard, not realizing how true this was.

'You said "the last day you kept tabs on him" – what's happened to him now?'

'He's vanished, sir. Three days ago our man arrived at his usual time in the morning, and as Hammersley's usual routine didn't materialize he made a few inquiries and found the bird had flown. The porter at the flats said a taxi had drawn up at half past seven, and that Mr Hammersley had left with two suitcases and a smallish wooden box about eighteen inches square and a foot deep, small, but apparently quite heavy. The taxi driver brought down the cases, and presumably he had been told up in the flat where to drive to, because once the cases were strapped on and Hammersley had got the box safely aboard, the driver climbed up in his seat and drove off without any further instructions.'

'May have been going on an early holiday, or convalescence after an illness,' mused the Commander, thinking of the three doctors. 'Or perhaps he's being blackmailed after all, and was running away from the blackmailer. In which case he needs our protection.' (Hammersley would have been touched by this solicitude for his welfare.) *'Is* he the Hammersley you knew in the old days? Have you made your mind up yet, Lingard?'

'I couldn't really swear to it, sir, he was always a rather shadowy blur in my mind. When I tailed him from Mortlake to Richmond the other night, I was in two minds about him – I couldn't honestly say I recognized him.'

'H'm! Wonder what he was up to?'

'He appeared to be watching a house in a quiet road near the river. When the lights went out some time after eleven o'clock, he went home.'

'Whose house was it?'

'To tell you the truth, sir, I haven't got round to that yet.'

'Check up on it. Any friends of Hammersley's will prove interesting, I'm sure. The Street Directory will probably help.'

'Oh, I've gone as far as that, sir – it's in the name of a wealthy widow who owns a number of houses in Richmond. But she can't live in all of 'em – most probably it's let to someone else. It would be too much to expect that Simon Good lives there with his very ancient typewriter!'

The Commander chuckled throatily. 'I won't keep you any longer, Superintendent, you've got a long job in front of you. That typewriter's going to be very difficult to find.'

Which was very true, for at that moment Mr Hammersley was pushing it over the edge of a two-hundred-foot cliff near the famous Commando Ridge at Hellsmouth. He watched the box bounce a couple of times on an outcrop of rock, and disintegrate; and then all the bits and pieces, and the typewriter, vanished into the boiling, seething cauldron below...

Lingard quickly put some men on the job of going round the eleven insurance companies which were involved directly on the eleven different burglaries, and before the day was out they were back with complete lists of the other companies which had reinsured each of them in respect of each different burglary. Some companies had been on more than one risk, and their names were naturally duplicated. There was only one company, however, which appeared as a reinsurer on the entire eleven different risks. The Tyburn & New York...

A very gently-handed inquiry also revealed that whilst Peter Meek was not employed by that company, Simon Good was...

18

Jiggery Pokery

Simon Good laid his plans carefully. One evening, after working late in the Shares Department, he said good night to Rumbold, and, ostensibly on the way out, made a call at a Gentlemen's cloakroom on another floor and waited in darkness in one of the cubicles until he heard the lift whine down the main lift shaft. He knew this would be Rumbold leaving after having locked up for the night, for the rest of the Shares' staff had left before Simon Good himself. He waited a few minutes more in case anyone came back for a forgotten umbrella, and then quietly made his way back up the stairs.

The building was now in darkness except for low-wattaged pilot lights at strategic points, and except for the vestibule below, where the night porter dozed in his cubby-hole, waiting for the housekeeper and one of the boiler engineers to return from their nightly visit to the Printer's Imp; on their return a cursory final check over the building would be made.

Good let himself into the Shares Department with the key he himself had cut in his garage at Richmond, and relocked the door on the inside. Groping his way over to the inner sound-proofed room which contained the Addressograph machinery, he felt for a shaded desk-light and switched it on. The room overlooked a building in course of construction, and the light was unlikely to be observed by anyone; nevertheless he pulled down the slatted blind to kill any reflected glow. He had one hour in which to complete what he had in mind, and he began to work swiftly according to a preconceived plan.

He went to the outer room, and with the aid of a small torch extracted from the stockholders' card index the card in the name of John Heathersedge Smith. The last entry on this was for £5,184, and against this amount was stamped the number of the dividend warrant which in due course would go out, No. 13402. In another part of the room were trestle tables on which thousands of prepared warrants were neatly stacked in numerical order. He extracted warrant No. 13402 and went back into the Addressograph room, closing the door behind him.

Dividend warrants issued by the Tyburn & New York were perforated across the middle; the top half showed the name of the stock-holder, the amount of stock held, the rate of dividend, the gross dividend, the tax deducted at source, and the resulting net dividend; the bottom half bore an Inland Revenue stamp, was in the form of a cheque, and showed to whom the net amount was payable.

The top half of warrant No. 13402 ran:

John Heathersedge Smith, Esq.,
Petherton Manor Farm,
near Montacute, Yeovil,
Somerset.

and indicated that a net amount of £5,184 was payable to him. The bottom portion read:

Pay Newquay & District Bank, Ltd,
Carbis Bay, St Ives,
Cornwall.
Cr. A/c John H. Smith – £5,184 only.

A little research in the special filing cabinets by the Addressograph machinery soon brought to light the two printing plates which had produced the warrant; he put them in an envelope in his case, and took out another envelope containing the metal blanks he had previously purloined. Carefully, he prepared two new printing plates on one of the machines. Then taking a blank warrant, also from his case, he printed a new warrant, the top half of which now read:

John Heathersedge Smith, Esq.,
C/o The Botallick Hotel,
St Ives, Cornwall.

And the bottom:

Pay Newquay & District Bank, Ltd,
St Ives, Cornwall.
Cr. A/c John H. Smith – £5,184 only.

He went into the outer office and brought back a heavy hand-numbering machine, carefully noting down the last number before altering the numbers so that No. 13402 would print next. He carefully stamped this number on the freshly prepared warrant, and then went out and placed it numerically in the pile from whence he had taken the other. In the course of the next few days it would be checked, counter-checked, sorted, re-sorted, and finally dispatched with thousands of others. Good hoped it would not fall to his lot to check it, as obviously he didn't want his initials to appear on the finished article. He put the new printing plates in their appropriate places in the cabinet.

He now turned his attention to printing a new record card. This entailed preparing a third plate, in the name of John Heathersedge Smith, but this time with a fictitious address – he made one up at random in Manchester. This was all he printed on the card, and having done it, he put the plate away in another envelope in his case.

Using purple ink to tally with a universal endorsement system, he ruled out the fictitious address and in small block capitals wrote 'c/o The Botallick Hotel, St Ives, Cornwall'. Opposite he wrote 'Pay Newquay & District Bank, Ltd, St Ives, Cornwall (cr. A/c John H. Smith)'. Against each amendment he now inscribed the word 'Mandate' together with a date fixed in accordance with a telephone call from Hammersley. The old card recorded two previous dividend payments, and Simon Good made similar entries, using two fountain-pens each with different ink, allowing the ink to dry naturally to simulate age. Adjusting the numbering machine, he printed against each entry the same warrant numbers as appeared on the old card, ticking each number with a blue pencil. He now added, using a ball-point pen, the current dividend amount of £5,184, once again manipulating the numbering machine and stamping No. 13402 against it. He did not tick this entry, of course, as this was done only when the cheque half of the warrant was returned to the company by their bankers, to indicate the operation was complete. The card was now finished, and he went back into the outer office and filed it away in place of the genuine one, which he laid aside with the genuine warrant.

His next step was to extract from the Bank Record files the two cards relating to the St Ives Branch and the Carbis Bay Branch of the Newquay & District Bank, Ltd. As he had previously discovered, the St Ives card reflected two stockholders, one in the name of Mrs E. Truscott and the other, the Botallick Hotel, Ltd; and the Carbis Bay card indicated only one stockholder, Mr J.H. Smith.

He went back to the seclusion of the inner room, and on a new card with the already printed heading 'Newquay & District Bank, Ltd', added 'St Ives Branch' in a round hand that could have been anybody's handwriting, and then added below, under each other, Mrs B. Truscott, Botallick Hotel, Ltd, *and* J.H. Smith. He put the two original cards aside and went out and in place thereof filed the one sham composite card in the appropriate cabinet.

He had one more job to do, and that was to prepare a false loose-leaf page for the Stockholders' Register. This was a handwritten job, and taking a blank sheet from a

257

cupboard, he commenced with the name 'John Heathersedge Smith', added the fictitious Manchester address, deleted it with another pen, and added in purple ink 'c/o The Botallick Hotel, St Ives, Cornwall'. Opposite this he wrote 'Pay Newquay & District Bank, Ltd, St Ives, Cornwall', and then added the date of the supposed authority to do this. He then added the previous dividend payments and warrant numbers, and also various stock transactions, purchases and sales, once again using several fountain-pens with different inks and allowing the writing to dry naturally.

He collected his impedimenta whilst waiting for this to take place, checked into his case the genuine warrant and various genuine cards he had removed from the indexes, together with the printing plates – two genuine and spare false one – pulled the covers back over the machinery, reset the numbering machine to the number it was at before he started, took a last careful look round to see that everything was in place, rolled up the loose-leaf sheet and popped it in a cardboard tube, switched off the light and made for the door to the corridor. Before opening this door he listened carefully, and then slipped cautiously out into the passage, relocking the door and pocketing the key.

He made his way quietly down the stairs, and when the coast was clear, slipped down to the basement to the fire-proof vault where the Stock Registers were kept overnight. It was the work of a few seconds to roll back the heavy metal door on its rollers, to switch on the light and find the right register. He loosened up the binding with the winding-key provided in a cavity in the thick cover, extracted the page in the name of John Heathersedge Smith, inserted the page he had just prepared, tightened up the binding again, and was soon on his way out of the building by a back door...

The Assistant Deputy Chief of the Sub-Research 'B' Laboratories of the Electricity Boards (Collective) Great Britain looked in at No. 3 Lab to see what progress was being made.

'Almost time for lunch, Freddy. How's it going?'

'Just finished,' said Freddy, putting a signature to a report form he had just completed. He folded the form neatly, and tucked it in the pocket for that purpose on a large linen tag-label which was attached to a shilling-in-the-slot meter on the bench before him.

'Positive or negative?' inquired the A.D.C.

Freddy sighed. 'Positive,' he said wearily, slipping out of his long white laboratory coat. 'Shan't be a sec!'

'Usual traces of rust in the coin-box?'

'Yep. Faintly but positively.'

'Who is it this time?'

'Some smart-Aleck out at Richmond.'

'He's got a fridge, of course?'

'So sayeth ye label on ye contraption.'

'Wonderful how many of 'em fall for it! They always think they're the first to do it. It starts with just one trial ice-'shilling' to see if it works, and then they dribble in one or two a quarter until they lose count and finally it becomes a shower. And if by chance they put a real shilling in you can hear the splash all the way to the Battersea Power Station.'

'What are you going to recommend doing with this joker – what's his name?' – he twisted the yellow tag round so that he could read it – 'Mr S. Good. Rope him in?'

'No, we'll give him a little more rope and he'll hang himself. Or, if I may mix a metaphor, the ice he's skating on is very thin, and he'll soon be up to his neck in hot water, if you see what I mean. We'll put the matter in the hands of the police, get them to take out a warrant, and then we'll watch at nights for his lights to go out. And when they come on again, with a bit of luck we may find an ice "coin".'

'You could call it ice "lolly".'

'–yes, with full-fruit flavour, unmelted in the coin-box.'

'And if he's just put a real shilling in?'

'We can still look at his refrigerator trays.'

'And if he hasn't a tray of ice lolly?'

'I said with a bit of luck. By the way, has he got gas laid on? If he has, I think we ought to let the Gas Board know. He's probably working the same dodge with them.'

'What do we get him for?'

'Stealing electricity – Section 10 of the Larceny Act, 1916. And wilful damage to the Board's property–'

'Wilful damage?'

'All that rust.'

'Bless my soul, etc.,' said Freddy. 'There was only the faintest suspicion of it, you know. The coin-box is still intact – the bottom hasn't fallen out!'

'Oh, quite. But it's just like trespass. The mere bending of a blade of grass may constitute damage amounting to trespass.'

'May it? Who says?'

'I do. And so does Justice Webster. And that gentleman knew his stuff. Before we've finished with Mr S. Good of Richmond, he'll wish he kept to the old-fashioned iceman and never bought one of our *de luxe* refrigerators – I suppose he's paid for it?'

'What a ridiculous question,' said Freddy. 'Even our best customers don't. Come on, let's get some lunch.'

Further discreet inquiries at Lingard's hard core of eleven insurance companies brought to light – in the more recent cases, where it could be remembered – the fact that the

Tyburn & New York had indeed asked for further information, plans and reports and so on, before coming on risk. – Oh, yes, it was quite clearly recollected – you see, such a request, generally speaking, was unusual. Yes, it was quite in order, companies were entitled to know all the available details of a risk, nevertheless, the request was unusual. – Was the request made by letter? – Oh, no, the Tyburn & New York's reinsurance man examined all the papers and took what particulars he wanted, before initialling the reinsurance slip signifying that the T. & N.Y. was on risk. – So that the request for fuller details need not have been an official one – Eh? Well, all the gen in the world wouldn't have been of much use to old Simon Good himself, would it? Not unless, ha-ha, he was going to commit a burglary!

The telephone rang out stridently, disturbing the peaceful post-dividend atmosphere of the Shares Department. The typist, who was in the act of placing Mr Rumbold's morning coffee on his desk and debating whether or not to cover it with the saucer, picked up the receiver.

'Mr Rumbold!' she called. 'Long distance.'

The Shares Department was wallowing in the aftermath of 'getting out the dividend', waiting for the complaints they hoped wouldn't materialize. Even with the intricate system of check and re-check, the human element was bound to enter, and in the course of preparing and dispatching many thousands of dividend warrants it was almost inevitable that a few errors of omission and commission would be thrown up in the cruel light of day.

Rumbold hurried out of the machine-room. 'Long distance?' he frowned. 'Did they say where?'

'It sounded like St Ives,' said the typist doubtfully, as Rumbold picked up the phone and announced his presence.

A tinny, disembodied voice answered him. 'This is the manager of the Newquay & District Bank, St Ives. Is that the Registrar of the Tyburn & New York Insurance Company? I wanted to check to see if a warrant for five thousand pounds odd, in the name of J.H. Smith, is in order.'

'Why shouldn't it be?' said Rumbold, scribbling the name on a scrap of paper and pushing it over to the typist. ('Get the record cards – stockholder's and bank,' he rapped, covering the mouthpiece.) 'What's the point? Are you questioning the validity of the warrant?'

'Not exactly. In strict confidence, Mr Smith wants cash quickly, and as he's only been one of our customers for less than a month, I'd be glad if you'd confirm the position.'

'It seems you're doubting the bona fides of

one of your customers,' commented Rumbold shrewdly, 'and if there's any confirming to do it will have to be at your end by you. All *we* do is to pay stockholders either direct or, within the terms of their special mandate, to the credit of their account at a named bank. It will be on your own head if there's any trouble over withholding payment – or *making* payment,' he added swiftly. He glanced at the stockholder's record card, which had been placed before him. 'What's the warrant number?' he asked.

'No. 13402,' crackled the phone.

'That's correct. We're evidently *ad idem* so far. The stockholder's name is John Heathersedge Smith (the warrant shows credit John H. Smith) the dividend payable, net of tax, is £5,184, and we hold a mandate to credit his account at the St Ives Branch of your bank.' Rumbold glanced at the bank record card. 'With this warrant you should have received two other warrants, in the names of Mrs E. Truscott and the Botallick Hotel, Ltd, all in the same envelope.'

'That's right,' agreed the bank manager, a shade unhappily, as if he really didn't know why on earth he was making all the fuss. 'It was just that I wanted to be sure in this case that I'd got the right man, as he wants this large sum of money at short notice.'

'Surely, if it's his money he's entitled to it,' said Rumbold practically. 'Are you suggesting that somebody heavily disguised as your client is coming to collect? When did he open the account?'

'On the eighth of last month.'

'We received a mandate to credit his account at St Ives on the tenth, two days later. His temporary address is, strangely enough, the Botallick Hotel.'

'That is so, but that's not so strange as you might think. The hotel manager recommended him to come along to us as we are their bankers. Well, I suppose if he's the same man who opened a temporary account with us *before* you received his mandate to pay it here, then the matter appears to be in order.'

'Only you can finally decide that,' said Rumbold thoughtfully. 'You haven't by any chance another account bearing the same name?'

'Definitely not,' said the bank manager.

'Just an idea,' said Rumbold.

'I appreciate it. Thanks for your trouble.'

'No trouble at all,' said Rumbold, 'it's a pleasure.' He hung up. 'Silly clot! My coffee's getting cold. I suppose we'd better have a look at this chap's mandate,' he said to Jackson, his second-in-command. 'Came in on the tenth of last month, according to the card.'

'That last batch is down in the vault – I'll slip down and get it.'

'Never mind. We'll look at the stock regis-

265

ter instead,' said Rumbold, and this they did. 'Seems to be in order,' he said a moment later. 'These entries agree with the cards. Wonder what he's beefing about? Perhaps he's worried in case we haven't enough money to meet the warrant.'

'Our stock isn't as bad as that!' grinned Jackson. 'Shall I nip down and get the mandate?'

'No, let it slide.'

Which was just as well for everybody's peace of mind, because Simon Good had forgotten about the actual mandate...

19

Banking for Beginners

Mr Hammersley, unrecognizable in a welter of ill-fitting dentures, a smart suit and raincoat, horn-rimmed glasses, dyed hair and a rather sombre homburg, ambled slowly down Tregenna Hill, St Ives, and turned thoughtfully into the bank a few doors from the corner of Tre-Pol-Pen.

'Good morning, Mr Smith,' said the counter clerk cheerfully.

'Er – good morning,' replied Mr Hammersley abstractedly. The manager popped his head out of his room, saw who it was, and hurried forward.

'Anything the matter, Mr Smith? You look a little distrait this morning.'

'I am rather worried, I must confess,' agreed the other. 'This house I've set my heart on at Carbis Bay. I hoped to come to an agreement with the owner by the end of this week – as you well know. So near, and yet so far! You will recollect that originally I hoped to purchase for something in the region of four thousand pounds cash. Cash, mind you. Not with any troublesome mortgage, but with good solid cash, not even a cheque. And then, as I told you last week, the owner, sensing no doubt my eagerness for the place, said he wouldn't think of anything under five thousand as a basis for negotiation.'

'What seems to be the trouble now, Mr Smith? You have, if I might say so, adequate funds deposited here. One of your dividends alone was for over five thousand pounds.'

'Yes, yes, I know,' fretted Mr Hammersley, 'but it seems someone else has entered the field and has bid five thousand eight hundred for it. I'd like to know how they knew about it. I suppose you haven't mentioned it to anyone?'

'Indeed, no!' exclaimed the bank manager hastily. 'Might I remind you that you didn't impart the information to me as to which house at Carbis Bay you intended buying?'

'Eh? Nor I did! You're quite right. My apologies to you. I thought of jumping in here with a bid for six thousand pounds to clinch matters, but that means making certain arrangements in London. You appreciate that when I had my pools win they almost turned me into a limited company, so I'll have to see what's floating around spare.'

'But surely you have enough on deposit here to clear six thousand,' said the manager helpfully. 'I'll check up.' He bustled away to a back office, and came back a moment later with an account headed *John Heathersedge Smith*. 'Here you are, sir, a balance of six thousand and fifty-four pounds.'

'Well, it certainly clears it,' agreed Mr Hammersley doubtfully, 'but it doesn't leave much to spare, does it? I particularly wanted to pay over the money before returning to town this week-end, because I shan't be down here for another month or so, and I wanted to make certain of things. Well, I've paid my hotel bill in advance – or best part of it,' (this the bank manager already knew for a fact) '–and I don't think there's much else outstanding, so it would leave the account open with about fifty pounds. It doesn't seem much. Would it be sufficient?' asked Mr Hammersley guilelessly.

'My dear sir, many accounts I have never *reach* fifty pounds!'

'In that case you've made up my mind for

me,' said Mr Hammersley. 'I'll try and clinch the deal today, I'll give you a ring and let you know when I shall require the money. You could get it by Friday, I suppose?'

'But certainly, Mr Smith. Thursday, if necessary.'

'Let us say Friday,' said Mr Hammersley offhandedly, 'assuming the deal goes through. You've taken a load off my mind, sir.'

'We aim to please,' beamed the bank manager, washing his hands with invisible soap and water.

'As soon as I've got my sisters settled at Carbis Bay,' said Mr Hammersley, 'I shall look forward myself to living in St Ives. The atmosphere suits my asthma, and everyone is so kind and helpful. The world would be a far happier place if one met the same friendliness everywhere. I mustn't detain you any longer. Good day to you all,' he said with quiet dignity.

'Good day to you, sir,' chorused the staff.

The bank manager escorted Mr Hammersley to the door and watched him amble on his way down the hill towards the harbour.

'The Registrar at the Tyburn & New York must have thought me a right Charlie,' he muttered as he turned back to the thraldom of banking.

The man they knew as plain Mr Smith collected the six thousand pounds on *Thursday* morning after all. He was full of suppressed excitement and they wished him luck.

'I shall need it,' he declared. 'If I'm successful you must all come to the house-warming. And now, if you'll excuse me, I must be off up to the Malakoff to catch the bus to Carbis Bay.' He glanced at his watch. 'I'll just about make it!'

There was a new sprightliness in his step as he climbed Tregenna Hill, and turned left past the church on the corner to the Malakoff. Smiling to himself, he ignored the bus station and took the road which dipped down again to the quaint little railway station overlooking the sea. With a few minutes to spare, he collected his luggage, tipped the porter lavishly, and caught a train which would give him a connexion to London.

The office of Messrs Swithin *&* Matthews, Ltd, stockbrokers of Finch Lane, E.C., was bustling with the feverish activity associated in the stockbroking world with a few minutes short of four o'clock. A jobber hurried in and reported to Mr Soames.

'I've managed to complete that last lot of Tyburn & New Yorks for Roag's Syndicate,' he rapped, not without satisfaction.

'Good. Then you'll be free to go out tomorrow and get some more.'

'Some *more?*'

'Some more.'

'Not for Roag's again?'

'For Roag's. Another order this afternoon.'

'What are they trying to do – get control of the Tyburn & New York?'

'They're a long way off doing that, but they're fast becoming mighty powerful stockholders. Whatever they're trying to do, you must exercise the greatest discretion in getting 'em.'

'Might be difficult – some of the brokers are beginning to talk. We're not the only ones after Tyburn & New Yorks for Roag's Syndicate. I heard an indiscreet word over a sandwich and a pint at lunch-time. Someone said the name should be changed to *Rogues'* Syndicate.'

'There's no need for the emphasis,' said Soames. 'I'm pretty quick on the uptake.'

20

Hans Wisselink

Jullien Fane, tightly clutching a well-filled brief-case, eyed the mean thoroughfare named Oude Amstelweg with marked distaste. He had wandered too far for his liking from the Ceintuur Baan district, where, if anywhere, he would have preferred to make his enforced purchase. The narrow lane in which he found himself was almost the last place in the world he would have considered purchasing anything, let alone thirteen thousand pounds' worth of diamonds. He consulted again the slip of paper in his hand, a purely nervous action, for by now he knew by heart the address he was seeking. The faded exterior of the little shop belonging to Hans Wisselink, Jeweller & Watch Repairer, in no way acted as a soothing balm, for the tiny fly-blown window, with its forlorn display of indifferent rings, bracelets and watches behind what seemed an unnecessary steel grille, carried with it a sad air of defeat.

Fane glanced casually over his shoulder as he stepped up on to the stone slab in front of the old-fashioned door. He could detect no one in that brief survey who might be either a doubtful character or a member of the Dutch or British police. The street was practically deserted except for two urchins playing with a ball. He had come alone, for this seemed to him to show a measure of good faith – if good faith could be brought into such proceedings – and in any event to have brought an escort would have scared off the blackmailer, who would then perhaps pursue a more unpleasant line of action in London. If there was any appre-hending to be done, it was going to be done in Holland, for Mr Fane was more likely to remain anonymous as Mr 'X' in Amsterdam than as Mr 'X' in London.

He pushed the door open and a bell tinkled somewhere at the back of the premises. The corners of the tiny shop were ill-lit and dingy. Even the silver-plated trays and trophies on the top shelves ('trash' in the trade and usually not for sale but merely for 'glitter') were barely visible. There appeared to be almost nothing worth buying. There was only one bright patch in this well of gloom, and that was a small glass-topped counter, running at right-angles to the shop window, bathed in a pool of brilliant bluish light cast downwards by a shaded high-powered lamp. There was nothing of note in the showcase beneath the counter, only a few diamond (or paste) bangles, a handful of rings and one or two gold watches. The glass top of the counter was scratched almost to opacity by years of wear; and there was a square of green baize with a watchmaker's glass.

An old gentleman, wearing a tasseled smoking cap and puffing away at an ornate pipe, shuffled into the shop from behind a heavy plush curtain.

'*Goede morgen, mijnheer,*' he said courteously; his voice was tired, as were his eyes which seemed to be expressing surprise that there should be a potential customer in the shop at that hour of the morning, let alone such a well-dressed one.

Fane replied in English. 'Good morning,' he said. 'My name is Jullien Fane.'

'So?' The other dropped easily into English. 'Welcome, Mr – Fane? You are one of our friends from England? What can I do for you? A little souvenir, a watch, perhaps?' he suggested hopefully.

'I've come to buy some diamonds,' said Fane, putting his brief-case on the counter, but still retaining a grip on the handle. The old man's face brightened.

'Diamonds, *ja, ja*. For your wife? A bracelet, a necklace?' An enthusiasm of long ago shone out momentarily, to be replaced almost immediately by confused apology. '*Mijnheer*, I regret. My stock is low, things are not what they were, you understand. Perhaps you will see some little trifle which attracts. The price, I assure you, will be moderate.' He shrugged his shoulders and moved his hands in a combined gesture of hope and despair.

'I want plain, unset diamonds of such a value that I can resell them for about eight thousand pounds.'

'Unset stones, *mijnheer*, now that presents a difficulty, I have none in stock. I can procure–' He broke off short, a look of utter incredulity spreading over his face. '*How* much did you say, *mijnheer*? Eight thousand pounds sterling?'

Fane nodded. 'To resell to bring back eight thousand pounds,' he repeated.

Hans Wisselink put his pipe aside on the counter. 'You make a joke, perhaps, Mr Fane?' he said slowly.

'I am perfectly serious. I have here the necessary money.' Fane tapped the briefcase.

'You are a long way from the big diamond houses of Cuypstraat, and the diamond cutteries of Tolstraat, Mr Fane. Why come to old Hans Wisselink, of Oude Amstelweg?'

'I was recommended to come here.'

'Recommended! Come, *mijnheer*, my whole stock is not worth more than a few hundred guilders.'

'Perhaps it was felt, therefore, that your margin of profit on such an order would be very moderate, and that as times are hard you would appreciate the order. I take it you can get the stones?'

'*Ja, ja,* I get the diamonds – in say a couple of days.'

'Today. I must have them today.'

'Say tomorrow?'

'Today, or not at all.'

'*Ja, ja,* I try. I haf to call on several friends, you understand? If I buy from only one, he say "Ho, ho, old Hans Wisselink is up to somethings" and the price, up she goes. The Dutch are hard business men, you understand? I do my best for you, *mijnheer*. Come back at three this afternoon. You are a diamond expert, Mr Fane?'

'I know practically nothing about them,' said Fane frankly.

'Then you will require to bring with you an expert to appraise what I have to sell you.'

'I shall come alone.'

'I prefer you to bring an adviser.'

'And I prefer to come alone.'

'As you wish, but should you change your mind, an appraiser will be welcome, Mr Fane. You are not buying – how do you say – "hen-food"? And this brings me to another point, *mijnheer*. Buying and selling are two different things.'

'I am well aware of that,' said Fane. 'I am a business man too.'

'Then, *mijnheer*, you will appreciate that the computation of the amount to be bought calls for careful thought. Even by taking as a basis the amount of stones I, in the trade, could resell for eight thousand pounds, and by adding to that my cost and profit, that total figure will not necessarily bring back to you – outside the trade – eight thousand pounds on resale.'

'Then arrive at a figure that will. I thought my original request made clear what I wanted.'

'Are they to be resold in Amsterdam or London?'

'I don't know. Would that make a difference? If so, take the worst position into account. Whatever you give me must fetch eight thousand pounds on resale, that's all I ask.'

'Then perhaps you personally will not be negotiating the resale?' said the old man reflectively.

'No,' said Fane shortly.

'I will do my best; my own profit will be small. I am near the end of the road, Mr Fane, and am satisfied with a little. And I would not want you to feel cheated on what to me seems a very strange deal. As time appears to be of the essence, if you will leave your address or telephone number I will contact you immediately if I succeed in getting what you want this morning.'

'I will call back at three this afternoon as you originally suggested,' said Fane. He turned to go, and was suddenly conscious of a slight agitation on the part of old Hans Wisselink. He arrested his movement towards the door. The old man coughed diffidently.

'I would expedite things, *mijnheer* – a little money on account – you understand? Although it is well known that Hans Wisselink owes not a single florin in Amsterdam, his credit only extends to the humble level of his establishment. *Mijnheer* understands?' he said anxiously.

'Of course. I should have thought,' said Fane, who actually found himself liking the old man. He extracted a large sum of money from his brief-case, and waited while the Dutchman fussed around counting it and making out a receipt. Fane put the latter carefully into his wallet, and was soon making his way along Oude Amstelweg to a main road where he caught a bus back to the centre of Amsterdam.

Hans Wisselink shortly afterwards locked up his little shop and shuffled off on his mission to the diamond quarter of the city. The detective sitting in the window of the dowdy café opposite took a final gulp at his thick black coffee, reached for his hat, and casually followed him. By lunch-time he was quite tired, for his quarry was very nimble for his age and appeared to hate all public transport. The mission was not finally completed till well after lunch, and by that time the old jeweller had visited five firms and had made three street contacts, haggling in doorways over the contents of intriguing little chamois-leather bags...

Jullien Fane meanwhile arrived at the city centre and walked slowly along Damrak looking out for the Pyx Travel Agency. He hadn't far to look, for his eye was soon attracted by a royal-blue neon sign which sprang into life and announced the agency every three or four seconds. He crossed over to it, and ostensibly reading the travel advertisements in the window, discreetly studied the well-lit interior. The Pyx Travel Agency was apparently a flourishing business, for although the tourist season had not yet opened up, there were several people at the booking counters. The agency dealt not only with air, sea and rail travel, there was also a counter for theatres, cabarets and restaurants. Jullien Fane approved the air of brisk efficiency which pervaded the place.

He pushed open the plate-glass door and made for a rack of brochures and handbills. This gave him an opportunity of studying the passers-by on the sidewalks. He knew he was being tailed by Dutch police (and possibly by an English representative of Interpol), and it was safe to assume the blackmailer or his representative was also watching his movements; but the hour was a busy one, everybody was intent on his own (and compared with his, Fane's, how trivial!) business, and it was impossible to single out anyone in the street who looked villainous enough to be a detective or innocent enough to be a rogue. Fane moved over to a vacant space at the counter.

'I am Mr Jullien Fane, from London,' he said in English.

'Yes, sir,' said the booking clerk, with no more than polite interest at the mention of the name. He spoke in English, for all the booking clerks at Pyx were expected to be fluent in at least two languages other than their own. 'What can I do for you, Mr Fane?'

'I want to book a trip along the waterways, in one of your own launches, for tomorrow morning,' said Fane. 'The one advertised in the window, which includes the visit to the Rijksmuseum.'

'It is by no means certain that that excursion will be running tomorrow, sir,' replied the clerk. 'It is rather early in the season, and we only have one of our launches in commission. Apart from the fact that it barely pays to run it at this time of the year, we had some trouble yesterday with the screw – it fouled a line in the river and the mechanics are working on it now. If it is the Rijksmuseum you particularly wish to see, sir, might I respectfully suggest a bus from outside the office here?'

'It was the waterways trip I particularly wanted,' said Fane, laying down his case on the counter and getting out his pipe from his greatcoat pocket.

'There are many interesting trips by ordinary public river-service,' said the clerk helpfully. 'Or we could book you a special river taxi – it would be more expensive, of course.'

'I would prefer one of your launches,' said Fane, somewhat in a quandary. He wondered how the blackmailer would cope with the revised circumstances – if he even knew that the Pyx launch was out of commission. 'I rather liked the advertised itinerary.'

'It is, of course, very popular,' agreed the

clerk. 'We have actually taken a few bookings on the understanding that if our own launch doesn't run tomorrow, then there will be an automatic transfer to one of our friendly rivals. Would *mijnheer* care to make a similar booking?'

Jullien Fane mused for a moment, absentmindedly withdrawing from his other pocket a brand new tobacco pouch, in crocodile skin, and he had pulled back the zip before he realized he had taken the wrong pouch from his pocket. There had been no time for Scotland Yard to do anything in the matter of tracing the sender of the new pouch, or checking up on Hans Wisselink and the Pyx Travel Agency, for the final instructions together with the pouch had arrived by special messenger as Fane was stepping on to the plane at London Airport. The Dutch police, however, had traced that the pouch was one of a special range made for the ultra modem *de Bijenkorf* departmental store in Rotterdam; further, nothing was known against Hans Wisselink, and the Pyx Travel Agency was a firm of repute. A sudden gleam came into Fane's eye as he was about to replace the new pouch in his pocket. Instead, he laid it on the counter beside his brief-case, and went on talking. 'I particularly wanted one of your morning trips,' he explained, 'because I want to contact someone who is doing the selfsame thing.'

'If *mijnheer* will tell me the name of his friend,' said the clerk, showing no interest in the tobacco pouch, 'we can check to see if a booking has been made.'

This almost caught Fane on the hop. 'Robinson,' he said at random.

The clerk reached for an order book, flipped it open at a certain page, and ran his finger down the names. 'Not yet,' he said. 'But all will be well, sir,' he suddenly beamed, 'for if our boat runs after all, you will both be on it, and if not, you will both be on our rival's, and you will make contact after all.'

'There is something in what you say,' agreed Fane. 'Book me a seat. When will you know for certain whether your launch will be running or not?'

'It is difficult to say, sir. We are doing our utmost, we don't like turning customers away. I'll have a word with the manager.' He went into a back room for a moment, and then reappeared. 'The manager suggests we ring you, if that is convenient to you, first thing in the morning, to let you know the position. If our launch is not in service, then it will be entirely up to you whether you use another itinerary or choose to have your money refunded.'

'That is very fair,' agreed Fane. He paid for his ticket, picked up his case, nodded good day and made for the door.

The booking clerk eyed the crocodile-skin

pouch left on the counter thoughtfully. He picked it up, weighed it in his hand for a moment. *'Mijnheer!'* he called. 'Your tobacco pouch!'

'Thank you,' said Jullien Fane, coming back to the counter. 'That was foolish of me.'

'Not at all, sir, just an oversight,' said the clerk, smiling. He added under his breath, as the General Manager of the Tyburn & New York went out into the street, 'Very foolish of you indeed!'

Fane made his way along Damrak into Rokin, where he found a fashionable café-restaurant and had a very good lunch. He wondered if he were still being tailed; if indeed he was, then both police and black-mailer were doing a good job, for nobody appeared to take the slightest interest in him. A glass or two of excellent wine mellowed him considerably, and he even found his thoughts turning towards Liselle, wondering whether he could fit in a quick visit. He decided after all that perhaps it would be wisest to neglect Liselle until Operation Blackmail (as he mentally named it) was successfully completed. He had been assured by a contact from the Dutch police that the blackmailer, when caught (not *if*, Fane noted) would be jumped on as from a great height, with the very minimum of publicity to Fane himself. Fane was intrigued as to the

283

identity of the blackmailer, and the glass of Dutch courage in his hand helped to cloud over the unpleasant possibility of much mud being stirred briskly.

A church clock chimed three o'clock as he made his way up Oude Amstelweg again. In the café opposite the jeweller's a small group of workmen were playing 'poor man's bridge' – *klaverjas*, in the window seat, and one of them facing the street favoured Fane with a toothy grin distorted into villainous proportions by the runnels of steam on the window.

The jeweller's shop was closed, but as Fane stood there trying the handle, Hans Wisselink shuffled out of the back room and unbolted the front door.

'Come in, *mijnheer*,' urged the old man, 'and I will bolt the door again so that we are not disturbed. I have been successful, although I have only just returned. Much of the casual trade is done in doorways in the lunch-hour. You have not brought a valuer?' he went on, as he locked up again and pulled down the blind. 'But have no fear, you will be well satisfied, and you know where to come in case of complaint.' He toddled over behind the counter, pulled the square of green baize into position under the one brilliant shaded light, and produced a chamois-leather bag from his side-pocket. Fumbling with the string for a moment, he tipped the contents out on to the baize, and

Jullien Fane caught his breath at the sheer sparkling lustre before him. The old man joggled the square of baize so that the diamonds became a kaleidoscope of eye-dazzle which made Fane blink, but not so much as to delude him into thinking that there were more diamonds there than he thought he would get for his money.

'There aren't many, are there?' he said critically.

'*Multum in parvo*,' said Hans Wisselink, 'much in little. That is why I wanted you to bring someone to appraise them,' he added. 'I assure you the value is there. Here is the calculation of the cost, I have written it down; the basic cost, my costs in obtaining them – *mijnheer* knows how it is, a little palm-oil here, a little there' (his hands undulated eloquently), 'plus a note of my actual profit, which I think you will agree is extremely moderate. Perhaps *mijnheer* will examine the list.'

Fane glanced at it briefly and grunted. 'Put them back in that little bag and I will count out the balance of the money.'

The transaction was soon complete, and he left amid profuse thanks for his welcome patronage. The men in the café opposite were still absorbed in their cards.

He had been given a number to ring from the privacy of his hotel room, and very soon a member of Interpol and a diamond expert, both of whom entered the hotel via the back way, were closeted with him. The expert examined the diamonds carefully, judged them genuine and so far as he knew, not stolen property, and expressed the opinion that the jeweller Wisselink had treated him fairly.

Hans Wisselink meanwhile felt he also had been treated very fairly. He had carried out his instructions implicitly, but nevertheless the fee of £2,000 in currency he had been instructed to deduct from the proceeds for his services was beyond his wildest dreams.

It had all been perfectly simple. It had been explained to him that someone would call with a request such as the English gentleman had in fact made. He had been told where to go to pick up the diamonds – to a firm which, whilst not now in the top flight, had once been very prosperous and was still a name to be reckoned with. Any qualms he may have had were soon smoothed out by several inquiries made of old friends in the trade who all assured him that the stones, if not recognizable as stolen property, were at least so well recut as to make identification of original ownership wellnigh impossible. The actual transaction with the English gentleman had been made without fuss or bother; the latter had the diamonds, and he, Hans Wisselink, had the money – which, he was happy to say, was as genuine as the diamonds, although he had no proof that it wasn't part of the proceeds of a bank robbery.

In fairness to Hans Wisselink he didn't know he had just handed over part of the stolen van Meyer diamonds to the general manager of an insurance company which was financially interested in the loss of them.

He carefully recounted the cash in his little back room, extracting first the authorized amount for his services rendered and reconciling the balance, which he packed up in a stout brown-paper parcel and tied with strong twine. He addressed a gummed label in block letters, and affixed it with care. Then once again locking up his shop, he ambled off to the post office in the main road and posted the parcel in the ordinary way, without registration...

21

Right up a Dutch Creek

At nine-thirty the following morning Fane received a telephone message from the Pyx Travel Agency. They were happy to inform him their own launch was in commission again, and they would be glad if he would pick it up at the appointed hour and place. He finished his coffee and rolls, and hurried out to the desk, where he asked for the small package he had deposited in the hotel safe the previous night. A sealed linen envelope was soon brought to him from the manager's office, and he hastened up to his room for his hat and coat, more than a little keyed-up with excitement.

He ripped open the envelope and extracted the zippered tobacco pouch with its small chamois bag containing so much wealth, and checked the contents before zipping it up again and placing it in his greatcoat pocket. He made certain he had his pipe, tobacco and matches, and also his boat ticket. He rang the police number again, and informed them he was on his way. They assured him their plans were well-laid...

He made the pier with a few minutes to spare, and was greeted by the counter clerk from the travel agency, whose job it was apparently to ensure that all the customers were accounted for and happy.

'*Mijnheer*, I regret – Mr Robinson has not booked with us,' he said, and this nearly caught Fane out, for he wondered who on earth Robinson was. Fortunately the clerk went on talking. 'Perhaps you will meet him at the Rijksmuseum.'

There were rather more passengers than Fane had expected, though how many of them were police 'bookings' he had no idea. As had been forecast in the first letter he had received, most of the seating on the launch was under cover, with side observation windows. There was, however, an open portion at the stern, with seating round the sides. It was to this part of the vessel that he proceeded with mounting tension. He was no coward, and now the hour had arrived, he was itching to get to grips with the creature who sought to ruffle his smooth existence. He sat alone hunched up in his overcoat, for there was a stiff breeze coming off the water. He eyed the backs of the passengers thoughtfully, wondering which were police and which was blackmailer – or blackmailer's runner. At length everyone was aboard, and the clerk on the quayside hailed the gnarled old man who stood on a low wooden box at the helm, hard by Jullien Fane.

'No more to come, Willem, you can cast off.'

With a juddering movement the boat drew away from the pier, and there commenced what normally would have been an intriguing excursion along the world-famous canals of Amsterdam. Jullien Fane, however, had no eye for the sedate charm of the merchant houses, for the sturdy arched bridges, all reflected imposingly in the age-old waterways.

The first part of the journey passed without incident, everyone seemed too intent on what lay ahead to take any interest in him. Although the sun shone bravely, Fane got desperately cold, especially when the launch chugged its way up certain stretches of water where a keen cross-wind caught him – in spite of his trying to crouch in the shelter of the gunwale. The old man at the helm once or twice turned and regarded him gravely, blowing into his cupped hands to indicate how cold it was, motioning Fane to take a place in the warmth of the covered seats forward. Pane shook his head, and the old man shrugged and paid him no more attention. He had done his bit to make the passenger comfortable.

Although Fane smoked furiously the whole time, the new tobacco pouch resting casually on his lap, nobody approached him or took the slightest notice of him. When, in due course, there was a stop convenient for either a brief visit to the Rijksmuseum, or for a warm-up and a black coffee in one of the numerous waterside cafés, Fane chose the latter, for by that time his throat was parched with smoking; he had his coffee laced with one of the various stimulants for which the Dutch are famous.

When he rejoined the launch, several people had decided to enjoy the crisp air in the open stern, and they were mostly kneeling on the seating and leaning over the gunwale. His seat had been taken, and it was on looking round for another position that he noticed the stranger – or at least, someone he hadn't noticed on the first half of the trip, someone who managed to convey the impression he had just joined the boat. The newcomer was middle-aged, well-dressed in the Dutch style, pleasant-looking with a healthy glow in his cheeks. He was casually leaning over the side, and his face was presented to Fane in profile. Fane's pulses quickened as the man turned, caught Fane's eye, and smiled a sort of half-welcome. Fane nodded back and took up a position near him. Out of the corner of his eye he noted two large men drift casually over and station themselves the other side of the newcomer, deeply absorbed in conversation.

The last passengers hurried aboard, a young Dutchman in his teens made a quick check, pulled in the short gangplank, gave the helmsman a shout and cast off. Once again the launch yawed away from the landing-stage, and was off on its homeward journey. The homeward leg was a short one, and it was apparent to Jullien Fane that if anything was to happen at all, it would have to be within the next twenty minutes or so. He filled his pipe, lit up, and puffed away mechanically, the smoke automatically wafting before the ruddy-faced Dutchman as it was caught up in the airstream of the vessel. The Dutchman's nostrils sniffed appreciatively. He pulled a pipe from his pocket, and the two men to his left eased in a little closer, still talking animatedly. Fane dragged the new pouch from his pocket and idly held it in his left hand so the Dutchman could see it. He managed to resist a wild desire to invite the other to try the tobacco, for he knew the first move must come from the Dutchman. That gentleman, gazing bleakly across the water, leisurely filled his pipe with his own tobacco from a tin, lit up with some difficulty in the breeze, and puffed away contentedly. For ten minutes or so, he and Fane stood side by side, leaning over the side of the vessel, without saying a word. Then, just as the home stretch came into view, the Dutchman said, *'Mijnheer is* from England?'

Fane nodded briefly.

'One can tell,' said the other. 'The cut of the clothes, an indefinable manner...' He tapped the dottle out of his pipe, and brushed some ash aside with his hand. 'A very enjoyable trip,' he commented.

'The best part was before you boarded the launch,' grunted Fane, staring straight in front of him.

'I have done it so many times before, *mijnheer*,' said the other, thrusting his pipe in his pocket, 'that I know every ripple.'

The old man at the wheel was gently edging the vessel nearer the shore. This, thought Fane, is going to be a last-minute grab, and away. Swiftly changing pouches, he filled his pipe again and lit up, puffing a veritable

292

volcano over the Dutchman; equally swiftly he brought out the crocodile-skin pouch.

'That smells very good tobacco, *mijnheer*, might I inquire the name of it?'

Fane told him. 'Why not try a fill?'

'*Mijnheer* is too kind. I will not insult him by refusing.'

The large men at his side stopped talking. Fane handed over the pouch containing the diamonds, doing his best to appear casual. The Dutchman felt the pouch curiously. 'This feels peculiar tobacco, *mijnheer*. Lumpy. Have you perhaps made some mistake?'

'I think you will find it to your satisfaction,' said Fane woodenly.

'But of course, *mijnheer* knows best,' agreed the other, fumbling clumsily with the little tag on the zip. He felt in his greatcoat pocket. This is going to be the switch, thought Fane, we're practically ashore. The two large men moved in and grabbed the Dutchman at precisely the same moment as the old man at the wheel jerked a cord and let out some almighty warning blasts on the siren as they came in to land. For a moment, all babel was let loose, for the well-dressed Dutchman, in his surprise at being apprehended, lost control of the pouch. Whether or not his arm was jogged was difficult to decide. Suffice to say that one moment the pouch was resting lightly in his right hand on the side of the boat, next moment it was overboard, and the two large men were shouting at him, and he was shouting at them, and Fane was shouting at them all, the old boy at the wheel tooting a merry accompaniment of ear-splitting blasts on the siren. By now there was a jostling crowd of spectators in the stern of the launch, and several bystanders gathered on the quay above.

'Fools!' thundered the Dutchman. 'What is the meaning of this? You have knocked *mijnheer's* tobacco into the water. Dolts!'

'You'd better come quietly,' suggested one of the men.

'My pouch!' shouted Fane. 'Get it before it sinks!'

'I personally will buy *mijnheer* another pouch if he will allow me the honour,' said the Dutchman grandly. 'If these clumsy dolts will only release my arms perhaps we can see what it is all about.'

'That pouch had the diamonds in it!' shouted Fane desperately.

'Diamonds?' said the Dutchman looking genuinely bewildered. '*Mijnheer* said tobacco! Willem!' he shouted authoritatively above the general hubbub. 'Willem! Hard astern! *Mijnheer's* pouch is in the water – it has valuables in it. Quickly!'

The old man reacted with commendable speed and brought the boat up, and gradually overcoming the forward impetus eased it back approximately to where they were when the incident happened. Under instruction he then slowly circled the spot in a fairly tight arc, all to no avail. By this time there was no trace of the wallet in the murky water, although in view of its rubber lining and light weight it might have kept awash for some seconds before sinking. After a few minutes they gave it up.

'And now, gentlemen,' said the Dutchman, who was still being held by one of the large men, 'perhaps you will be good enough to explain all this to me. This Englishman invites me to have a fill of tobacco from his pouch and you descend on me like a pack of wolves.' A sudden gleam came into his eye. 'I see it all,' he said severely. '*You* knew he had diamonds, and *you* were after them! The authorities shall know of this!'

'We are the authorities,' said one of them, producing a card.

'Then kindly act like them, and let go of my arm.'

'Not flaming-well likely, you're coming along with us to answer a few questions.'

'How very true I shall come along with you, but *I* shall be asking the questions and demanding the explanations.'

'You know very well there were diamonds in that pouch.'

'Nonsense! *Mijnheer* told me it was tobacco and asked me to have a fill of it. You must have heard him. And was it not I, who feeling

295

the lumpy nature of the contents, suggested that the gentleman had made a mistake?'

'That is so,' agreed one of the men doubtfully. 'Nevertheless, we are being met by a superior officer on the quayside, and you can make your complaints to him.'

They were in fact met at the landing-stage by a superior officer who hurried aboard and greeted the prisoner in some surprise. '*Mijnheer* Strookman, what is happening?'

'I wish someone would tell me. I have been arrested for – I know not what – either accepting a smoke of tobacco from a stranger or for letting these thickheads knock his diamonds into the canal. But why blame me? You are aware of my reputation.'

'But certainly, *Mijnheer* Strookman.' He turned to the plainclothed policeman. 'This is the manager of the Pyx Travel Agency,' he explained to him. 'I fear there has been some mistake. Let us talk it over reasonably and without heat, we are on good terms with *Mijnheer* Strookman...'

When Fane left the police station an hour later, he knew he ought to be convinced that a mistake had occurred, and yet somehow he wasn't. He couldn't quite see how Strookman came into it, and in any event the diamonds were now lost in the mud at the bottom of a canal. If Strookman *were* the blackmailer (and that seemed doubtful) would he now be scared off making further claims? If he was only the intermediary, then the principal obviously wasn't going to be satisfied. It was very depressing. If all had gone well, Fane's intention had been to seek consolation in Liselle, perhaps to pay a visit to the Femina 55 Club for dinner and cabaret. Now, for all he cared, Liselle could go to the Vondel-park and jump in the biggest lake...

Later that afternoon, the manager of the Pyx Travel Agency, Rip Strookman, was working with old Willem in the stern of the launch, when the senior police official who had recognized him earlier on happened to be passing on the quay above. He paused and watched them for a moment, and then gave Strookman a shout. 'Having trouble with your boat, *Mijnheer* Strookman?' he called.

Rip Strookman and old Willem, who were both hanging over the stern, whipped round together and looked up searchingly at the policeman.

'*Ja, ja,*' grunted Strookman. 'The boat has been out of commission – it fouled a line the other day and we thought it had been put right, but Willem tells me the engine was dragging again this morning. I think there must be a strand of hemp winding round the shaft.'

'Life is very irksome,' agreed the other.

'It was this morning,' countered Rip. 'If you hadn't appeared on the scene I would now be languishing in jail for throwing a customer's diamonds in the canal, or some such rubbish – I haven't got the hang of it yet!'

'Ridiculous, of course! My men were over-zealous, and we must once again offer our apologies, *Mijnheer* Strookman.' The police official deemed it wisest to be on his way, and the two below watched him out of sight before they resumed fishing for the thin nylon thread they knew was fixed securely to the side of the vessel below the water line. Old Willem, with the aid of a crooked stick, found it first, and gently pulled up enough for Rip to get hold of. Rip took over the operation, and still pulling gently until he had quite a length of slack, he moved over to the off side of the vessel where his move-ments were least likely to be observed; and whilst Willem kept a look-out to see there were no casual bystanders, he continued to haul away until on the end of it there appeared a sodden tobacco pouch. There was a small snap spring-clip on the end of the line, and this retained the pouch by means of the eyelet hole in the brass tag of the zip. Strookman unhooked the pouch, pressed its sogginess to ensure the contents were still intact, and slipped it into his side pocket. He instructed Willem to dispose of the nylon line and clip. 'You did a good job, Willem, you've earned another bottle of brandy for Anna. Mr Jullien Fane was, as they say in England, right up the canal.'

Leaving Willem to make things shipshape, Rip Strookman strode briskly back to his Travel Agency in Damrak, whistling a happy little tune. The van Meyer diamonds had been a very good 'buy' despite the work he had had to put into the re-cutting...

A brown-paper parcel had arrived for him by the parcel post, and he took it into his private room with instructions that he was not to be disturbed. The parcel was from Hans Wisselink of Oude Amstelweg, and contained quite a lot of money in currency. He checked it over carefully and found it in order. Then he reached for the telephone and instructed the gentleman at the other end to buy another block of Tyburn & New York stock on behalf of Roag's Syndicate... Oh yes, the van Meyer diamonds had been a very good 'buy' indeed.

22

Organized Chaos

About a week after Hammersley returned to London Simon Good made surreptitious nightly visits to the Shares Department with the aid of his duplicate key to check the record card of John Heathersedge Smith, until one evening he found what he was looking for – a blue tick against No. 13402. This meant that at long last the cheque half of the warrant had been cleared and returned by the bank. Good began to work with speed and efficiency. He took out from his case the genuine warrant – which had never been sent out, the various genuine record cards and printing plates he had previously taken away, and laid them all out in order. He then went to the cabinet where the returned warrants were kept in neat numerical bundles of a hundred, held together by rubber bands.

He found No. 13402, examined the rubber-stamped 'Paid' and the perforated date made by the bank, and grinned happily. The stamping machines were evidently standard equipment in use at all branches of the Newquay & District Bank, for both markings were similar to those appearing on the warrant returned from Carbis Bay Branch in respect of the previous dividend; there appeared to be no branch identification other than the clerk's initial through the amount.

From his case he took out a rubber stamp, an almost dry ink-pad (to simulate the faded purple he had observed on the previous returned warrant he had borrowed for matching-up purposes) and a small date-perforating machine. Taking the current genuine warrant No. 13402, he tore off the bottom half, stamped it 'Paid' (praying that Carbis Bay Branch hadn't changed to a green or red ink-pad), impressed the date of payment with the perforating machine (craftily operating across the corner of the warrant in such a way that it looked as if it had been done in a hurry, the actual day of the month just missing the paper) and finally put a somewhat nebulous biro squiggle through the amount of £5,184. He put the thus-treated document in place in the bundle of returned warrants and snapped the rubber band back, returning the bundle to the cabinet. He retained the false warrant which had been cleared at St Ives.

With a blue pencil he added a tick to John Heathersedge Smith's genuine record card, and put it back in place of the dummy one.

He similarly replaced the bank index cards and also the metal printing plates. Then collecting his surplus impedimenta, he took a last quick look round, locked up and made his way quietly down the stairs to the basement, picking his opportunity carefully at ground-floor level to avoid the porter. He had one thing more to put right – the Stock Register. He made for the fire-proof vault.

Unhitching the cleat, and noiselessly sliding back the heavy metal door, he slipped inside, switched on the lights, found the right register, loosened up the binding, quickly extracted the sham record sheet in the name of John Heathersedge Smith. The genuine one he took from a cardboard cylinder which just fitted diagonally in his case. Unrolling it and smoothing it out, he quickly replaced it in its rightful position in the register, tightening up the binding again with a few turns of the key. He had already made the necessary tick against the warrant number here, so that all that remained to be done was to replace the register, roll up the dummy sheet and put it in his case, switch off the lights, push the metal door back into place, and then leave the building by a back door used by the maintenance staff.

All of which was just as well, because the following morning the company received a rather sharp letter from an important stockholder complaining that he hadn't received his dividend...

Mr Rumbold, the Registrar, hurried along to the Secretary's room in answer to the buzzer. Mr Earnshaw Withers's attention seemed to be divided between two matters before him.

'Ah, Mr Rumbold! I notice Roag's Syndicate has bought another block of our stock.' He pushed a letter with several important-looking enclosures across the desk, and Rumbold skimmed through them quickly.

'H'm, they're fast becoming very important stockholders,' he commented. 'This last purchase will just about put them – if I may coin a phrase – in the top ten.'

'If they continue to buy at this rate, it's probably just as well their voting power is limited by the Articles of Association, otherwise' (he permitted himself an acid grin) 'we might find ourselves voted out of a job. And now a complaint. A Mr John Smith, who lives near Yeovil, writes to say his bank at Carbis Bay in Cornwall hasn't received his usual dividend warrant yet, and as it's a good bit overdue, what about it?'

'That's strange, sir,' said Rumbold, puzzled, 'this is the first year for some time that our Stock Account at the bank has been cleared – there's nothing outstanding in respect of this dividend. How much is it for?'

'Mr Smith says £5,184,' said the other, mildly.

'What!' cried Rumbold. 'There must be some mistake!'

'There must be,' agreed Mr Withers. 'Let me know what it is.'

Rumbold hurried back to the Shares Department and called his second-in-command. 'Jackson, have a look at this. A stockholder's written in from Yeovil to say he hasn't received his dividend yet, and Withers wants to know all about it.'

'He must have had it, the Stock Account balances,' objected Jackson. 'There must be some mistake.'

'Exactly what I told Withers, but he still wants to know about it.'

'How much is he screaming for – a couple of quid?'

'No. Five thousand one hundred and eighty-four pounds.'

'Phew! No wonder Withers is withering. Sounds as though the bank has slipped up, they've passed the warrant through their books and cancelled it out, and have forgotten to post this merchant's account. What's his name?'

'Here we are – John H. Smith.'

They went over to the card indexes and found the card in the name of John Heathersedge Smith, of Petherton Manor Farm, nr. Montacute, Yeovil, Somerset.

'The warrant number's been ticked,' said Jackson, 'so he must have had it.' He went over to a cabinet and produced Warrant No. 13402, and pointed out the rubber-stamped 'Paid', the perforated date and the squiggle in biro through the amount. 'It's been through the bank – there's their cancellation. "Pay Newquay & District Bank, Carbis Bay, St Ives. Credit John H. Smith. £5,184." They've forgotten to post his account.'

'This sort of rings a bell,' said Rumbold thoughtfully. 'Wasn't it the Newquay & District Bank which rang up from St Ives?'

Jackson had produced another card from a neighbouring index. 'Here you are – here's the bank card. Newquay & District Bank, Carbis Bay, St Ives.'

'I suppose that must have been it,' frowned Rumbold doubtfully. 'How many stockholders are paid at that branch?'

'Just the one. J.H. Smith.'

'I seem to remember there were several.'

'Wait a minute, though,' said Jackson, 'here's another card – Newquay & District, St Ives. Must be neighbouring branches. Couple of stockholders on this one. Mrs E. Truscott and the Botallick Hotel, Ltd.'

Rumbold grabbed the card. 'I remember those two names,' he said. 'And I remember this other bloke, John Heathersedge Smith. My recollection is that these three warrants were payable at the same bank.'

'I don't see how they could have been,' pointed out Jackson practically. 'There's the evidence of the two separate bank cards. Let's check up the cards of Mrs Truscott and the Botallick Hotel.'

'I'll have a look in the registers,' said Rumbold, vaguely disquieted.

Everything, however, appeared to be in order.

'I reckon this Mr John Smith is trying it on,' said Jackson.

'He's had other dividends before this,' pointed out the other.

'When you start on the downward path there's always a first time.'

'Nobody would be stupid enough to imagine they could get away with such a try-on. No, I think your first guess was right – the bank have forgotten to post his account. We'd better write and tell him the warrant has been returned through the bank clearing house, and that he ought to take up the matter with them.'

'Wait a minute, though,' frowned Jackson. 'Surely there was a question of a mandate to pay a local bank whilst the stockholder was temporarily resident at – at a hotel – wasn't it the Botallick Hotel?'

'That's what I was thinking. But it can't be, can it – there's no mention of it anywhere in the records.'

Jackson scratched his head in puzzlement. 'I've thought of something else – I was going down to the fire-proof safe to fetch up the mandate, but you decided to let it slide, don't you remember?'

Rumbold suddenly smiled happily. 'Yes, I remember. That's proof positive this couldn't have been the case there's absolutely no mention of any such mandate here; if there had been, it just wouldn't have vanished off the card overnight. No, we're mixing this up with something else. We'll write Mr Smith and tell him to sort it out with his bank.'

The bank did in fact sort it out – quickly, and in no uncertain manner; and in view of the

306

sharp exchange of acrimonious telephone calls and the ensuing aura of confusion, Mr Rumbold was dispatched post-haste to Cornwall, armed with all the bits and pieces to clarify things.

After close collaboration with the bank manager at Carbis Bay, things became even more muddled. It was soon apparent that no warrant for £5,184 had been received at that branch. Nothing was reflected in any of their books, and consequently nothing had been credited to Mr J.H. Smith's account. Rumbold politely asked *where* then had the warrant been paid if it hadn't been paid there, seeing that it had been returned through the bank clearing house purporting to have been paid there. This indeed set a poser, for nobody in that very small branch had the faintest recollection of ever having seen that particular warrant.

It was then suggested that as the branch was known as the Carbis Bay (St Ives) Branch, and that there was also a plain *St Ives* Branch, perhaps the confusion had arisen there.

And so Mr Rumbold made his way over to Tregenna Hill, St Ives, and was soon ensconced with the manager of the branch a few doors from the corner of Tre-Pol-Pen. The manager was waiting for him, obviously as a result of a telephone call from Carbis Bay, and they got down to cases right away.

He told Rumbold that the warrant had in fact been met at that branch, and said that it had been definitely made out for the St Ives Branch to the credit of John H. Smith's account.

Rumbold thereupon produced the cheque portion of John H. Smith's warrant, and this, of course, clearly said Carbis Bay Branch. The bank manager remained unshaken.

'Mr Smith had a temporary account here, and he was staying at the Botallick Hotel,' he said precisely, 'and it was because of the very temporary nature of things that I took the trouble to ring you in London.'

'I must confess that owing to the stress of subsequent work I only have a hazy idea now of what was said,' said Rumbold, 'but I would like to show you now the actual printing plates which produced that warrant, and you will clearly see that Mr Smith's address was not the Botallick Hotel, St Ives.' He fumbled in his case for the envelope containing the plates.

'Don't forget, I *saw* the warrant,' said the other, still unshaken. 'The top half definitely showed the stockholder as being Mr Smith c/o the Botallick Hotel.'

'That's what *you* say, but you're already wrong about the branch, it's clearly Carbis Bay. Take a look at the plates.'

'Well, I can't prove now what I saw, because that part of the warrant is sent to the customer with his account. Anyway, Carbis Bay Branch denies having had it. What does Mr Smith say?'

'He says he hasn't received it – nor the money.'

'We can't be talking about the same man. He collected £6,000 here in the front office – that took into account the dividend of £5,184.'

'Well, I'm going to Yeovil to discuss his complaint – we'll see what he has to say about *that!*'

'Yeovil?'

'Yes, that's where he lives – here's the printing plate. Petherton Manor Farm, near Montacute, Yeovil.'

'I gathered he came from Manchester. Won the Pools.'

'There's something very mysterious going on here. What was he like?'

The bank manager described him. 'Altogether a very charming man,' he concluded. 'Created an excellent impression at the hotel – I know the manager. What do you intend to do?'

'I shall have to report the whole thing to my Executive,' said Rumbold non-committally.

23

Roag's Syndicate

Hammersley caught a tram-car at the Gare du Nord in Brussels and made his way round the main boulevards to the Porte de Namur, where he alighted and crossed the road to the narrow Rue du Dépôt. Looking from left to right, he walked slowly down the hill.

The Golden Fleece proved to be quite a large café jammed between the entrance to a hotel and an exclusive-looking restaurant. Pushing his way through the door into the heavy atmosphere of cigar smoke and coffee, he went over to the counter, behind which sat a girl whose vital statistics were more than usually vital, appearing to defy the laws of gravity. In accordance with instructions, he asked for the proprietor, adding the magic word 'Syndicate'.

The look of studied indifference in the girl's eye was instantly replaced by one of marked interest, and the movement of her knee against a button under the counter was quite imperceptible as she got down off her high stool.

'This way, monsieur,' she smiled, indicating an arched doorway, through which – one gathered from a pointing finger painted on the wall – one reached the hotel. Apparently the hotel, the café and the restaurant were all part and parcel. As they reached a door with a neat little plate marked *Directeur*, a well-set man, not old, not young, emerged smiling at Hammersley and dismissing the girl with a wave of the hand.

Hammersley's mind went skidding back over the years, and his jaw sagged a fraction. 'Sergeant Blake!' he gasped.

'Come, come, my dear Hammersley, all that was over a thousand years ago! You're on holiday now. Welcome to one of my hotels. You haven't changed a bit. The others are waiting.'

'The others?' stuttered Hammersley, allowing himself to be pulled gently by the arm into *Monsieur le Directeur*'s room. And if his mind had skidded back into the past a moment ago, it was now positively screeching along in the supersonic ranges. In this quietly opulent room was a polished table, seated at which were three men who greeted him vociferously. He recognized Rip Strookman instantly, although that gentleman had put on considerable weight since the lean years. Of Dutchy he was doubtful; the build was there, the face was not quite there – or more than there. Simon Good – Peter Meek – he knew only too well.

'I had me face lifted, Hammersley, me old china,' said Dutchy. 'I know what you're thinking.'

'Bless my soul!' said Charles Hammersley, at length. 'Where did you all spring from?'

'Like you – we're on holiday,' said Rip.

'Tell me more – what are you all doing for a living?'

'I run a string of hotels,' said Blake. 'I bought 'em out of sandwiches and hard work after the war.'

'I still sell me bulbs and plants in Leatherwick Way,' said Dutchy. 'And I've also got a stall in the Veerdijk market in Holland.'

'I run a travel agency in Amsterdam,' said Strookman, '–among other things. And what about you, my dear Hammersley?'

'Hammersley's my insurance adviser,' put in Simon Good quickly. 'On the claims side, you might say.'

There was a ripple of merriment at this remark.

'He's like Blake – he likes a good safe job,' said Strookman slyly.

'Safe!' grunted Dutchy. 'Blimey, the last good safe job he did he nearly blew up, or burned down, 'alf of Reigate!'

The party fell to reminiscing over some excellent liqueurs and coffee. Simon Good produced a pipe and lit up. Hammersley's eye fixed on it instantly.

'You recognize it, Charles? I smoke it here

every year on the anniversary of the day that Peter Meek vanished, on the day of the annual general meeting of the Syndicate. Meet the Syndicate.' He waved his hand expressively. 'You recall the pipe – do you recall anything else about that day in relation to the five of us?'

Charles Hammersley stared back into the past for a moment. 'Yes,' he said, 'I do. You asked us what our jobs were in Civvy Street, and commented what a wonderful set-up it was for roguery. As I remember it, you didn't ask me about my job, I suppose you already knew all about it.'

'Your memory does you credit, Charles. You see before you – you are facing the mirror – a pride of rogues. Perhaps a 'prey' of rogues would be more apt.'

'Bless my soul!' exclaimed the other again.

'It can probably do with it,' agreed Simon Good. 'Now this is the first meeting you've attended, and you'll find we dispense with formality. In introducing Charles Hammersley to the Syndicate, I would like to say that his activities have already stepped up our considerable holdings in Tyburn & New York stock. In that connexion I would inform you I have looked into the question of voting power under that company's Articles of Association, and it might be to our advantage to break down the holding into several nominee holdings. Our position has never been stronger, even if we are forced into an honest living from now on, and in that connexion I must bring to your notice that for some reason the police are beginning to take an interest in Peter Meek. Why, I don't know. Where I've slipped up, if slipped up I have, I know even less. Suffice to say I feel it advisable to recommend suspension of all activities from now on till further notice. The dividends from the Tyburn & New York alone will save us from penury. Any questions?'

'No questions,' came the united response.

'Then before we begin to enjoy ourselves,' said Simon Good, 'it only remains for me to remind you of the rule that none of us inquires too deeply into the jobs and occupations of other Syndicate members. And if anything goes wrong, we each stand alone. Before we adjourn, perhaps I should report on the good work of our new member. I set him the formidable task of analysing a number of insurance contracts with a view to finding the flaws, if any. Before these wordings reach the public, counsel's opinion is usually sought, and to be able subsequently to find any flaw or ambiguity is something of a feat. Nevertheless, Hammersley has come up trumps on a clause on a marine contract, which we might be able to use to our advantage; he has found a definite flaw in an Aviation policy-wording – only I don't suppose any of you is prepared to be involved in an air crash to test the strength of his reasoning with the company concerned; and finally he has found a loophole in the conditions of a bloodstock policy – I think his research was stimulated by the recent unfortunate horse-race where the young jockey, Larry Lemon, was thrown against the rails and killed, and his mount, Sanda's Boy, had to be destroyed on the course. You will recollect it was insured for twenty thousand pounds, and whilst Hammersley's scheme is by no means so ambitious, it should provide in due course a steady augmentation to our funds.' Simon Good lifted his glass. 'And now a toast. "Roguery with caution – Roag's Syndicate."'

'Please don't break the glasses,' said Blake hurriedly, 'they came from the Duke of Chalfont's place.'

24

'Causes of Which Remain Unknown'

They never got to the bottom of the strange affair of the dividend warrant, although the police, who took over the inquiries, secretly felt Simon Good had something to do with it. But it was a different thing feeling it and proving it. And although Hammersley had disappeared at or about the same time as John Smith appeared at St Ives, the descriptions of the two characters so widely differed as to make it highly improbable they were actually the one and same person. The bank officials clearly remembered Mr Smith going off to the bus stop at the Malakoff en route for Carbis Bay, whereas a porter at St Ives railway station even more clearly recollected a man of Mr Smith's description asking how to get a connexion to Yeovil, which, of course, was where the real Mr Smith lived. The porter's memory had been considerably assisted by the one-pound tip Mr Smith had given him. In fact, he was never likely to forget Mr Smith, who talked of spreading a little happiness with his football pool win, which talk tallied with what he had told the bank and the hotel. The police checked up an address in Manchester, which address Mr Smith used to speak of with tears in his eyes as being the house of his birth, and when it turned out to be a police station, they judiciously let the matter drop. The 'Dividend Warrant Case', as it was called, subsequently developed into a most intriguing three-cornered legal battle between the Tyburn & New York, the bank and the real Mr Smith, who not unnaturally still wanted his money.

It was all very confusing.

The van Meyer diamonds were never recovered, the insurance companies paid up and looked big, and Jullien Fane, who ordered an intensive Burglary Insurance advertising campaign on the strength of it, never realized he'd actually had some of them in his pocket in Amsterdam.

The General Manager, talking over with Mr van Meyer one evening the question of placating Mrs van Meyer because of the loss of the diamonds, mentioned confidentially that he knew a very good jeweller in a small way in Amsterdam from whom one could get stones at a very reasonable cost. Mr van Meyer visited Hans Wissclink, and in due course purchased some diamonds which were as near to the original ones as he was ever likely to get. Indeed, he was amazed at his astounding luck in picking up gems of the same pellucid quality as the ones he'd lost, and was more than pleased with his purchase. Hans Wisselink was quite happy with his low margin of profit (after all, he was even nearer the end of the road) and Rip Strookman was pleased to get the van Meyer diamonds finally off his hands, having sold them twice.

No further blackmailing demands were made on Mr Fane, so he kept his fingers crossed and hoped the blackmailer had been scared off by the strong police activity in Holland.

Quenella Mansfield kept strictly out of his

way, but not before she told him she thought it best for both of them if she left the Tyburn & New York as soon as she could find another post. Jullien Fane inwardly breathed a sigh of relief, outwardly agreed with her with great reluctance, and with even more reluctance made a show of pressing a cheque on her by way of solarium. Miss Mansfield made an even better show of allowing herself to be talked into accepting it, and Mr Fane immediately cast his eye round for a new secretary whose speed at shorthand-typing was not necessarily the most important qualification.

The tie-up (as betrayed by the typescript) between the unsigned blackmailing letter that Fane had received and the signed letter smacking of blackmail that Hammersley had dropped, presupposed that Simon Good was the blackmailer of Fane, and a very careful watch had been kept on him. As, however, he had been going earnestly about his humdrum business in London whilst Fane was losing an awful lot of money in Amsterdam, there was nothing the police could hang their hats on. And so they quietly pursued their inquiries at the other end of the chain – Hammersley.

A deceptively shy young policeman called on that gentleman to return the letter Lingard had picked up in Fetter Lane. He explained that in view of the somewhat threatening contents they wondered if he wanted any help, or if he could tell them anything about the Simon Good who had signed it.

'Where is the envelope?' asked Hammersley, at a tangent.

'Presumably there wasn't one,' replied the shy young policeman, 'else we wouldn't have needed to read the letter, would we? I mean, it could have just been posted on to you, and we wouldn't have known anything about the contents.'

'Ah. When was it found?'

'I don't really know, sir. Recently, I assume – I'm really only a messenger-boy. When did you lose it?'

'I don't really know,' said Hammersley.

'Ah,' said the shy young man. 'And what about this Simon Good?'

Charles Hammersley was also deceptively ingenuous. He straight away denounced the epistle he had received as being not merely a joke in bad taste, but one which sought to incriminate Simon Good.

'Do you know Simon Good well?'

'Not particularly, now. In the old days I was his batman.'

'Was he known as Simon Good then?'

'Oh, no! I knew him as Major Meek. Peter Meek. I met him for the first time since the war only recently.'

'Was that by accident?'

'Well – no. More by appointment, I would say. You see, he received a letter couched in similar terms to mine, only his purported to come from me, and was signed "Charles Hammersley". And so we met.'

'Had either of you any reason for fearing exposure in respect of – um – some indiscretion in the past?'

Hammersley laughed easily. 'Not to my knowledge,' he said. 'I'm quite happy. The only thing I wondered about the Major was why he had changed his name, but I gather he was merely fed up with the old one of Meek. Whether he did it by deed poll or only adopted it, I couldn't say. Anyway, although we each wondered what the other was up to, the letters at least brought us together again.'

'Do you know if Mr Good still has his letter?'

'No, I have it.' Hammersley fished in his wallet. 'Here it is.'

'And why have you got it, sir?' asked the other curiously.

'I was going to compare the typing – I dabble in photography and intended blowing up a couple of prints, but I never really got round to doing it. By the time I got the urge to tackle the job I discovered I'd lost my letter.' He smoothed out the letter alleged to have been sent to Simon Good, and compared it with the one the policeman had returned. 'It looks very much like the same typing, doesn't it?'

'It does indeed, sir.'

'The *e* and the *f* are out of alignment – see?'

'Quite so. Do you think Mr Good would mind if we borrowed his letter for a while?'

'I'm quite certain he wouldn't mind,' declared Charles Hammersley. 'Only too pleased to help. As a matter of fact, as both letters were posted in Fleet Street, he wondered if someone where he works – an insurance company in Fetter Lane – did it for a joke.'

'Could be,' agreed the shy young policeman, without conviction or hope.

It came to pass in the fullness of time that a City firm of insurance brokers offered the Tyburn & New York an interest in a large burglary insurance which had come their way. A sizeable country house was involved, and one of the principal items at risk was a priceless collection of diamond bracelets, bangles, clips, and pendants belonging to the actress wife of the actor-manager who owned the place. The vulnerability of the risk lay in the haphazard periods of unoccupancy brought about by their professions, although it was stressed on the proposal form that the great wealth was kept in a Lumm safe. The Tyburn & New York accepted a share of the insurance, the bait was nibbled, and in due course Simon Good called at the brokers' office for more detailed information about the risk...

Superintendent Lingard rubbed his hands happily, and went about the task of intensifying the watch on Good, Hammersley and Dutchy. It was whilst quietly posting two men in the crowd at the latter's stalls in Leatherwick Way and indicating the man who was to be kept under observation, that Lingard suddenly spotted young Jim Laker buying some plants. He sidled up to the boy, gave his most good-natured grin, and asked how much the plants were. Jim told him.

'You can't beat Dutchy,' commented Jim, pulling the newspaper back and exhibiting the sturdy young seedlings.

'Too true,' agreed Lingard. 'You're like me, I buy a lot here – I've seen you here before. I remember a while ago you brought back some dud bulbs from an old friend of mine, Simon Good.'

'You know him?' said Jim, with new-found interest.

'He's an old acquaintance of mine. I suppose you're from the Tyburn & New York in Fetter Lane? What on earth Simon wants with hundredweights of bulbs I just don't know – he never was much of a gardener.'

'Oh, he gets 'em for a friend of his, a chap named Blake. D'you know him too?'

'Blake – not old Blake? Haven't seen him for years! D'you know where he lives?'

'Somewhere out at Denham, I think. Mad on gardening.'

'Oh. Used to run a snack-bar, when I knew him,' said Lingard.

'Still does. In Chelsea. I think it's called the Golden Porcupine. The customers come out in prickles when they see the bill.'

Lingard laughed heartily. 'Watch out for your plants,' he warned, 'that paper's a bit wet, you'll lose the lot. Get some more newspaper.'

And by the time Jim Laker had re-wrapped his plants, Lingard wasn't there to be asked what name should be mentioned to Mr Good.

Blake was now traced with comparative ease, but though he was watched almost night and day, all that could be said for the gentleman who had once been one of Lumm's safe experts was that during working-hours he worked like a nigger managing his Chelsea restaurant, and in his spare time lovingly watched his garden burgeon.

A report came to Scotland Yard via Interpol concerning the loss of Fane's pouch of diamonds from a launch owned by Rip Strookman. In all the circumstances, Lingard was not surprised that the Dutchman came into the picture somewhere, but as he apparently hadn't made a single Dutch cent out of the peculiar incident (indeed, by all accounts the diamonds were now buried in the silt of one of Amsterdam's colourful waterways) it was difficult to see what the game was and who was committing the fouls.

Rip Strookman generously took no further

action against the Dutch police for involving him in the fracas on his launch, and the police judiciously kept out of his way so as not to remind him of the unfortunate incident.

An attempt was actually made to crack the Lumm safe containing the jewellery of the actress wife of the actor-manager, and it was patently obvious by reason of the very close police surveillance that neither Simon Good nor any of his friends had anything at all to do with it, their alibis being provided by the police themselves. In actual fact the robbery had been attempted by an American cracksman in England on holiday. He was literally amazed at the speed with which he was picked up, and when asked by the learned judge who was about to lengthen his stay here if he had anything to say, he replied, 'I think your policemen are wonderful.'

The shy young policeman called on Simon Good, showed him some photographs of the American cracksman, and asked if by any mischance he, Mr Good, had accidentally imparted any gen to the American regarding the Lumm safe or the layout of the country house. The shy young policeman said he understood Simon had made a particular point of asking the brokers for certain information, and wondered if he'd talked about it, say in a pub, and had been overheard.

'Certainly not, my dear bobby,' Simon declared virtuously. 'I would never dream of being so incautious. The only reason I asked for the information anyway was because I was instructed so to do by my head of department, a certain Mr Moran, who particularly wanted further details of the risk.'

And this indeed proved to be the case. Mr Moran, following Mr Earnshaw Withers's recent questioning as to whether the Guarantee & Reinsurance Department ever asked for additional information before accepting guarantee risks, felt there might be an ulterior motive in the questioning, perhaps even a mild reproach, and therefore decided henceforth to ask for plans and reports left-right-and-centre. Indeed, such was Mr Moran's sudden enthusiasm for obtaining extra details that he even laid claim to some of those cases where Simon Good had acted purely on his own behalf. All of which, whilst greatly adding to Mr Moran's sense of never missing a trick and being on top of the job, also added considerably to the general confusion.

It was all very regrettable.

Simon Good, Hammersley, Blake, Dutchy, and Rip Strookman went assiduously about their individual blameless ways with a steadfastness that was remarkable. None of them made contact with any of the others, and they appeared to be the unfriendliest friends in all creation.

25

Down the Hatch

Late one evening, Good had occasion to leave Shepherdess Walk (where, in addition to Quenella Mansfield's house, he owned five other bijou residences) to pick up some private papers inadvertently left at his modest bachelor establishment at Richmond.

He had been in the latter house studying the documents rather longer than he imagined, when suddenly the lights went out. With a growl of irritation he felt in his pocket for a shilling, without success, and then groped his way to the kitchen. With a slice of luck the refrigerator might have had enough time to help him out of the difficulty. It obliged, and in a few moments he had the lights going again.

There was a knock at the front door, and Simon answered it curiously, for he received few calls in the evening other than by appointment. Two men were on the step, and another stood back a little.

'Good evening, sir, we are police officers,' said the larger of the two, showing his credentials, 'and I have a warrant to search this house. This gentleman with us is a technical expert.'

'Technical expert?' said Simon Good, his mind flying to the typewriter which he hoped had been bashed to pieces by the cruel sea. 'Does your warrant extend to him?'

'No, sir. Have you any objection to his coming in with us?'

'Not at all, come right on in!' said Mr Good, puzzled, caught on one foot and wondering what it was all about.

He soon found out, for they made straight for the kitchen and the refrigerator, wherein they found a tray of ice 'shillings' with just one missing. With the aid of the man from the Electricity Board, who opened up the meter, they found it just beginning to melt in the coin-box. The detective in charge, acting on instructions from Scotland Yard, also looked round and found a typewriter, an old one, and made a test sample on a sheet of paper. He compared this with a sample folded in his notebook, and even he could see it wasn't the machine they were looking for.

Simon Good was taken to Richmond Police Station and charged, under Section 10 of the Larceny Act, with fraudulently abstracting electricity...

Mr Justice Meddlisome gazed down sombrely at Simon Good.

'Peter Meek, you have been found guilty

of committing a felony within the terms of Section 10 of the Larceny Act, 1916. That section lays down that any person who maliciously or fraudulently abstracts, causes to be wasted or diverted, consumes or uses any electricity, shall on conviction be liable to be punished as in the case of simple larceny. Have you anything to say before I pass judgment upon you?'

'Not really, your Lordship, except that having listened closely to all the evidence I'm inclined to agree with the jury.'

'We have a way of dealing with flippancy in these courts,' remarked the Judge without any trace of emotion. 'I have been giving considerable thought as to what to do with you. Your learned counsel saw fit to put your character in issue. It would probably have been wiser from your point of view to have left it buried in obscurity, for the suggested bad side of you brought out in skilful cross-examination appears to outweigh the known good. The latter includes a superb military record of service given unstintingly in your country's hour of gravest need; it also includes an excellent testimonial generously given by your employers in *your* hour of need. The obverse side of your character, however, brings to light a side so mean and bitter as to make me ponder whether it is psychiatric, rather than judicial, treatment you require. The meanness, for example, of deliberately failing to put postage stamps on letters; this from a man owning an expensive automobile and several houses in the heart of Mayfair, a man who purports to be kicking against a humdrum existence earning but a few pounds per week with an insurance company. That, Meek, gives me pause to think. Your precise means were not brought out in cross-examination, but I suggest the Inland Revenue authorities pay earnest attention to your file. The day of reckoning must always come, Meek; in this life you only get what you pay for, and ultimately the account is rendered for anything owing. Now I am disturbed, Meek, by the allegations – not of prime importance in the case at issue – of your seeking private information regarding burglar alarms and the like, information not – in the instances to which I refer – required by your employers, the implication being that in some way you used this knowledge to your own advantage, to the detriment of your employers and the people who put their trust in them. You will not be unaware Meek, of the Latin phrase *uberrima fides* – 'utmost good faith'. The public are entitled to expect precisely that from the employees of any insurance company they choose to patronize. I am disturbed, Meek, by rumblings of blackmail, by mutterings of forgery. I am suspicious of the fact that you have been living under an assumed name, not being satisfied with the one given you by parents to whom you were doubtless the whole world. The name you have adopted has brought you no better fortune. Perhaps the number you will be allotted shortly will prove to be a lucky one. Meek, I am disturbed by the fact that a man of your upbringing and apparent wealth can bring himself so low as to obtain a few coppers' worth of electricity by fraudulent means. It is the latter point that inclines me to believe that it is in fact psychiatric treatment you need – you look puzzled, Meek.'

'I am indeed, my Lord, quite apart from this talk of psychiatry. I realize, of course, that I myself elected to go for trial before a jury, but I am wondering why in any event I have had to come before you on such a frivolous charge, when so many other things have now been suggested, things which, if true, must have been committed *before* this trivial accusation I am now facing, and which anyway have obviously received the attention of the police. Equally obviously the Director of Public Prosecutions couldn't make any of it stick, and all these innuendoes must therefore remain, as your Lordship has so wisely described them, *merely* implications, suspicions, rumblings, and mutterings. I am nevertheless intrigued as to what started the police on my trail. There seems to have been a spirit of vindictiveness about the whole thing, an attitude of "get-him-at-all-costs".

330

These unfortunate smears on my character may have repercussions on my Insurance career, and I should like to know who was responsible so that I may consider what legal action to take.'

'Don't exasperate me too much, Meek,' warned the Judge in measured tones, a little pulse beginning to quiver in his jaw. 'For your guidance, it is a principle of these courts that the police are not obliged to divulge the sources of their information, and in your case they particularly wish to keep in the background the alert officer who has a long memory for people's faces and for the foolish things those people say in unguarded moments. Circumstance caused your paths to cross, and one might say that the merest glimpse, a retentive memory, and a chain of events leading from what I believe is called a hunch, have put you in the dock, Meek, and have been your undoing. I want you to remember that the same officer will be on your tail in future. In the meantime I feel your enforced absence from public life will benefit not only the public, but you, and will have the salutary effect of bringing you down to earth. Psychiatric treatment often includes shock treatment. It is not generally appreciated that the maximum term of imprisonment I am permitted by law to prescribe for a simple larceny is as much as five years.'

'Seems a very long time, my Lord.'

'It is, it is meant to be, and don't interrupt.'

'I beg your Lordship's pardon, but all this is new to me, I am not fully conversant with procedure. It does seem though, bearing on the point you've just raised, that that's one of the reasons why our prisons are so full. I'm all in favour of the shorter, sharper sentences advocated by the Lord Chief Justice. Quicker turnover, if your Lordship pleases.'

'His Lordship doesn't please, and he is rapidly losing his temper.'

'Forgive me if I talk too much, my Lord, I am naturally of a friendly disposition, and I really am interested in all that you have to say, and all that is going on.'

With an almost visible effort the Judge controlled his fierce displeasure, and gazed reflectively and coldly at the man before him.

'Peter Meek, you have exasperated and angered me almost beyond endurance. Throughout these proceedings you have displayed a flippancy amounting to contempt. I sentence you to twelve months imprisonment. Did you say something?'

'No, my Lord, although my lips may have been moving. A friend of mine recently promised to show me how to get a drink without paying for it. It rather looks as if I may be disappointed.'

'You *will* be disappointed,' said the Judge, his breathing quite constricted.

'I shall, of course, with respect, appeal.'

'By all means do. You have your legal advisers. I shall be interested to learn, in due course, the grounds.'

'Well, I can tell you the gravamen now, my Lord, purely from the lay viewpoint, and on a strictly friendly basis. The legal advisers you so kindly remind me of will, of course, have to work on it.'

Mr Justice Meddlisome looked slowly round the court in a very unfriendly manner, dwelling for a moment on the foreman of the jury. The foreman had been caught in the middle of a particularly fatuous grin; he made one or two twitching movements with one side of his mouth to prove he was always like it. The court became very quiet.

'Pray go on, Meek,' said the Judge between his teeth.

'In the first place, my Lord, I feel your attitude to this case has been coloured by those unproven factors which you yourself have been pleased to call implications, suspicions, rumblings, and mutterings, and your detailed references to them seem to indicate the weight you have placed upon them, as compared with your almost non-existent reference to the thing that has brought me here – my boyish prank of experimenting with an ice "shilling". (Of course, I know there was rust in the coin-box of that meter, there's rust everywhere down by the river.) Secondly, and it pains me to mention this, surely in view of your Lordship's obvious anger and your Lordship's admissions in court on the subject, would it not have been wiser to defer judgement till another day? I feel sentence was unduly harsh because it was pronounced under a sense of exasperation. I wouldn't know, of course, I haven't a legal mind, but that's how it strikes a layman.'

All breathing in court was suspended, and no pins were dropped.

Mr Justice Meddlisome looked down at Peter Meek for a moment with eyes of ice, perfectly motionless, like a hawk carved in granite, his mind flitting ahead to the Court of Appeal, visualizing all that would be said, all that would *not* be said. Perhaps, after all, the sentence *was* harsh, perhaps he had made the unpardonable error of being goaded into a hasty decision. After all, he was only human, and therefore fallible. Suddenly the grimmest little smile touched his lips for the most fleeting of all moments. The loophole was the amount he had added for contempt, yes, that was the loophole! He made a brief note in the book before him. Shades of Judge Jeffreys, he was becoming as specious as the man Meek, perhaps it was infectious! Ah, well, it was too late to do anything about that sentence now...

'Send the prisoner down,' he said bleakly.

The publishers hope that this book has given you enjoyable reading. Large Print Books are especially designed to be as easy to see and hold as possible. If you wish a complete list of our books please ask at your local library or write directly to:

Dales Large Print Books
Magna House, Long Preston,
Skipton, North Yorkshire.
BD23 4ND